S0-ABD-692

Wayne G. Woodford
5/4/77

A THREE-PIPE PROBLEM
A THREE-PIPE PROBLEM
A THREE-PIPE PROBLEM

BOOKS BY JULIAN SYMONS

FICTION

NONFICTION

Julian Symons

A THREE-PIPE PROBLEM

Harper & Row, Publishers
New York, Evanston, San Francisco, London

A HARPER NOVEL OF SUSPENSE

FIRST U.S. EDITION

Designed by C. Linda Dingler

Library of Congress Cataloging in Publication Data
Symons, Julian, 1912–
   A three-pipe problem.
   I. Title.
PZ3.S9927Tj3   [PR6037.Y5]   823'.9'12   74–20421
ISBN 0–06–014193–X

75 76 77 78 79 10 9 8 7 6 5 4 3 2 1

For Ngaio Marsh,
who gave me the title

"What are you going to do then?" I asked.

"To smoke," he answered. "It is quite a three-pipe problem, and I beg that you won't speak to me for fifty minutes."

The Adventures of Sherlock Holmes

THE FIRST MURDER

The crimes known to the press first as the Karate Killings and then as Sherlock Holmes's Last Case began one New Year's Eve. On this evening of rain and blustering wind the usual things happened in central London, where the gaiety was, as always, partly synthetic and partly real. The people swarming up the pavements of Regent Street and Oxford Street, straying all over the road, stopping cars, kissing their occupants and wishing them a Happy New Year, could be said to be looking for reality or desperately maintaining illusion. The young men and women who plunged naked into the Trafalgar Square fountain appeared to be enjoying themselves, although one had to be rushed off to hospital, suffering from exposure. At parties people, some of whom had met for the first time, sang "Auld Lang Syne" and then embraced warmly before driving home, often with more than the permitted amount of alcohol in their blood. In thousands of houses people with nowhere to go watched comedians on television wearing paper hats while they sang sentimental songs.

It was a New Year's Eve like any other. The police remained good-humored in spite of the sparklers and bangers thrown at them. They turned a blind eye to motorists who had had one too many, except when they became involved in accidents. There was an average number of telephone calls from householders who returned home, after singing "Auld Lang Syne" with tears in their eyes, to find that burglars had not only forced locks and taken jewel cases, but also scrawled obscene messages on bedroom walls. Several cases of incendiarism relating to shops and stores were reported, three of which proved to have been set to collect the insurance. There were a number of assaults, the result of quarrelsomeness through drink. And there was a murder.

The dead man's name was Charles Mole. He was forty-three years old and he lived in Streatham, which may now be counted as one of London's inner suburbs. The body had been found just before eleven o'clock on Streatham Common, a few yards away from one of the lighted footpaths that cross it. He had been killed with one or more blows on the back of the neck. His wallet had not been touched, and no attempt had been made to search the body. Beside him there lay an unopened bottle of nonvintage port.

Mole had worked for the past ten years in the research department of Fact Consultants Ltd., a firm that organized opinion polls. He lived in the upper part of a Victorian house just off the common, with his wife, Gillian. They had no children. The case was in the hands of Chief Superintendent Roger Devenish, and it was Devenish who talked to the widow. He knew that most murders are family affairs. Play the variations on a triangle of wife-husband-lover, or on a quartet of two married couples, and you soon came up with the right answer. But Sergeant Brewster's inquiries in the neighborhood had revealed no entanglement on the part of husband or wife, and certainly Gillian Mole gave little encouragement to such thoughts. She was a thin, dark woman of forty, with a strained, intense expression accentuated by the way she wore her hair pulled away from her forehead. She told Devenish the story he had already heard from his sergeant. It was usual for the Moles to celebrate the New Year with a glass of port, and at ten o'clock they discovered that there was none in the apartment. Charles had said that he would go out and get a bottle. He had not taken the car, because it was not worth the trouble of getting it out of the garage. He had walked across the common, and then— Devenish, who knew that Mole had been to a local pub, had one drink and bought the bottle of port, nodded.

"Mrs. Mole, did your husband have an enemy? Or had he quarreled with somebody recently?"

"No enemies. We keep ourselves to ourselves."

"He didn't have any affair you know of with a woman? Or drink too much? Or have any trouble at the office?"

"Three questions. Three answers." Devenish had dropped ash from his cigarette on the corner of a small table. Mrs. Mole leaned forward and carefully pushed it into an ashtray. "There was no other woman in Charles's life. There was no other man in mine. We have no children, which was a sorrow to us both, but we were happy together." She indicated the gleaming empty screen across the room. "We watched a great deal in the evenings. Charles said it was important for his work; it helped him to understand the way people react to advertising.

"The second question. Charles drank very little. We should have had two small glasses of port each if he had come back. No more." She looked as though she might be about to add to this, but went on. "Charles didn't say much to me about his work at the office. So far as I know there was no trouble of any kind, but you would have to talk to the head of his department, Mr. Mantleman."

"I'll do that." Devenish gave her the rueful, worried smile that had charmed a good many women into rash remarks. "The problem is this, Mrs. Mole. As you put it, there seems absolutely no reason for your husband's death. It looks like an absolutely unprovoked attack—there's no sign of any preliminary fight. Of course, such things do happen, but generally a gang sets on to

3

one man for some reason. Nobody saw that happen and, as I say, there's no sign of it on the ground. Apparently a man simply went up to your husband and made a murderous attack on him for no reason, and that seems very unlikely."

"I understand what you are saying, of course, but it is more important to you than to me."

"Really? I should have thought you'd want to know who killed your husband."

She said impatiently, "Of course. But I have to get used to the idea that Charles is dead. And since his life was not insured, and I imagine his pension will be small, I have to think about making a living."

"You don't know of anybody who hated him, perhaps somebody from the past?"

She looked at him levelly. "Charles and I had no enemies. And very few friends. Perhaps we are not very interesting people."

The view that Charles Mole was not somebody likely to have made enemies was shared by Mantleman, a big, bluff man with an apparent taste for extravagant ties. Mole's work had been the correlation of statistical material, he said. Devenish looked slightly baffled.

"A lot of the work we do is for companies who are making tests of reaction to a new product. Let's say a new line in aftershave or baby powder is being put out in selected areas. When the results of this area testing come in they need detailed analysis. That's the kind of thing Mole did, and he was good at it. He was careful, the sort who never gets to the office late or leaves early."

"Did he do confidential work of any kind?"

"You're thinking of industrial espionage, selling secrets?" Mantleman laughed heartily. "The kind of thing we do isn't that important. If anybody really wanted to get hold of information about reactions to product X, they could do it without too much trouble."

"Women?"

"I suppose he knew they were different from men, but he never showed any sign of it."

"Drink? Anyone at the office dislike him?"

"He'd have a drink or two, hardly ever more than two. He got quite skittish at the firm's Christmas party after two or three sherries, but don't get me wrong: I've never seen him drunk. What was the other thing you asked? Oh, yes, trouble at the office. No, nobody disliked him; you couldn't dislike him." Mantleman leaned forward. "Mole was the nearest thing you can get to a cipher, and how can you have strong feelings about a cipher? If it weren't for his empty chair, I'd have forgotten by now that he ever existed."

So Mole had been a cipher. In Devenish's view most people were ciphers, and there must still have been a reason why this particular cipher was wiped out. The reason, however, was not apparent.

The material gathered about Charles Mole made a slim file.

THE SECOND MURDER

Sir Pountney Gladson stood five foot three in his socks. He had a high, slightly shrill voice, and handwriting so large that he rarely got more than a dozen words on a sheet of writing paper. His friends called Sir Pountney a character. His enemies, who were more numerous, used words of which "mountebank" was the kindest. His activities were multifarious, and they only began with his work as a Member of Parliament for West Dorset. He was not seen often in the constituency, but when he did appear the occasion was always newsworthy. There was the time when his Lamborghini had joined the Fords and Jaguars of local farmers in blocking a main road as a protest against a reduction in farm subsidies, the day when he had given away a hundred fivers to a hundred inhabitants of a village, telling each of them to put the money on Pountney Special, which couldn't lose the Wokingham Stakes. The horse had duly won, and Sir Pountney's name went into village legend.

Sir Pountney was—what else was he? The list of his directorships filled half a column in *Who's Who*, he was the president of the Union Jack League, chairman of the Motorists' Society and of the group that called itself Britain's Heritage. In the

House he made few speeches, but asked a great many of the kind of questions that make news. "Is my right honorable friend aware that his rigidly sectarian policies in relation to education have made him the most execrated man in public life in this country?" was the kind of thing. Sir Pountney was much against the creeping Communist menace, and opposed also to long-haired students and to spineless intellectuals who brought the sewer waste of the Continent to England's green and pleasant land. He was in favor of fast cars and Rugby football and fox hunting, as representative of the British way of life. "There's not much wrong with a man who drives fast, tackles clean and doesn't flinch at a five-foot hedge," he said once.

At 4 A.M. on the seventh of January, Sir Pountney was found dead in Hamborne Mews in Mayfair, a hundred yards from the Over and Under Club, where he had ended the evening. He was at the steering wheel of his Lamborghini and he had been killed by a blow on the gullet, succeeded by one on the back of the neck.

The death of Charles Mole had been worth no more than a paragraph in the national press. Sir Pountney Gladson, in death as in life, made headlines. It was natural that crime reporters should notice that the murder method was identical, that they should connect the two cases and that they should ask questions of Roger Devenish. The superintendent, who did not regard himself as vain but still got a warm feeling in the pit of his stomach when he saw his name in the papers, was friendly but noncommittal. His most persistent questioner was Phillips of the *Globe*.

"Can you confirm that just the same karate chop was used in both cases?"

"Karate is your word, not mine. Both men were killed with blows on the neck; that's right."

"Do you know of any link between Mole and Sir Pountney?"

"Obviously we're working on the assumption that there is a connection between the two cases."

"But so far you haven't discovered it?"

"I said we're making that assumption."

"It might be, though, that the two murders are completely unconnected? It might be some madman going around practicing karate?"

"I don't think I'll comment on that suggestion."

"Leaving the first case aside, do you have any leads to Gladson's killing?"

Devenish smiled. "I have a dozen."

A reporter from the *Enquirer,* a sensational tabloid, leaned forward. "Has it struck you, Superintendent, that there was just a week between these murders? So that if it were a sequence, we might expect the next one on the night of the fourteenth or the early morning of the fifteenth?"

"I had noticed the length of time between the two cases."

"You don't think it's of any significance, that there will be another—"

"I don't go in for that sort of speculation," Devenish said sharply. "And now if you'll excuse me."

"If it were strangulation, I know who I'd put my money on," the *Enquirer* man said afterward to the man from the *Mirror.* "Thumbs himself." Devenish's thumbs were indeed gigantic, quite out of proportion to his well-shaped hands, and they had earned him the nickname, which he did not much like. The *Mirror* man responded with a jibe about the size of Devenish's thumbprint. They agreed that he obviously had no real lead.

They were right, in the sense that the inquiries had turned up no connection of any kind between Mole and Gladson. On the other hand, there were a good many people who had reason to dislike Sir Pountney. One was the actress with whom he had spent the evening before his death, Sarah Peters. Brewster had talked to her in her Paddington flat. The sergeant was a painstaking, methodical man, an opponent of the permissive society.

"Just let me go over it again, miss. Sir Pountney called for you here at about seven o'clock, you had a drink here, and then he took you out to dinner at Veglio's restaurant, Dean Street. Have I got that right: V-e-g-l-i-o? Good. Then you met two friends of his, Mr. Lancelot George and Mr. Wilmer Traven, and you all went to the Over and Under Club. Mr. George and Mr. Traven were American, and you say they were keen to see what this club was like because they were interested in getting into gambling over here?"

Sarah Peters was tall and dark. "Right. They were all joking about it. Pow owned part of the Over and Under; I don't know how much."

"And these two gentlemen weren't too impressed?"

"They liked the club but they kept saying it didn't give enough scope, they'd need half a dozen like it."

"Then they left at about 2 A.M. and after that you quarreled with Sir Pountney."

"For God's sake, I've told you all this."

Brewster's face was square and red. The eyes, large, brown and reproachful, might have belonged to somebody else, even some other species, perhaps an ox. "I didn't quite understand why it was you quarreled, Miss Peters."

"Pow was in a filthy temper when they'd gone. He wanted to leave at once and go back to my place. I was on a winning streak at baccarat and I said no. Do you know, from that moment I began to lose." She looked at her nails, then up again. "At the Over and Under I played with Pow's money. It was understood that if I won I kept it, as long as it wasn't too much. If I lost I gave an IOU, but I never paid them. Once a month Pow would tear them up."

"Very generous."

She looked at him sharply, continued. "But that night he said I was on my own. I asked what he meant, and he said I could pay my own losses. I was more than fifty pounds down then, and five minutes later it was a hundred. I stopped playing and told Pow what I thought of him."

The sergeant looked at his notes. "Ferguson, the manager,

said you told Sir Pountney you had friends who would look him up. Did you say that?"

"I might have."

"What did it mean? Who are the friends?"

Her gaze slid away. "Just words. I was angry because he was so bloody mean. Then I cleared out and left him to it, and went home."

"That was just before 3 A.M. After you got home, what did you do? Ring up your friends?"

"Of course I bloody didn't."

Inquiries showed that some of Sarah Peters's acquaintances might have been ready to look anybody up. She knew Jack and Harry Claber, two brothers who ran the best-organized of South London's gangs, and when she was not working she sometimes went to race tracks with them. Harry Claber was said to have been sleeping with her, but it was a long step from that to ordering the death of a man as well known as Gladson. Devenish did not think that Claber would have done it. And in any case, why would Claber have wanted Charles Mole killed?

A lot of other people disliked or detested Sir Pountney Gladson. He was on the extermination list compiled by a group who called themselves the Black Beastlies, a man named Reed had threatened him after losing a court case in which he claimed to have been cheated in relation to an agreement for the commercial development of a disused Cornish tin mine, there was another recent case in which Gladson had driven his Lamborghini up onto a pavement, injuring an old woman. All of these were investigated. The Black Beastlies expressed pleasure at the extermination of this particular rat, but denied any connection with it. Reed was living down in Cornwall and had a convincing alibi, and the victim in the car case could not say too much in praise of Sir Pountney. Devenish saw her himself. She was the wife of an old-age pensioner named Page, and they lived in a couple of rooms in North London off the Marylebone Road.

"A real gent," Mr. Page said. "One of the old school. Out of his car in a flash, he was, 'ad the wife in 'is arms, got 'is suit all bloody. There was a lot of blood."

Mrs. Page took up the theme. "And traveled with me in the ambulance to the hospital. Sent flowers. Oh, yes, a real gentleman, Sir Pountney." She indicated her leg, which was in a cast. "Of course, they say it'll be a long time before I can walk again properly. I mean, you have to expect it at my age."

"What exactly happened?"

"I was at the bus stop, see, and Bert was just a few feet away, when this car came round the corner like *that*, and then it seemed to go out of control like, and the next I knew I was on the ground, with Bert and Sir Pountney bending over me. I recognized him at once, mind you, from seeing his picture."

"What sort of speed was he going at?"

"I don't know, but it was fast. I should say—" A warning glance from husband to wife.

"It was inside the limit," Page said. "I saw it. The thing was, 'e skidded, that's what caused it, a greasy road, couldn't 'elp it."

"That's what you said when the police came? You didn't want to make a charge?" Page muttered something. "What's that?"

"I said we didn't want any trouble. Not with someone like him. I mean, I belong to the Union Jack League myself. There's too many foreigners here already."

"What did he pay you to keep quiet?" When the man started to protest, Devenish said, "You may as well tell me; I'm not saying you did anything you'll be in trouble for."

A glance between the two of them, then he nodded. Mrs. Page said in a hushed, reverential tone, "Two hundred."

The trouble with the working class, Devenish quoted afterward to Brewster, is the poverty of their desires. And their ambitions, he added. If they'd put it into a solicitor's hands, Gladson would have been pleased to pay a thousand to avoid a charge of dangerous driving when he'd knocked somebody down. Brewster, who thought the workers were too uppity anyway, and also that Gladson had had some good ideas, did not comment.

In any case, it was clear that Page was not in the running as an executioner. And there was no other obviously suitable candidate.

3

ENTER
MR. SHERLOCK HOLMES

Sherlock Holmes closed the door of the living room, walked along the passage, opened the door of his Baker Street rooms and walked down the stairs to the world outside. On the way he paused, as he often did, to look at the mementos of the past that lined the walls. Here, preserved under glass, were the crumpled piece of paper, the key, the metal disks and the peg of wood that were reminders of almost his first case, that of the Musgrave Ritual. There was a letter of thanks from James Ryder, whose felony he had forgiven in the affair of the Blue Carbuncle, the small sealing wax knife used in the matter of the Golden Pince-Nez, and—upon the whole most pleasing of all—relics also of half a dozen cases unrecorded by Watson. Among them were the envelope involved in the Tropoff affair, which if it had been opened at the time of its receipt would have meant death. The seal was still intact, although of course the poison that impregnated the envelope had long since lost its venom. Here was a fragment of the curiously flexible crutch that had played a part in the unveiling of the Austrian Monster, a newspaper picture of Vigor the Hammersmith Wonder, a photograph of Baron Maupertuis, inscribed: "To Mr. Sherlock

Holmes, who brought about my ruin. With undying hatred. Maupertuis." The great detective contemplated this last with something between a smile and a frown. It was satisfying to possess a unique relic, regrettable that the story relating to it would never be told.

As he descended the stairs he reflected how attractive and tellingly descriptive was the word "rooms" in relation to his lodgings. "I left my Baker Street rooms"—splendidly appropriate. Why did wretched house agents insist upon using not the word "rooms," nor "apartment," nor even "flat," but the atrocious "maisonette"? "I left my Baker Street maisonette"—abominable!

Within the rooms, double glazing restricted the traffic noise to a continuous but not unpleasant hum. Now, however, a blast of sound from Baker Street met him as he opened the door. He stood in the street for a minute, taking it all in, hating it. The cars were bad enough, sleek, vulgar vehicles filled with vulgar people, heavy-jowled men reminiscent of that worst of blackmailers, Charles Augustus Milverton, or hard-faced women with hair of brass, all of them maneuvering for advantage. But worse, because noisier, were the shiny red buses, cattle trucks going from nowhere to nowhere, and worst of all the great thundering lorries with their cargoes of mechanical rubbish, much of it blessedly unknown in Holmes's day. He stood there as he did every morning, soaking it all up, and the grim reality of modern Baker Street had its usual effect. The image of Sherlock Holmes faded, and he became again Sheridan Haynes.

The day was frosty but fine, and he decided to walk to the rehearsal rooms in St. John's Wood. Such a walk was almost always a pleasure. It was common for him to be stopped by somebody who recognized him as the actor playing Sherlock Holmes in the TV series. Sometimes they called him Mr. Haynes, sometimes they asked if he was Sherlock Holmes, a suggestion he did not exactly deny. On half a dozen occasions people had told him of troubles and problems in their own lives, and although he had been able to do nothing more than offer advice, experiences like these warmed his heart.

But first, as he turned the corner to get out of Baker Street, he was greeted by a man wearing a blue jacket and serge trousers. On the jacket was a yellow patch that said "Traffic Warden" and gave a number. A peaked yellow-and-blue cap completed an outfit familiar to all Londoners. The man's name was Cassidy. He had a long horseface that accorded well with what seemed a miserable disposition. Traffic wardens were often regarded as snoopers because part of their job was giving parking tickets to motorists, but most of them seemed happy in their work.

"Morning, Mr. Haynes. And a cold one."

"Good morning, Cassidy. *That* doesn't seem to get any less." He jerked a thumb behind him at Baker Street. "I wonder we have any hearing left. Filthy things, belching out poison."

"Nothing wrong with cars, just too many of them, that's all," Cassidy said gravely, as though enunciating a profound truth.

"If I had my way I'd have special roads made. All these things could go along them, but they'd never be allowed to move off. Don't ask me how we'd manage; we managed very well without cars in the past." He smiled. "Back in my day."

"Things were different back in Sherlock Holmes's day, right enough."

"And better, Cassidy."

"I daresay you're right. Are you off to rehearsal, sir?"

"I am. First day."

"I'll wish you luck, then. Not that you'll need it, no fear of that." The warden had been glancing at meters as they strolled along, and now he stopped beside one, wrote out a ticket, put it under the windshield wiper. "Twenty minutes over. People complain, but we're only carrying out the law."

"Exactly. If they don't want to be fined, let them park their cars for the right time. Or get rid of them." He walked on. Cassidy raised a hand to his cap in what could almost have been interpreted as a salute.

The rehearsal rooms had formerly been a Christian mission. On the ground floor a blackboard said, "Sherlock Holmes, The Naval Treaty," with an arrow pointing upward. In the room upstairs, the studio area was marked out with tapes on the floor, and a group of actors huddled around a table with the producer of the series, an energetic little Pole named Willie Lowinsky, and Richard Spain, who was directing this episode. Willie flung his arms wide in greeting.

"Sherlock is here; now we can solve the problem." He came close to Sheridan Haynes, whispered, "The puzzle is, what has happened to the central heating? We are all freezing." He rolled the *r* emphatically. At that moment a young man with a small face lost in a forest of hair put his head around the door and said in a hoarse voice, "Okay now. It was an air bubble. We've bled the rads."

"Ron, you are an angel." Willie blew a kiss to the face, which vanished, and beamed around the table. "Now that you are all warmer, or you will be in a minute, let's get on. If you'll sit here, Sher, we'll read it through. Ready, Basil? Go ahead."

" 'Listen to this, Holmes,' " Basil Wainwright said. He began to read the letter from Percy Phelps. " 'My dear Watson, I have no doubt that you can remember "Tadpole" Phelps, who was in the fifth form when you were in the third. . . .' "

Sheridan Haynes read the script almost automatically, but as it continued he found that he could not help being annoyed by Basil. In appearance Basil Wainwright was a perfect Watson, with a square, honest face framed by muttonchop whiskers, a splendidly bewildered look when Holmes made a surprising deduction, and a general air of dogged stupidity that was just right. When he was Basil Wainwright rather than John H. Watson, however, he camped about outrageously. Sheridan Haynes had met a lot of queer actors in his time, and told himself that he didn't mind them, but during this read-through Basil seemed to go out of his way to try to make the story sound ridiculous.

He was annoyed also by the introduction of Irene Adler. When the series began, the idea had been that they should stick to the themes and characters of the original stories as closely as possible. Through three series of thirteen episodes that plan had been adhered to. When the fourth set of thirteen was planned, however, it was decided that the formula must be varied to provide Holmes with an opponent, who should appear in several stories. Moriarty had been considered, but Irene Adler was preferred. She was played competently enough by Sarah Peters, but her presence in stories where she had no place set Sher's nerves jangling. Irene had been turned into an international spy, who in this story was the agent to whom Joseph Harrison hoped to sell the secret of the naval treaty. At the end of the reading, when Willie asked for comments, Sher could not refrain from saying something.

"I hope Basil won't go on talking like that when we rehearse."

The Watsonic look of bewilderment appeared. "But, Sher love, it was only a read-through. You didn't expect me to *act.*"

"If we all camped about, there'd be no point in reading through at all."

"Well, Sher, *you'd* never camp it up. We all know that."

Willie intervened. "Remember you're a straight man, Basil. Anything else?"

"I'm still worried about Sarah. That scene where I try to kiss her and then Basil comes in—it's right out of character. In fact, her whole presence is wrong."

"Thanks very much," Sarah said.

Willie waved an arm. "We'll talk about it. Any queries, Richard? No? Right, then. Break for lunch. All back at two o'clock, please."

Most of them went to the local pub for lunch. Willie steered Sher and Sarah to the table he had booked. The men drank pints of beer, Sarah a Bloody Mary. Over nondescript food,

Willie deployed his smoothing-over technique.

"Darlings, I love you both. I hope you aren't going to cause any fuss and bother for Richard."

"Am I causing it?" Sarah pushed away her plate and lighted a cigarette.

"Sher, I have to tell you. It's very naughty of you to say things like that in public. Very naughty indeed."

"I'm sorry," Sher said, and meant it. "Sarah, I apologize. I let Basil get under my skin, and I shouldn't have done so. But, Willie, I've told you before how it does outrage my sense of what's right for a Sherlock Holmes series to have a master spy appearing in half of them. We made a success by sticking to the originals, and now—"

"Sher, I'm not going to let you go on." Willie's smile was still there but his voice was brisk. "One, viewing figures were falling at the end of the last series. That's a fact, and you can't get round it. And two, all this was settled at the planning conference."

Sher was silent. It had been put to him by the director of programs almost in the form of an ultimatum, although such a word had of course not been used. Phrases had been used like "the old formula getting a little worn," "marvelous show but it needs new blood," "Sherlock's superlative but Sherlock alone can't carry an hour on the box." He had argued against this but in the end he had accepted it.

Willie said softly, "Let's remember something else, too. You aren't Sherlock Holmes."

"Don't be ridiculous."

"It isn't so ridiculous. I've been in from the beginning, remember, I wanted you, I said you were the one who could do it. It was a plus that you knew all about Holmes and the stories. But don't push it too far, don't start kidding yourself."

From the bar came Basil's high-pitched laughter, the clank of glasses, the persistent yapping of the manageress's toy poodle, a rumble of altercation from a group playing darts. Everything was too noisy; it was impossible to think. And outside in the busy street, permeating the pub noise, was the whine of cars. He became aware that Sarah had spoken.

"What was that?"

"I said I wish you were Sherlock. Then you might be able to solve these Karate Killings and stop the bloody police from pestering me. They seem to think that just because I've let Harry Claber take me around, I asked him to have old Pow knocked off. I don't do that, not even when people say my presence is wrong."

"I said I was sorry."

"Okay, I don't hold it against you. It would be nice if you cleared up the murders, but being questioned wasn't so bad. The sergeant was just a clot, but the chief or super or whatever he's called was quite civilized. And a knockout to look at; one of the dishiest men I've seen for a long time. Present company excepted, of course." She ducked her head. Willie smiled and looked more than usually like a pixie. There came into Sher's mind what Conan Doyle said about Irene Adler: "To Sherlock Holmes she is always *the* woman." Well, he reflected, Sheridan Haynes certainly couldn't say that about Sarah Peters. Beautiful in her way, but for him not half as attractive as Val. "You're supposed to go in for Sherlock Holmes deductions, though. All right, then, deduce."

"That's a parlor game," he said, although that was not quite how he regarded it. "If I *were* Sherlock I might go round examining the hands of all the suspects and see which of them looked as if they could kill somebody with a karate chop, but I'm just myself. And don't worry, I'll be good from now on."

"Me, too." Her lips brushed his cheek.

Willie stayed for an hour of rehearsal, then slipped away. After the first day he left things to the director, reappearing at the rehearsal rooms only once, when they had been at work for a week. Then he would come to the last couple of days, when they were in the studio.

That afternoon everything went smoothly for Richard Spain. Basil was suitably solid, gruff and bone-headed, Sheridan Haynes forgot some lines as usual but was finely Sherlockian, Sarah played her part with verve. By the end of the day another Sherlock Holmes episode was promisingly under way.

THE GREAT MAN AT HOME

4

"He's here. In the showcase." He heard Val say this outside, and then she put her head around the door. When the company had created the rooms in the image of those occupied by Holmes and Watson, there were certain diversions from the canon on which both he and Val had insisted. They had replaced the spare bedroom occupied by Watson with a study that Sher used for learning parts, and Val had flatly refused to have the mock-Victorian kitchen the company wanted, complete with electric cooker made to look like an old kitchen range. In the end they had settled for recreating the living room, making a bow window to conform with the original and reproducing the room that had been made for the Sherlock Holmes exhibit at the Festival of Britain, although they had to use smokeless fuel on the fire because of the clean-air restrictions, and the room inevitably contained personal things of their own. Even so, Val often referred to it as a showcase.

"I'm going out to shop. You'll be better off on your own."

It was true that he did occasionally feel uneasy when talking to an interviewer in Val's presence. She had a disconcerting air of knowing exactly what he was about to say.

"What's he like?"

She wrinkled her nose. "The usual."

Val was right, as he saw at first glimpse of the young man, who wore a shirt with fashionably long collar points, and casual clothes that still managed to look elegant. Adrian (or perhaps it would be Francis or Christopher) would be polite, even deferential, and would listen attentively, but then he would go away and write a piece that showed he'd been laughing at you all the time. This particular interview had been arranged by the company's press officer, and was guaranteed to be something different. It would be, the press officer had said on the telephone, a treatment in depth of the whole Sherlock Holmes phenomenon.

So Adrian, this general Adrian, sipped a glass of sherry, and sat in a wing chair, and looked appreciatively at the Sherlockiana—the slightly bent poker and the items under glass, cigar ends, orange pips carefully mounted in a case, and the rest.

"I know the poker, from 'The Speckled Band.' I see you didn't bend it quite straight, in spite of what Watson said. And the five orange pips—I recognize them, of course. But what's this pamphlet, 'Obscure Nervous Lesions,' by P. H. Trevelyan, B.Sc.?"

"It comes from 'The Resident Patient.' "

The young man clicked his fingers in annoyance. "So it does. And the cigar ends, no doubt. I've read it, you see, I just wasn't quite quick enough. And that's as good a point as any for me to start asking questions." He produced a reporter's notebook. "I suppose I might as well go in at the deep end." He smiled the engaging Adrian smile. "How much do you identify yourself with Sherlock Holmes?"

"Sherlock Holmes was a character in fiction. I'm pleased to be playing him, and I admire him, but that's all."

"That's the orthodox answer, I know. But surely there's a bit more to it. I mean, there's the names. The same initials. And you'd expect Sheridan to be called Sherry for short, but you're Sher. How did that happen?"

"I told you I admire Sherlock Holmes."

"But when you took the name of Sheridan—"

"I didn't take it. My name is Richard Sheridan Haynes. Richard Haynes sounded dull, so I used my second name. I've been called Sher for years, long before the series began."

"Somewhere in our files it says you read the Holmes stories first when you were ten or eleven years old, but when did you first start collecting?"

"If you just mean books, first editions and so on, when I was about fifteen. If you mean these souvenirs, some of them came from the special Sherlock Holmes exhibition in 1951. One or two are studio props from our own shows, like the orange pips. Others I've had specially made."

Adrian wrote in his notebook, using the flying characters of genuine shorthand, not the usual abbreviations of reporters.

"Sherlock Holmes must have made a lot of difference to your life." The young man tossed back an unruly strand of hair. "I mean, you were always a well-known actor, but since the series started you've become positively identified with one of our national heroes. And then you've moved from—Weybridge, isn't it?—to this flat in Baker Street, so that in the eyes of lots of people you *are* Sherlock Holmes."

"I don't think it's surprising that an admirer of Sherlock Holmes should want to live in Baker Street."

Adrian smiled. "I think it's wonderful. Now, I'm sure you'd agree that the success of the series, as half a dozen TV critics have said, isn't only because you're the perfect Sherlock. It's also because the productions have been so faithful to the stories. How much was that your idea?"

He had been asked the question before, although in a different form, and now he fielded it easily, with a smile that belonged to Sheridan Haynes and not to Sherlock Holmes. "I can claim a bit of credit, perhaps. I've always believed that it's a mistake to try to improve on the Holmes stories by adding extra bits. Here are these wonderful characters, Holmes and Watson, fixed in a wonderful period when life was slower and quieter, and the combustion engine wasn't threatening to defile everything agreeable in our lives. To an old-fashioned man like me it was a better world, but the point is that it's complete and perfect. Why spoil it by introducing modern psychology and that sort of thing, when they just don't belong in the stories? So I might claim a little credit, say ten percent. But the other ninety goes to Willie Lowinsky, our producer. I'd worked with Willie before, on the stage and the box, and when he told me that what he had in mind was Sherlock Holmes played absolutely straight, I was delighted. So it was Willie's idea, and Willie who sold it to the powers that be—which was the great achievement."

The young man said, not exactly asking a question, "I've been told that the pilot script was done as a send-up. I expect you've heard that yourself."

Of course he had, but he was not going to admit it. "What an extraordinary idea. But it isn't for me to comment. You should ask Willie about it. I know what he'd say."

"Feeling as you do about the original, what's your attitude to the new series? They're not sticking faithfully to Sherlock, are they? I mean, you've got Irene Adler in several stories. That's not according to Doyle."

"Again, I don't think it's for me to comment. You should talk to Willie Lowinsky."

Adrian nodded, looked at his notes. "You've been asked this kind of thing before, I know, but it does seem that you've developed something like Holmes's powers of observation. I wonder if you can tell me anything about myself?"

Now he was pleased by Val's absence, because he knew that she would have been watching his response to this question. As it was, he savored the reply. "Apart from the fact that you dressed in a hurry this morning, and that you probably didn't sleep at home, nothing. Oh, yes, one thing. Your accent tells me that you went to a good public school, but I doubt if it was followed by a university."

"Remarkable," Adrian cried.

Sher smiled. "Elementary, as the master said. Your socks are a pair, but one is inside out, something that I can't imagine a man as careful of his dress as you obviously are doing unless he was in a hurry. And you're wearing orange cuff links that jar with your elegant blue shirt. It's possible that they're your taste, but possible also that you slept away from home, took a clean shirt with you but forgot to take another set of links."

"Absolutely right. And about the university, too. But how—"

"You write genuine shorthand, which you must have been taught. It isn't likely that you would have taken a shorthand course after three or four years at a university."

"Thank you for the demonstration. Just one or two more questions. You say that the Holmes world was better. Would you like to get back to it?"

He gave Adrian the Sheridan Haynes smile, wistful and a little sad, that had melted a thousand hearts on tour, although it had not gone down so well in London. "You're talking about the impossible. But when I look round at all the noise and clutter, at our secondhand pleasures and our dependence on machines—yes, I'd like to be back with Sherlock in those London fogs. Everything now is mechanical, even police work. Sherlock Holmes solved cases by his own logical powers. Nowadays, I'm told, the police feed their information into the computer and it comes up with the answer."

"Not always."

"What's that?"

"They haven't come up with an answer in the Karate Killings, have they? Do you think Sherlock's logic might do better?"

Sheridan Haynes leaned back and put his fingertips together. "In any case there must be clues, clues left by an individual that are capable of interpretation by another individual, rather than a machine." He looked directly at Adrian, an incisive Sherlock look. "If Sherlock Holmes were here today, and allowed to apply his method of inductive logic to the Karate case, I have no doubt that he would solve it."

SOMETHING ABOUT KARATE

Investigation of the people connected with the Karate Killings continued, but with little result. Mrs. Mole and Mantleman appeared to have no connection at all with Pountney Gladson. Very well, Devenish said, they would check out again all the people known to have a reason for wishing Gladson out of the way. It turned out that George and Traven, the two Americans Gladson had talked to in the Over and Under, were associated with a front organization for the Mafia. They were indignant at being mixed up in a murder case, and convinced Devenish that they had no reason to kill Gladson. They longed to return to their native land and he let them go. He talked to Sarah Peters, but although she did not impress him as somebody naturally truthful, he could not believe that the events would have been a sufficient reason for wanting Gladson dead. Still, he was interested in anyone connected with Harry Claber. Devenish went down to see the Claber brothers at the youth club they ran just off Streatham High Road.

When he arrived, Harry, who had been a middling good professional welterweight, was in the ring with a gawky youth half a head taller than himself. He easily avoided the punches telegraphed at him, and offered advice as he ducked and wove.

"Left—left—use it *quicker*, Dave. A bleeding nursemaid wheeling a pram could get out of the way, you're so slow. Now, one-two, get your right over, what's happened—paralyzed, is it? Christ, no, don't drop your guard like that or you—see—what—will—happen." He beat a tattoo on the boy's face, then peppered his ribs when he raised the guard. "Okay, Dave. You'll have to sharpen up if you're coming anything but second next week. Off you go now.

"How about it, Thumbs—you want to try a round, just one, just to show me? That's if we can find a pair of gloves big enough."

Devenish shook his head, smiling. Harry Claber jumped lightly from the ring and went to the dressing rooms. Five minutes later he was buying Devenish tea at the bar. "Can't offer you a beer—strict TT." He waved a hand at the table tennis and billiards tables. "Just look at 'em enjoying themselves; keeps 'em off the streets and out of the pubs. You got anything against it?"

"Nothing at all, Harry."

"But still you're hard on me; I don't understand it." Harry Claber had a broad, flat face, with just the end of his nose askew, the only evidence that he had been a professional boxer. The effect was to give him a slightly comical look, an effect enhanced by the jokey way he often talked, and the smile that seemed fixed permanently on his mouth. All this was deceptive. Harry would have thought no more of ordering a man to be cut than he would of calling a taxi.

"Where's Jack?" Devenish asked. Harry was the clever brother, Jack was not so bright. Some said he was downright simple.

"Over there playing snooker." Harry was drinking milk. It left a rim of white around his upper lip, which he licked off. "No use pretending you've come to see the club, is it? What's up?"

"You're good with your fists, Harry. How are you with the

chopper?" Devenish made a chopping movement. Harry stared, then laughed.

"Do me a favor, will you? I've never been in a karate club in my life."

"You did your national service."

"Where one of the things they did *not* teach us was how to dispose of an enemy at a blow. I mean, what would have happened to the officers? All this because I took that girl around hither and yon—the actress. *I* don't know, you've just got it in for us." He raised his voice. "Hey, Jack. Here's Thumbs Devenish come to pay us a visit."

Jack Claber racked his cue and came over. He was a bigger version of his brother, but his face was not illuminated by the intelligence that sparkled in Harry's eye. His look at the chief superintendent was hostile. "What's he here for, then? If he wants to see us, why don't he come to the garage?"

The Clabers owned a couple of garages in Streatham and Brixton, which, like the club, were run perfectly straight.

"It's okay, Jack, everything under control." Harry was smiling.

"What's he want to poke his nose in here for? This is our place where we help the community, ain't that right, Harry?"

"Right. Were you going to say something sarcastic, Devenish? Sarcasm is the lowest form of wit is what they taught me at school, but then of course I never had the benefit of your education."

"I'm just a grammar school boy myself. And something else. I've got a handle to my name."

"I thought we were friends," Harry said, smiling. "Sorry, Chief Superintendent."

"Mr. Devenish will do. All I want to know is, what was your connection with Gladson, and why did he get done?"

Jack stared with his mouth slightly open. Harry said, "Look, we're British."

"I've noticed. With regret."

"Sarcasm, see; I knew you couldn't resist it. Thing is, old Pow may have been a bit of a bastard, but he stood up for Britain. He wanted to send the nig-nogs and the Pakis back where they belong, in the jungle. That Union Jack club and all that—he had the right ideas. We contributed to the club, Jack and me; it was no secret. Pow appreciated that. And he used to give me a tip or two when we went racing. Not that many of them came up."

"Did he like it when he saw you going around with his girl?"

"Sarah, you mean? Don't be bleeding stupid; she's nobody's girl. She's had more men than you've had hot dinners."

"Supposing I told you I knew she'd rung you that night."

Jack made a growling noise. Harry answered, with undiminished good humor, "You'd wouldn't try to plant that on us, Mr. Devenish. If you want to know who killed Pow, ask the nignogs, those Beastlies. Not that I've got anything against 'em, mind you, only you can't trust 'em. Jack here had a black girl friend who was supposed to be a virgin, and what happened? He caught a dose."

"Okay now, free sparring," Riverboat Jackson said. The thirty young men and half a dozen women advanced toward each other, making chopping gestures and every so often kicking up their right legs in a balletic manner. There was a minimum of bodily contact, although the flying kicks delivered barefoot landed occasionally on thigh or backside.

Half of them were blacks, and Riverboat was black, too, a big Negro who was said to have got his name from working a gambling boat on the Mississippi, though for all Devenish knew that might have been a romantic invention. The place was called the Anglo-American Fitness and Athletic Club. It was used a good deal by blacks, and Riverboat occasionally dropped a bit of information about black militants.

He was calling out words of encouragement and criticism. "Number fourteen there, don't twist your body, you'll lose balance. Balance, balance, remember what I said, I didn't give you a technique for falling over, but that's what half of you have got. Number twenty-six there, good, that's good, got a bit of style. Remember what I said about blocking, as well as the punching techniques. *Uke-waza* now, *uke-waza,* you defend as well as attack." He winked at Devenish, murmured, "A bunch of rubbish," then clapped his hands. The free sparring stopped. "That's it, boys and girls. Remember now, technique's the word, you got to have it. For the strike, *uchi-waza.* For the kick, *keri-waza.* The punch, *tsuki-waza.* The block, *uke-waza.* Remember." He demonstrated, and Devenish admired the grace with which he performed punch and kick. Riverboat raised a hand and the group left him for the changing rooms. He shrugged. "Rubbish, but it's money, you can't deny it."

Devenish was looking around. They were in a hall near Euston, a former Methodist chapel turned over to physical instead of mental health. Another part of the hall, separated by ropes from the rest, was used as a gymnasium. A vaulting horse stood in one corner and parallel bars in another; ropes looped from the ceiling; there was a boxing ring. Riverboat followed his gaze.

"Tonight's karate class, but I teach everything. Judo, kwang-fu, the noble art of self-defense. Riverboat's an expert in them all. Just wait while I change." Like the class he was barefoot, and wearing loose white jacket and trousers. "It's karate that interests you?"

"Right."

"Thought it might be. You can buy me a beer."

In the saloon bar of the Three Chairmen up the road, Riverboat drank two pints of beer quickly, and shook his head to suggestions that the Beastlies might have used karate as a killing method.

"What would they be doing that for? Some of those boys got guns, all of 'em got knives. What'd be the point?"

"Fooling policemen like me."

"Man, you're too subtle." He showed his splendid teeth, laughing. "Subtle those kids ain't."

"Say one of them had karate training in the army, became an expert; how about that?"

"Mr. Devenish, you don't know much about karate." Devenish agreed. "You know what 'karate-ka' means? It means karate player. It's a sport, you understand."

"Oh, come on now. You mean those boys in there were learning it as a sport, like cricket or tennis?"

"Not cricket or tennis, but I'm telling you they're not going out to kill anybody. Self-defense, yes, it's useful. Attack, not so much. In the army they don't teach karate, just unarmed combat. Turn around. I'll show you." Devenish unwisely turned and found an arm immediately encircling his neck, so that he was gasping for breath. The barman put down a glass he was drying and came up. Devenish waved him away, dug in thumbs below the arm, levered his hand in, broke the grip and moved away. Riverboat's grin split his face.

"See? Unarmed combat. Garroting, like the Indian thugs. Karate, no."

"Are you telling me there's no such thing as a karate chop?"

"Yes, there's a karate chop, all right. But you know anyone who's ever used it to kill? I don't, not me, not old Riverboat. I tell you what I reckon. You want to kill somebody with karate, you use a straight punch on his throat first. Like this—thrust, then twist." The meaty fist came within an inch of Devenish's throat. "Throat or jaw, those are the points. I hit you like that, believe me you're helpless. Not for minutes, but for seconds, you're helpless. Then I push down the head." The chief superintendent allowed his head to be lowered. "And then the chop. Maybe once, maybe twice, maybe we have to chop three times." A hand hard as a board just touched his neck. He straightened up. "And for this chop you need practice. Don't you try it, Mr. Devenish. All you'll say is, Oh, ah, that hurts."

Riverboat shook his hand in mock agony, drained his glass. "You have one with me?"

"No, thanks. I must go. You're not saying it's impossible, only that he'd have to be skillful."

"Right. Something else. Trying to kill with a karate chop—a professional wouldn't do it. You punch just a little bit wrong first, you hurt him but not enough. To escape from somebody, yes, the punch is fine. For an attack, no. Too difficult, not sure enough. I'm not saying it can't be done, you understand, only that a pro wouldn't try it. What you're looking for, Mr. Devenish, is an amateur."

THE HAYNES FAMILY IN THE MORNING

6

Sheridan Haynes, his long form wrapped in a dressing gown, sat drinking hot black coffee, eating slightly burnt toast, reading the *Times*. Val, wearing a twin set, was doing the same thing while reading the *Daily Telegraph*. They were both papers that had been there in the past, when Holmes smoked his before-breakfast pipe while studying the agony column.

A continuous hooting outside seeped through their consciousness. He went to the window. Two cars had collided. A green Ford Capri, coming from a side street, was locked with a Jaguar that had been going along Baker Street. The fenders of both cars were crumpled, rather as though they were bulls locking horns. The owners of the cars had jumped out of them and were moving militantly toward each other. Seen from above they looked like puppets. Another puppet, Cassidy the traffic warden, ran to separate them as they seemed about to give battle. The hooting, presumably from one of the cars' horns that had got stuck, stayed in Sher's ears as he moved away from the window.

Val spoke without looking up from her paper. "If you don't like the heat you should get out of the kitchen."

"I don't know what you mean."

"I think you do." She took a cigarette, lighted it carefully, puffed. He knew that it must be ten o'clock, which was when she had her first cigarette of the day. Val was a woman who lived by her habits, the first cigarette around ten o'clock and never more than fifteen a day, the first drink after midday and never more than two before lunch or dinner. Many women looked untidy at breakfast, but Val would have been ready to receive royalty. She had been as composed and practical when shows he was in folded as she was when they got the news that the Sherlock Holmes contract was going to bring in more money in a single year than they had seen before in five.

"If you don't like the noise, why come and live here? What was wrong with Weybridge?"

Outside, miraculously, the horn stopped. He went to the window again. A toy policeman was on the scene, talking to the militants. Cassidy had vanished. The collision had caused a holdup. The cars looked like beetles, filthy little dung beetles, as they nosed their way inch by inch toward—toward nothing, that was the truth. Dung beetles at least had an objective but the purpose of these creatures was simply movement, the result a smearing of their excrement over everything civilized. The whole of Baker Street was filled with these objects; they were crawling all over the world. He could feel them on his skin.

"Nothing was wrong with Weybridge." He moved back again, sat down. "But you know how pleased the company were when we agreed to make the break."

"Don't give me that." She tapped ash carefully into an ashtray. Val was a great ash tapper. "You know very well you were mad keen to do it, once Willie made the suggestion. Weybridge suited me perfectly. Near enough to London to get up in half an hour for a play or a film, a nice easy suburban social life. I'm a suburban woman, as you've said."

"I didn't say that."

"Oh, yes, you did," she said implacably, and he knew that if he argued she would be able to tell him the date and the time at which the words had been spoken. "And you were right. Coffee mornings and that antique shop; it suited me very well. I like it here, I can even take the Sherlock stuff, I'm adaptable. I don't want you complaining, that's all, or thinking that Sherlock will last forever. It won't."

"Val. Darling."

She submitted to his embrace rather than returning it. "I've got to go to a sale in Croydon." She had bought a small antique shop of her own in Greenwich, which she ran with an assistant, and it was flourishing. She had a nose for the kind of sale at which the Victorian bric-a-brac she specialized in might be going at reasonable prices. As she was opening the door she added, "Besides, Sherlock Holmes had no time for women; you've told me that often enough."

Left alone in the apartment, he settled down to learn his lines, something he had found increasingly difficult in recent months. The post came through the door, later than usual. There were three letters for him, and a magazine. One letter was from their son, Charles, who had taken a job on an Australian sheep farm after a year at an agricultural college. The gist of his six pages was that he was well and the sheep were even better. Another letter asked Sher to open a new store in Highgate. The third began, "Dear Mr. Sherlock Holmes, I hope that you can help me. . . ." It went on to say that the writer's husband had disappeared, and that it was difficult to tell him all the circumstances in a letter, so that she would be grateful for a personal interview. There was no indication whether the woman thought that she was writing to Sheridan Haynes playing Sherlock Holmes or to the detective himself. He received one or two letters like this every week, almost all of them from women. At first he had answered them, but then one of the women had come and accused him of kidnapping her baby daughter. Since then he had had a card printed, which read: "Mr. Sheridan Haynes thanks you for your letter, but regrets that he cannot deal with any queries in relation to Sherlock Holmes."

He put one of these cards in an envelope, addressed it. Then he rang up his agent, Desmond O'Malley, and arranged that Desmond would fix a fee for the store opening. On Desmond's advice, and with the company's agreement, he refused all offers to appear in advertisements, because it had been decided that they would be bad for his image. This, however, was different.

"That was a lively piece in *NewsTime*," Desmond said. He had taken care never to lose his soft Irish brogue. "Beautiful, Sher boy. You really told 'em."

When Sher had rung off, he opened the magazine. It was *NewsTime* and the story covered nearly three pages. The headline read:

SHERLOCK COULD SOLVE KARATE KILLINGS
SAYS TV'S SHERLOCK HOLMES.

RISE AND SLIGHT FALL
OF A GREAT DETECTIVE

It was not quite true that the pilot script had been done as a send-up of Sherlock Holmes, nor was it altogether false. At the beginning Willie Lowinsky had expounded the idea to the director of programs over lunch at the Connaught.

"We play the stories absolutely and totally straight, you understand me. We recreate this wonderful lost Victorian world and the monsters who inhabited it. Such villains. Such heroes." Willie gave his *r*'s an airing as though he were gargling.

The director nibbled thoughtfully at his whitebait and did not comment. Impassivity had taken him a long way. The assistant director, who wore a green corduroy suit and an enormous red tie, voiced doubts.

"It's bound to be comic. Wouldn't do as a series. Might try a one-shot, play it for the laughs."

"No no no no." Willie spoke with passion. "We must be absolutely serious. If people laugh they laugh, but it will be *with* the Great Detective, not *at* him. I stake my reputation on it." He put a hand on his heart. Willie was a great staker of his reputation.

"Who did you have in mind?"

"Sheridan Haynes."

"Not much of a name," the assistant director said. The director nodded agreement. He had never heard of Sheridan Haynes.

"And not such a great actor," Willie agreed cheerfully. The director took a piece of brown bread and butter, and raised his eyebrows. "A bit of a ham, a bit out of date. But for this he is perfect. He looks wonderful, that tall, ascetic look that is so very English. And he knows Sherlock Holmes, he has read all the stories, he is soaked in the Holmes saga like a baba in rum. What do you think he is called? Sherry would be the natural name for Sheridan, isn't that so? But for him it's Sher, and why? Because it could be a shortening of Sherlock."

"Sherlock Holmes was never called Sher," the assistant director pointed out.

Willie beamed at him. "Precisely. Don't you see that the thing about Sheridan Haynes is that he *must* identify with Sherlock Holmes? Or are you just kidding a poor foreigner?"

They went on talking, and in the end it was agreed that they would try a one-shot of "The Speckled Band," perhaps the most famous of all Sherlock Holmes short stories. Willie insisted that it should all be absolutely straight, with Dr. Grimesby Roylott a terrifying Victorian ogre and Helen Stoner a quivering maiden in distress. The assistant director thought that it would look as uproariously old-fashioned as the Folies-Bergère. They may both have been right. Some critics praised the faithfulness of the production, others ribbed it, but they all agreed that in Sheridan Haynes the studio had found a splendid Sherlock. And the rating figures were high.

So Willie got his series. And before the series was halfway through its thirteen programs, the ratings were astonishing. For three dizzy weeks "Sherlock Holmes" reached the top of the charts, and was removed only by a new soap opera of supreme asininity. During the whole thirteen episodes it never sank lower than fifth. The series was sold in America, West Germany and elsewhere. When it ended, there was a general clamor for more, and a *Times* editorial headed "The Return of Sherlock Holmes" praised the network for adding to our stock of innocent gaiety on television, and making no concessions to the shoddy violence of the modern world. "Through narrow gaslit streets our hero walks with his foolish but invaluable friend the Doctor. He succors the innocent and brings wrongdoers to book, and we are all the better for it," the editorial said. "And with all due respect to Eille Norwood and William H. Gillette and the other distinguished actors who have played the part in the past, it does not seem too much to say that in Sheridan Haynes our newest form of visual art has found the perfect Sherlock."

It was after the first series ended that the publicity department had the brain wave about Sherlock Holmes living again in Baker Street, and Willie went down to Weybridge to sell the idea. Willie knew Sher and Val as well as most people did. He had been the producer on a couple of tours in which Sher had played, had done the social problem play that had been the actor's one real West End success, and had used him occasionally on TV. He regarded Sher as a nice but old-fashioned man, distinguished only by his passion for Sherlock and his hatred of motorized traffic. Val he put down as an attractive, basically discontented woman. It was Val to whom he would have to sell the package rather than Sher, and on a warm afternoon in the garden of their solid Edwardian semidetached house he did just that. When he had finished she softly clapped her hands.

"Bravo. A fine performance."

"I don't know what you mean. It's just an idea. You're free to say no."

"When you talk about the advantages of living in London you're getting at me. You know there's nothing Sher would love more than to live in Baker Street."

Sher got up. "I don't care for being referred to in the third person when I am present. I'm going in to mix some martinis."

"But it's true, isn't it?"

"Val darling, you know I'll be happy with anything you want." Then he was gone, tall, thin, with sloping shoulders.

"You see," she murmured lazily. "He longs for it. And the way you've talked about it has just been getting at me, hasn't it? Don't bother to deny it. Just tell me why I should leave Weybridge. I know the company's coughing up a lot of money, but why should I move? Lots of friends, nice cozy life. I like it. What's in it for me?"

The impressive thing about her, Willie thought, was her total composure. He felt certain that she wanted him to make some advance or proposition, and yet he knew that if he said nothing she would not show annoyance. He said tentatively, "Are you so completely happy here? I shouldn't have thought so."

"I asked the question and you haven't answered it. What's in it for me?"

"We could see each other more often."

She shook her head, laughing. "Oh, Willie."

He had always found her attractive, and he believed in the effectiveness of a direct approach. "I should like to go to bed with you. I think you'd like it, too. In London it would be easier, much easier."

"Oh, dear me, Willie." She put her handkerchief to her eyes. Sher came out with the martinis. "Willie's convinced me," she said through her laughter. "He's a most persuasive man. Let's go to Baker Street. If you want to."

Sher's smile was rare, but singularly sweet. He smiled now. Willie looked from one of them to the other, and wondered who had been fooling whom.

That had been at the end of the first series. The second had been almost equally successful, and so had the first episodes of the third. With the last half dozen, however, there was a decline in viewing figures, and although the decline was not steep it was steady. Willie found himself lunching again with the director.

There was a new assistant director. He wore huge horn-rims, a jacket that buttoned up to his neck and flared trousers. He used words like "viable," and was much in favor of what he called "drama in the image of the modern." He was also fond of the expression "Let's face it," which received considerable play now.

"Let's face it, Willie—this Holmes series has had it. The marvel to me is that it's stayed up as well as it has, when you consider the outdated image in which it was conceived."

The director was eating coquilles St. Jacques. He paused between mouthfuls to look inquiringly at Willie.

"What you call the outdated image is just the reason it got those terrific figures."

"Not any more. You simply have to face it—something that's right outside the modern idiom like this can't last. The way I see it, you've either got to modernize it somehow or pack it in."

"Ridiculous," Willie said. "Just a few episodes that are not so good—you can always get those at any time. Because of that you want to stop one of the most successful series ever made."

"Modernize or—" The assistant director glared through his horn-rims. Both of them turned to the director, who was finishing his coquilles. He swallowed the last mouthful, dabbed his mouth with his napkin, looked from one to the other of them and sighed.

The result of this luncheon, as of many similar luncheons, was a compromise. The fourth Sherlock Holmes series was commissioned, but concessions were made to the image of the modern, specifically that Irene Adler should appear as a permanent antagonist to Sherlock Holmes, and that the original stories should no longer be sacrosanct. The new series had been launched with a publicity campaign in which the lead article announced: "Sherlock Holmes versus Irene Adler. Has the Great Detective Met His Match?" Would the publicity have an effect on the viewing figures?

8

AN AFFAIR OF THE HEART

At the Croydon sale Val bought a couple of figures which she thought were very good Staffordshire, a Pembroke table in excellent condition, and what might with some generosity have been considered two Morland watercolors. The pictures were in any case extremely cheap, and perfectly salable in the Greenwich shop.

On the way from Croydon to Greenwich she drove, as she almost always did, with zest and determination. In her experience, men hated to be passed by women drivers, and when she could pull out and pass a fiercely trilbied man, or a man with a cigar pushing out at an angle from the corner of his mouth, she felt a small surge of pleasure.

Come on now, she thought as she drove up the Croydon Road to Beckenham at nearly twenty miles an hour beyond the speed limit, come on, my beauty, get past that Rover with the thick-necked stockbroker rhinoceros at the wheel, yes, you're past, and now a quick dash by the greengrocer sheep in his Jag, show him what life's like, rub his nose in it, teach him women drivers aren't all just placid cows who make way for men on the road. Going up Beckenham Hill and into Bromley Road the traffic was nose to tail, with no chance of passing, but on the turn into Brownhill Road she got in the lane going straight ahead, turned right and cut in on a Mercedes coupe driven by an elegant young man. The Merc flashed, which made her feel good, because she had always wanted to own a Merc. As she came up to traffic lights the other car drew level. The young man wound down his passenger window and used a number of four-letter words. She used some similar language back, before turning away from him down Burnt Ash Hill. *Such* behavior, Val, my girl, she said to herself. You should be ashamed.

The Val Haynes who sat behind a steering wheel was a different person from the composed, middle-aging woman who sold antiques and ran a household efficiently. She drove as though she were in competition with every car that drew level with her, and indeed she often thought in this way, saying to herself: Car in front at Spratt's Corner [or next road junction, or next roundabout] is the winner. Driving in London gave her limited opportunities, and she did not much like it. Her favorite driving was on motorways. There she flashed cars that stayed in the fast lane and refused to move over, and overtook them from the inside lane if she had to, or engaged in races against sports cars. She would return from a trip to a sale at Nottingham or Bristol sated as a cat who has illicitly swallowed cream.

The shop was off Romney Road, near the Maritime Museum and the Naval College, in an up-and-coming area that was still not quite fashionable, so that she had been able to get a lease cheap. Fritz, who ran it for her, was a German in his fifties who had been a prisoner of war in Britain and never gone back. He was a skillful repairer of slightly damaged pieces. His knowledge of antique furniture was scrappy, but this meant that he did what she told him without question, and this suited her very well. If she made mistakes occasionally, they were not pointed out to her.

She spent a couple of hours in the shop, and then drove sedately back to central London. At four o'clock she was in a flat not much more than a mile away from the rehearsal room where a troublesome scene in which Sherlock Holmes discovered that Irene Adler was behind the theft of the naval treaty was being played, in bed with Willie Lowinsky. They had made love, and she was smoking, tapping out the ash in her careful way.

"You know, Willie, I often wonder why I'm doing this."

"Because it's nice."

"I don't think so. I mean, it is nice but that's not the reason."

"Because you're nice. Because I adore you. Didn't I say so that day in Weybridge?"

"That was just a ploy in the game to get Sher to Baker Street."

"Darling, I don't know why you don't believe it when I say I adore you. I always have."

She laughed. "If you meant a word of it, you'd sound ridiculous. For that matter, I don't see why you do it. With me, I mean, when there must be so many younger birds available." She put out the cigarette, propped herself on an elbow and looked at him. "Except that you're losing your hair and getting fat, so perhaps there aren't all that many available."

"One of the things I love is you are so frank," Willie said without conviction. He patted his stomach. "I am not so fat."

"And there must be plenty who get much more excited in bed."

"They are so silly. I love you, Val darling, because you are not silly. I have told you many times I want you to come and live with me."

"I've heard you say so; yes."

"And I mean it."

She took another cigarette, considered it, put it back. "I suppose what I get out of it is some kind of release I don't get with Sher. He's not too much in bed, you know; he never was. But I sometimes think what we're both doing is getting back at him. Because he's so successful, because he loves it so much."

"You're talking nonsense."

"I am not, and you know it. But I'll tell you something else. I've had almost enough of Sher. I married Sher, but now I'm wedded to Sherlock. I used to think it would be better when it all ended; now I'm not so sure."

He made an irritated gesture.

"Tell me, Willie, is it going to stop, will this be the last series?"

"You know I can't answer that. When you're working on a series you don't start talking about whether another one will follow it."

"You mean to tell me there wasn't an argument about whether to pack it in when the last lot ended?"

Willie jumped out of bed and stood glaring at her, a radish not only forked but hairy. "I love you, my darling, but one thing I must tell you. I don't go to bed to have a business discussion. That I keep for the office." He began to put on his clothes. She watched him with the total composure he envied, then said that it was time for her to be going anyway. Sher would be home soon.

"You have been very clever, Mr. Holmes," Sarah Peters said. "My congratulations."

"Madame, if I may return the compliment, your own skill and ingenuity were very great. You erred, if I may say so, only in choosing so altogether foolish— I'm sorry."

The continuity girl said, "You erred, if I may say so, only in your choice of such an inferior collaborator."

Sher repeated the lines correctly, took two hesitant steps toward Sarah. "Good-by. In future, keep out of my way. Next time—"

The prompt girl said, "I advise you to keep out of my way."

"Good-by. I advise you to keep out of my way. Next time—"

Sarah took her own two steps toward him. They were very close. She was wearing a chocolate brown trouser suit, and she was tall enough to be only a couple of inches below him. She smelled of cigarette smoke and gin. "Next time, Mr. Holmes? Is that a threat or a promise?"

They looked into each other's eyes. Then Sher turned and strode from the room, opening an imaginary door. Sarah stood looking after him with an enigmatic half-smile.

"Fine," Richard Spain said. "That's it for today, loves. Tomorrow morning, ten-thirty, and let's all of us be here on time, okay? Still lots to do."

The cast began to talk to each other. Their voices buzzed in Sher's ears like the humming of insects, Basil's rising above the others with mosquito shrillness. Outside a heavy lorry ground its gears. He felt as though a band of steel had been put around his forehead. "Richard."

"Sher. I wanted to have a word."

"I'm sorry about the lines. The trouble is they're so wrong. 'I advise you to keep out of my way.' Holmes could *never* have said that; it's totally out of character."

"Is that why you look at me at the end as if I were Myra Breckinridge?" Sarah asked cheerfully.

Richard smiled nervously. He was young. "Let's huddle in a corner and talk about that last scene, shall we?" They sat around a table on small, hard chairs. "Sher, you're meant to be half in love with Sarah, but she's right: from the way you play it nobody would know."

The band was clamped a little tighter. "In love—that's absurd. We know Sherlock Holmes never fell in love with anybody. What does Watson say? 'He never spoke of the softer passions save with a gibe or a sneer—'"

"Bugger what Watson says. Sher, love, we're working on a script, remember? If you say you actually can't speak the lines, they'll have to go. But they're important, and something will have to go in instead. It's no good referring me back to the sacred texts."

It was all perfectly reasonable. With an effort he controlled himself, and said gently, "I see that, Richard. I'll get the lines right tomorrow. But there's one other thing. The ending. You roll the credits at the end as usual, right?"

"Right."

"And you always roll them over a picture of me—walking down Baker Street or taking tobacco out of the Persian slipper, or sitting by the fire with Watson. You're rolling this time over the picture of Sarah standing there after I've gone out. You must see that's wrong. Nothing to do with you, Sarah. It's just that the stories are about Sherlock Holmes, and they have to begin and end with him, like the Maigret series."

"Oh, for God's sake." Sarah got up.

Sher flung out a hand in a commanding Holmesian gesture. "Just a moment."

She turned and faced them, tall, dark and elegant. "As far as I'm concerned, you can roll your credits over whatever you fucking well please, Mr. Sherlock Holmes."

She walked away. Richard got up as though to call her back, then sat down again. Sher put a restraining hand on his arm and said, still in the Holmesian vein, "Let her go." He disliked women in trousers, and it disturbed him that she was so tall. He was five foot ten, not quite tall enough for the ideal Sherlock, but it was surely stupid to choose an Irene who was only a couple of inches shorter. He thought of mentioning this, but decided against it. After all, the casting choice had been Willie's.

"You shouldn't have said that."

"She ought not to be so touchy. It's absurd. And I must say I do dislike hearing women use that word. Old-fashioned, I daresay." To his surprise he found himself saying the very thing about which he had been going to keep silent. "And she's too tall for the part."

"Sher, there's no point in arguing about that, and you know it. And the next time you've got something to say which affects another member of the cast, I'd be glad if you'll say it when we're alone. I'll speak to Willie about rolling the credits if you really want me to; it was his idea to have an occasional variation. But you've got to get more into that last sequence. And there's a passage in Act One I'm not happy about. It's when you see Irene for the first time. . . ."

They talked about it for nearly half an hour. Then Sheridan Haynes went out into the dark cold January afternoon, a wind blustering and biting against him. A hint of snow was in the air. He wrapped his overcoat around him as he walked back to Baker Street. The traffic was dense. The yellow lights above him shone like flowers on concrete stalks and the car lights were different flowers, yellow or winking red, but all of them poisonous, staining the atmosphere and turning the people who drove them into robots, little mechanical figures going through jerky motions with hand and foot. It was a pleasure, and it was a gift also, to be able to transform this world in his imagination so that the monstrous electric flowers became soft yellow gaslight, and the people crowding the pavements turned into the decorously clothed men and the gracious women of long ago. The mystery of that world was recreated for him, the present faded away. When a voice said, "Good evening, Mr. Sherlock Holmes," he heard the words without surprise.

It was Cassidy, and with him another traffic warden, a little apple-cheeked man who wore the same uniform but with two stripes on the patch at his shoulder. It was this man who had spoken. "Have I got the quotation right, sir?"

A surge of pure pleasure went through him. It was like meeting a compatriot in a strange country. "Yes, but you're not the person who should be saying it. Still, I'm glad you study the master."

"It was Irene Adler in disguise, I know."

"This is Mr. Johnson," Cassidy said. "He's the controller for our area."

"That's right. Joe Johnson's the name. I go around the area keeping an eye on things, and when Cassidy here told me he often passed the time of day with you, I thought: If I ever see him I'm going to chance it and speak. I hope I haven't offended."

"Of course not."

Cassidy blew his nose. "He's always talking about you. Now if you'll excuse me, I ought to be moving."

Johnson looked after him. "A very good man, honest as the day. In the army once, then in the police. The right type, though he's a bit of a miserable devil." He dismissed Cassidy. "Mr. Haynes, it's true that I'm a great admirer of yours as well as of Sherlock Holmes. I wonder whether you'd do me the honor one day of coming round and having a cup of tea or a glass of beer with me at home. I'm a bit of a Sherlock Holmes collector myself, and one or two of my things might interest you."

It was the kind of suggestion he had often refused, but the pleasure he had taken in the greeting and their brief conversation made him say yes. Johnson wrote down an address in Shepherd's Bush and they fixed a date.

Sher arrived home in a good temper. Val was already home, and greeted him with the calmness that was one of the things he valued most in their relationship.

THE THIRD KILLING

9

Sue Devenish did not exactly think of herself as a perfect wife, but she tried to behave like the perfect wives she had read about in women's magazines. "When your man comes home with the look on his face that means he's had a terrible day, *don't* start off by telling him the fright you had when Johnny fell and cut his knee. Sit him down in his favorite armchair, mix him a good strong drink, have one yourself, and settle yourself to *listen*. Your turn will come later." So on this particular evening when Roger came home with that certain look, she did not reproach him for being late without phoning to tell her, but brought him a large whisky and herself a gin and tonic, sat on the arm of his chair and asked him what was up.

"Does it show that much? Sorry. Just that the Assistant Commisioner bawled me out this morning, in the nicest possible way, about what they call the Karate Killings. What lines were we following, had I considered the possibility that Gladson's murder had nothing to do with the first one, or that it was politically motivated, and all that. As though we hadn't talked all that over fifty times. He's a nice bloke, the A.C., but not too bright."

Although other wives were almost always impressed when they learned that her husband was a chief superintendent in the CID, Sue had the feeling that there was something not altogether nice about being married to a policeman. However, she knew that a wife must keep up with her husband's work, and she was interested in the Karate Killings because, like many of their neighbors in Wimbledon, she had had a certain admiration for Sir Pountney Gladson.

"Are you *sure* it's nothing to do with politics? I should have thought—"

"I'm not sure about anything, not even that it was a karate chop. A lot of people are pleased he's out of the way, all sorts of lefties and Maoists and blacks. But that's different from knocking him off, and in his own car, too. If there wasn't a link with the other killing, through the way it was done, then my bet would be that it was a personal job. He was pretty much of a bastard, and he seems to have had a finger in some odd pies. He was mixed up with the Claber gang, and I wouldn't be surprised if they had something to do with it. But that would just be instinct, no facts." He looked gloomily at his whisky, drained the glass and patted her backside. "How are the kids?"

"John stayed up hoping to see you. He got a star at school today for reading. Jean's a bit whiny; I think she may be sickening for something. Nothing to worry about." The perfect wife does not burden her husband with petty domestic problems. "I've made something special for dinner, boeuf Bourguignon with red wine and brandy in it. Lucky I chose a casserole; it won't be overdone."

"You shouldn't have troubled. Eggs and bacon would have been fine."

"For a starving man coming home after a hard day's work? I hope I can manage something a bit better than that."

"You're the most angelic wife who ever lived," Roger Devenish said with a sinking heart. Sue was an erratic cook at any time, but particularly fallible when she attempted something ambitious. And so it proved now. The beef was certainly not over-done, yet it managed mysteriously to be so hard that it almost bounced off the fork. The sauce resembled mulled wine and brandy strongly laced with pepper. She herself ate little, but she had piled his plate high, and he was struggling when the telephone rang. He jumped up eagerly. When he came back three minutes later he was looking grim.

"I've got to go out. No use complaining, love, they had to call me. It's another Karate Killing. Soho this time, in a dirty bookshop. And it's beginning to look as though my bet about the Clabers is right." He looked at his plate and said with relief, "Wonderful meal, love; just can't stay to finish it."

She was interested enough to forget about the boeuf Bourguignon. "Why do you say it looks as though you're right?"

"The boy who's been knocked off belongs to another gang. They run the porn shops. The Clabers may be trying to move in."

"So they've killed the chief of the other lot?"

He patted her cheek, laughed. "They don't kill each other. It's some poove who's been done, named Sonny Halliwell. He's not important, only the method—the good old karate chop."

The date was the fourteenth of January.

Sonny Halliwell got his first name partly because he looked so boyish, partly to distinguish him from his father, Billy, who had been a frightener for a firm of property developers named the Fifth City Company. A frightener's job is to get unwanted tenants out of houses and flats by making their lives uncomfortable. Billy Halliwell would set trip wires on stairs, empty rubbish in front of doors, rent apartments above and below unwanted tenants to tarts, with injunctions not to worry about noise. After a few weeks of Billy's attentions, most tenants were ready to accept an offer from Fifth City of a small sum of money to terminate their lease.

Billy's career as frightener ended when he was badly beaten

by a group of tenants who resented the electrical devices he had been using to give them shocks when they turned on the landing lights. He emerged from the hospital shaky and nervous, in no condition to frighten anybody ever again. There are no pensions among villains, but Billy hung about the Brompton Gaming Club, took messages and ran errands for important people, and scraped a living. His father's career was a lesson to Sonny, who was not physically equipped for the part of frightener, and in any case disliked violence. He had been employed by Sporting Ventures of Great Britain, which might be called a companion company to Fifth City, as croupier, club manager and then club director, which meant that he was responsible for all the managers in Sporting Ventures' eighteen clubs.

Sonny had done very well, but we all have weaknesses, and he had two. He used LSD and on occasions got distinctly wild under its influence, and he was not only queer but sentimental with it, liable to make unfortunate emotional attachments. On the other hand, he was honest, a characteristic so rare in his circles that he was bound to rise high. When Fifth City and Sporting Ventures decided to diversify their interests into the field of literature by starting a chain of pornographic bookshops, it was natural that Sonny should have been chosen to look after them. He had been doing this efficiently for three years.

On the day of his death, Sonny made the usual weekly round of the group's shops in his latest car, an MGB-GT. Nothing is easier for the managers of such shops than to put a large part of the takings into their own pockets, since the business proceeds by loan and exchange. A little thieving is customary, but Sonny's job was to make sure that the managers were not stealing their employers blind. Just before eight o'clock he paid his last call, to Contemporary Books, just off Lisle Street in Soho. He had told his current boyfriend, an actor named Charlie Reynolds, to phone him there at eight-thirty so that they could make plans for the evening. Just after eight-thirty Charlie called. The receiver was picked up.

"Sonny, hallo, it's me."

"And who's me, when he's at home?"

"Oh, Sonny, you're just too much." Charlie giggled.

"You're altogether too much yourself," Sonny replied. The conversation might have continued in this flirtatious way for some time, but Charlie then heard a bell ring. "Who the hell's that?" Sonny said. "The shop's shut. Just a minute, Charlie."

What Charlie heard after that proved of great interest to the police. There was a murmur of voices, the words indistinguishable. Then Sonny said, "What *do* you want, then? I don't understand. I've told you we're shut."

A man's voice replied, "You're not shut to me."

A pause, then Sonny said, "Oh, all right." There was the sound of the door being opened, and Sonny said, "Well, what—"

"I want *you.*"

There was the sound of something being knocked over. Sonny's voice came high, squealing. "What are you doing? You're not—" Then a strangled cry and a thud. Charlie called Sonny's name and heard breathing at the other end of the telephone. The telephone was replaced and there was a decisive click.

Charlie spent ten minutes in painful reflection on the trouble he might be causing, both to himself and to Sonny. After that he telephoned the police.

The shop was like a hundred others. There were girlie magazines in the window, with a sign saying: "Full Range of Adult Reading Within. Adults Only." Around the walls inside there were more girlie magazines, together with postcards of women. A wooden partition and a curtain led to the inner room, holding the hard-core stuff. The body lay near this partition, on its side, the face suffused with blood. A rack of books had been pulled down, and copies of *Spanking Sessions, I Was a Transvestite Mormon, Love Laws of Ancient Greece* and similar works lay on and around the corpse. The photographers had gone when Devenish arrived, but fingerprint men were still busy. A red-haired detective inspector named Millard, from West End Central, greeted the chief superintendent.

"Sorry we didn't contact you straight away. Only realized it might be for you when the quack looked at him. Whoever did it hit him in the throat first, see. But he was killed by a chop, or anyway a blow on the back of the neck."

"What time?"

"That's one thing, we can fix the time. I told you he was a poof." Morgan's look conveyed his distaste. "He was speaking to a poof friend on the phone when he got it. The shop was shut. The friend heard it on the phone, rang us. I thought you'd want to talk to him."

Devenish took the piece of paper with the address. "This boy worked for Freddy Williams, right?"

"Had done for years. Never been inside. And he'll never go in now, that's for sure."

"What makes you think it's the Clabers?"

"Williams has had a clear run with this stuff till now. Handled ninety percent of everything that came in. Most of it's Scandinavian, a bit from Germany. Four months ago the Clabers fixed up their own sources of supply from West Germany and opened a dozen shops. A couple of weeks back three of their managers got done, shops smashed up. This will be a comeback. The Clabers don't give up easy."

Devenish looked down at the figure on the floor. "The shop was shut; that means he opened the door. Must have been someone he knew. You don't know how much this friend of his heard? Right, then, we'll ask him."

"You're sure about what you heard this man say. 'I want you' —you're certain of those words? Good. Now the voice. Any accent—foreign, Irish, northern, midlands, public school? Just think."

Charlie Reynolds's room was in a part of Fulham not yet fashionable. It contained a bed that served as a sofa, a cardboard wardrobe, a curtained-off kitchenette. None of it was in good condition, and at the moment Reynolds himself did not look in good condition either. He was a slight, delicate young man with prominent eyes. His pale face and his very short legs made Devenish feel sorry for him. "It just sounded like an ordinary voice. Remember I was hearing it through the phone, not direct. It wasn't public school. Nor foreign. I suppose I'd call it BBC English, rather rough BBC English."

"What age?"

"Not young. And not really old. Somewhere between thirty-five and sixty. I'll tell you something else. I only heard a few words, and it's just an impression. But it was rather as though he were playing a part."

"Playing a part?"

"I was in a telly series once called 'Drong the Avenger,' and Drong had to say things like 'Bolts cannot keep me out, bars shiver at my touch.' It was rather like that: 'You're not shut to me.' A bit ham." He gave a giggle, cut it off, put a hand over his mouth, made a dash for the curtain.

There were sounds of retching, then a tap running. Charlie Reynolds came back, looking even paler. "Sorry. The loo's on another floor, communal, and so's the bath. Stupid to get upset. It was just that we'd been talking on the phone, making jokes, you know."

"You were close friends?"

"I don't know what you want me to say. You're fuzz. People like Sonny and me, you don't like us."

"I'm not interested in your private life unless it affects his killing. I want to know who killed him and why, that's all. How long had you known him?"

"Three months. We met at a club off Shaftesbury Avenue called the Carrousel. We knew about each other straight away."

Love at first sight, Devenish thought, and then asked himself why queers couldn't feel it just as much as heteros. He knew they could, but why was it so hard to acknowledge? He looked around the shabby room. "You didn't live together?"

"Sonny's always lived with his mother and father in Finchley. We talked about being together all the time, but his mother's ill, and his father is—well, a dead loss was the way Sonny put it. He had to look after them, or so he felt. Sonny was a sweet person, very gentle." He dabbed at his eyes. "Sorry. Would you like a cup of tea? It would be no trouble to make one."

"Thanks." Reynolds pulled aside the curtain to reveal a small cooker, a sink and a couple of battered cupboards. While he made the tea Devenish prowled about, looking at the few books and ornaments. A head-and-shoulders photograph of a fair, wavy-haired young man looking pleased with himself stood beside the bed, hardly recognizable as the body on the bookshop floor.

Reynolds came out of the kitchenette. "Isn't he sweet?"

"He wasn't in a sweet business."

"He never talked about that; I don't know anything about it."

The chief superintendent was reminded of several wives who had given him similar assurances about their husbands. Often the assurances were true. The teacup had a chip out of it. He sipped from the other side.

"Acting doesn't pay too well, from the look of it. Don't bother to answer. Sonny was a user, right?" Reynolds's face seemed to be fixed in a fascinated stare at the teacup. Then Devenish realized that the actor was looking at his thumbs. "What was he on?" Reynolds hesitated. "I can get it from someone else, but if I have to I won't like it." He put down the teacup and the thumbs appeared in their full power.

"Speed mostly. Sometimes acid. We never used H. And there was never a problem."

"You mean you could always get it. At this club, the Carrousel, right?"

"We could always get supplies. Of course, Sonny was well placed, but anyone can if they've got money. Sonny wasn't hooked."

58

"He paid for your habit as well as his own."

"That's not fair." The teacup rattled as Charlie Reynolds put it down. "It wasn't something that worried Sonny."

An implicit reservation struck Devenish. "What did worry him?"

"His family. He wanted us to be together, you see. He'd have paid for a woman to live there all the time and look after his mother, but she didn't want that. And then . . ."

"Yes?"

"Sonny's dead now; I wouldn't have said anything while he was alive. Sonny had an accident. In his car. A TR-6 he had then. We hit another car."

"You were with him. What happened to the other car?"

"It was a Mini. Pretty well a write-off."

"And the driver?"

"He was badly hurt. Something to do with his spine. But it was his fault; he crossed when the lights were red for him. Sonny was charged, but when the case came up he was cleared."

"You gave evidence?"

"Yes. And there were two independent witnesses."

"When did this happen?"

"September. The case came up early this month."

"Why was Sonny worried, if it was all the way you've told it?"

"I said he was a very sweet person. The whole thing upset him. He hated anybody getting hurt."

The chief superintendent nodded noncommittally, got some more details of the accident and left. When he closed the door Reynolds had picked up the photograph of Sonny and was looking at it forlornly.

The Halliwells lived in a semidetached house in West Finchley, a house that duplicated all those in the rest of the street and in the streets parallel on either side. It was midnight and bitterly cold when Devenish and Brewster escorted Billy Halliwell back to his home. Frost gleamed on the pavements and rimed the windows of the cars that lined the streets.

They had picked up Billy at the Brompton Gaming Club, where he had been drowning his sorrows in whisky. He protested then and he protested now, even as he put the key in the lock.

"This'll be the death of his mother, I can tell you that."

"We've already informed your wife," Brewster said. Halliwell shook his head.

"No, no; I mean having the fuzz in the house." Inside the door he raised his voice mournfully as a baying bloodhound. "Kathie my love, are you there?" There was a bay in reply. "She's in the lounge."

The lounge contained a three-piece suite, a glass cupboard with silver in it, a range of Toby jugs on the mantelpiece. Mrs. Halliwell sat in one of the armchairs, directly facing the blank eye of the television set. She was very fat. Her balloon head, dark eyes buried in it like currants in a pudding, topped the larger balloon of her trunk. Two surprisingly slim legs looked incapable of maintaining the formidable structure.

"You're drunk. Your son's dead and you get drunk," she said to Halliwell.

"My love, how are you? It's her heart that's wrong, you see, it's the old ticker. And the shock of it— Will you be having a drink now?" He said apologetically, "I should have told you, these gentlemen are—"

"I can see what they are. Which of you was it spoke to me on the phone?"

Brewster said, "I did."

"And you'll be the one they call Thumbs. Well, they're big enough and ugly enough."

A gas fire, full on, hissed softly. It was very hot in the room, an airless damp heat that had its own smell, with which was blended the smell of Mrs. Halliwell.

"There are a few questions," Devenish said. She laughed, showing small white false teeth.

"What's the use of questions? Sonny's dead, isn't he? You haven't come to say you've brought him back to life."

"Don't you want to know who killed him?"

"We can deal with the one who got Sonny. In our own way and our own time we'll do it."

Halliwell belched and sat down. "We can do it, all right, don't worry. We look after our own."

"What could you ever look after?" the woman said bitterly. "It was Sonny kept him at that club, though he did nothing but booze and quarrel there. And Sonny paid the rent here, too, and lived here, though he'd sooner have been away. He was a good boy, good to his old mum and dad, and now they've killed him."

"Who've killed him?" Brewster asked.

"Who d'you think?" Her little eyes glared at him. "If you've got anything between the ears you know who did it."

"A good boy." Halliwell had mysteriously conjured up a glass of beer. "A good boy, Sonny was."

Devenish wiped his forehead and intervened to check this Pinterian keening. "You mean the Clabers."

"Who else? Who else would want to kill a boy that never hurt anybody?"

"He wouldn't have hurt"—her husband sought for the telling phrase and triumphantly found it—"a fly."

"Except in his TR-6."

Halliwell looked blearily at his wife. "Ah, that was different. Mother of God, it was an accident; it wasn't Sonny's fault. I mean, Freddy Williams just looked after it for him, didn't he now? And there was no hard feelings."

"Billy Halliwell, you be quiet." Though the fat woman spoke softly, Halliwell flinched. She got out of her chair, a formidable operation but one in which she refused help. "I'm for bed. I'll say good night to you and see you out."

Devenish got up, too. He looked half her breadth and twice her height. "I'd like to see his room. I'll get a warrant if you make me." She lumbered toward the door. "Mrs. Halliwell."

"I heard. I'm showing it you. You don't suppose I'd let you turn my boy's room over without keeping an eye? You'd plant stuff just to blacken his memory."

Sonny's room was at the back. She moved toward it uncertainly on her thin legs, swaying and bobbing like a yacht in a wind. Her husband brought up the rear, murmuring under his breath. When they reached the room she stood beside the door and watched while they went over it.

The room held nothing for them. It was small, neat, the room of a quiet man. On the walls were half a dozen watercolors of London scenes—Swiss Cottage, Piccadilly Circus, London Bridge. From the door, where he stood behind his wife, Halliwell told them that Sonny had won prizes at school for art and had thought of going to art school, but they decided there was no future in it. Devenish looked up from a drawer containing socks, handkerchiefs, shirts in restrained stripes and delicate colors.

"There wasn't too much future in working for Freddy Williams either."

He ignored Halliwell's obscene reply. Beside the bed there was a photograph of Charlie Reynolds, and beneath it clippings praising Charlie's acting in a TV play.

Halliwell commented. "An actor named Reynolds, a friend of Sonny's, a nice young feller."

"Did Sonny have any other friends like him? Anyone who might have been jealous."

"That's a filthy insinuation, a terrible thing to suggest." The words bubbled in the man's mouth. He wiped away spittle.

"It's too late at night to play games. We're not worried about Sonny's morals." Devenish moved quickly across the room, brushed past the bulk of Mrs. Halliwell, gripped her husband by the shoulders. "I want to know if somebody had a personal reason for knocking him off."

"You're hurting me, Super, you don't know your own strength."

"That was an assault," Mrs. Halliwell cried. "I saw it. You try it again and I'll see a lawyer."

"You do that"—Devenish glared at her—"and I'll see this old lush inside a cell. By God, you'd think I was putting you through some sort of torture instead of trying to find out who killed your son."

"I don't like the smell of police. They make a house stink."

Brewster was smelling a small tobacco jar. He held it up. "Pot."

"He used it sometimes," Halliwell said. "And why not—there's no harm in it."

"We're not looking for pot." Devenish was not looking for anything in particular, just to see if there was an obvious personal reason for Sonny's death. He didn't expect to find it, and so was not disappointed. There was nothing to contradict his belief that this was a gang killing, possibly the first move in a war.

To get out they had to pass the fat woman. "You've finished. And you've found nothing." Her voice was triumphant.

"Thank you, Mrs. Halliwell." The detectives were in the narrow hallway. She came close to Devenish. He could smell her.

"You turn over my boy's things, prying. Snooping and prying, it's all you do, shoving your filthy great thumbs into everything." They began to move down the hallway, Halliwell with them. Her voice followed, rising as though caught in a wind, with only phrases audible. "Filthy dirty police . . . trailing their slime . . . my boy's memory . . . never again without a warrant . . . his sacred memory . . . shut the door." And then an eldritch screech. *"Don't let them in again."*

"I'm sorry for that," Halliwell whispered as he opened the

front door on a night of frost and wind. "She gets excited, you know, and that's bad for the old ticker. Sonny used to see that she never got excited. He was a good lad."

In the car Brewster said, "He must have been, to live in the same house with them. It's the Claber brothers and Williams, wouldn't you say, sir?"

"Looks like it. Certainly a chat with Freddy Williams is indicated."

FREDDY WILLIAMS

In the morning Devenish got a report on the accident in which Sonny had been involved. It had taken place at night, at a traffic junction near Marble Arch. His car had been in collision with a Mini driven by John Jarvis, an advertising copywriter who lived in Islington. The cars had met in the center of the junction, the TR-6 catching the Mini broadside. A charge had been brought against Halliwell of driving dangerously while under the influence of drink or drugs. At the trial two witnesses had given evidence that they saw the Mini cross after the light was red, although Jarvis maintained that it was green. Charlie Reynolds, Halliwell's passenger, confirmed this. The two witnesses had turned up after the original police court hearing, at which Halliwell had chosen to go for trial. Both of them said that they had read about the case in the papers and had come forward to prevent a possible miscarriage of justice. The medical evidence was not conclusive. The police doctor was emphatic that Sonny had taken a sufficient quantity of some drug, probably amphetamine pills, to make him unfit to drive. On the other hand, Sonny's own doctor said that his story of taking a pill for a mild migraine attack was perfectly consistent with what he had found, and that Sonny was quite fit to drive.

The jury was out for over an hour before bringing in a not guilty verdict.

Devenish sent Brewster to see Jarvis and visited Freddy Williams himself. The two men had met a couple of times, once in connection with a raid on a gaming club and once at the Lord Mayor's Summer Banquet, where they sat opposite each other. He suspected that the table placing had somehow been arranged, and was not overly pleased by the sophisticated badinage to which Williams subjected him. It gave him a feeling of inferiority, and he did not like feeling inferior to a crook.

Freddy's criminal kingdom was not run like that of the Clabers. In one part of his operations he was not a crook at all but a legitimate dealer in works of art. He specialized in nineteenth-century painters, French and English, and was the author of a standard work called *English Painting from Crome to Turner.* He was very proud of his expertise and of his unflawed reputation. Yet there was no doubt that, if you used such old-fashioned phrases, Freddy had emerged from his good public school and his subsequent five years with a City finance house to become a "king of crime." He was Fifth City and Sporting Ventures and Contemporary Books, although it would have been hard to get behind the fences of interlocking companies and dummy directors put up by his accountants, so that you could prove it. It would have been difficult, indeed, to prove Freddy's direct connection with anything except his art gallery. His secrets lay in Bermuda-based companies and Argentinian multiple trusts. He had never been in prison, never even been charged, and it was unlikely that he had ever raised a hand in anger when somebody displeased or defied him. Devenish thought he might have liked the man better if he had. He wanted a crook to behave like one, and really preferred the Clabers to Freddy Williams.

The gallery was showing an exhibition of nineteenth-century

English watercolors. Devenish glanced at the paintings, which seemed to him quite pretty but rather wishy-washy. Did people really pay a lot of money to put such things on their walls? He had a feeling of being conned, which was not dispelled when he was shown into the black-and-white study upstairs, in which all the furniture was egg-shaped. Williams also looked like a benevolent egg. He had a bald head, which narrowed at the top, pinkish, well-shaved cheeks and a swelling bulb body that tapered down to elegantly shod small feet. He wore gold-rimmed glasses with large lenses, which gave him an innocent expression.

"A glass of Madeira, Chief Superintendent? I always take one at this time in the morning. An old-fashioned taste, but the Victorians knew what they were doing. Something sweet in midmorning, a dry apéritif before a meal, spirits not on any account until after food. To be properly in period I should be offering you a slice of cake, but I'm afraid there are only these water biscuits."

The glasses had cut-glass stems; the decanter was cut to the same pattern. Devenish would sooner have had beer, but was determined not to be put down on a matter of taste. Williams sipped, nodded approval, waited attentively. There was a slight smile on his rosebud mouth.

"You've got an interest in an organization called Contemporary Books."

"Have I, now? That's something you would find it hard to prove."

Devenish took a sheet of paper from his pocket. "Your nominees are a man named Sebastian Harris and a Polish-born crook named Soltyk, who managed to get himself naturalized. They're also on the board of Fifth City and Sporting Ventures, together with a very smart accountant named Quinn and a couple of stooges. Your connection is through your solicitor, Evelyn Prinkish. He controls a company called—"

Williams held up a hand soft as a baby's. "Let's concede for the sake of conversation that I have an interest. You said on the telephone that you wanted to see me about something important."

The room and the man annoyed Devenish, the ridiculous room with its black ceiling and white carpet, its two black walls and two white ones, its low chairs with their wide curved bases and almost pointed tops, and the complacent man dressed to tone with the room, an untouchable crook with soft white hands. He knew that part of his annoyance sprang from his feeling of inferiority, inability to understand how people even thought of rooms like this, or why a man like Williams was allowed to exist. Why didn't everybody want to live comfortably in suburbs like Wimbledon? He controlled the annoyance, but let it show.

"A man of yours named Halliwell was knocked off last night in Soho. He was killed because the Clabers have been trying to move into your territory by opening up shops selling films and hard porn. Three of their shops have been done over by your boys, and this was a way of getting back at you. I've come to tell you not to start a gang war with the Clabers." Williams began to speak. Devenish's voice overrode him harshly. "If you do, I'll personally see to it that life is made so uncomfortable for you that you'll be glad to get out to Bermuda or the Argentine or wherever it is you've piled your dirty money."

The art dealer had stopped smiling. "A policeman with moral feelings about money—that's something new. Has it occurred to you that if what you say is true, and what you call a man of mine has been killed, you should be talking to the Clabers and not to me?"

"Don't try to tell me my business. You knew Sonny Halliwell."

"Yes, I knew him." The smile came back. "He was a painter of sorts; not a good one, I'm afraid, but I gave him a little encouragement."

"I'm not talking about paintings. He worked for you."

"Not for me. It was Sebby Harris who employed him."

"But you approved it."

"I liked Sonny. He was a pleasant lad. I did what I could for him. He had a father who was employed by one of Sebby's companies. The old man had fallen on bad times, from what I heard, and Sonny looked after him. It was rather touching."

"Did he have anything to do with smashing up the Clabers' shops?"

"Sonny? You can't have known him. Sonny was timid and easily frightened. A gentle person. That's why I liked him."

"You looked after him when he was in trouble?" A crease lined Williams's brow. "He was in a car accident with a man named Jarvis and a case was brought against him. He was acquitted."

"Oh, that. Yes, I remember. Fortunately two witnesses appeared who happened to have been on the spot. Wasn't that lucky?"

"Very. No doubt they were both respectable."

"I should be disappointed if they were not. What's that got to do with Sonny's death?"

"I don't know that the accident has anything to do with it. I just wanted to clear it up. I'm warning you, Williams. If I find you or Harris or anybody else is making more trouble with the Clabers, you'll be sorry. I won't have it, you understand. You leave them to us. You get the message?"

He got up. Williams got up, too. He looked a little quizzical, a little sad.

"You're a forceful man, or do I mean a forthright one? Both, perhaps. Anyway, I admire that. I've had the pleasure of entertaining members of the force at select little dinner parties, some of them even your superiors in rank. I don't suppose that would interest you? No, I see it wouldn't. I'll pass on what you say to Sebby, but he's impetuous. Forceful, rather like yourself. Of course, you know what would be the very best thing for every-body concerned? Putting somebody in prison for killing poor Sonny boy."

"It was a put-up job," Brewster said. He had seen Jarvis, who was still wearing a steel brace to support his back. Jarvis insisted that the light had been green for him when he crossed, and also that the witnesses had not been there at the time of the accident. He said some bitter things about inefficiency and corruption. Brewster had also talked to the witnesses, an electrician and an out-of-work garage mechanic, both local men, neither of them with a criminal record. The electrician's name was Arnold Dollman, and Brewster had remembered that a bouncer named Gus Dollman worked at the Brompton Gaming Club. It turned out that he was Arnold's brother. Arnold Dollman had admitted nothing, but he was shaken.

"We'll soon have it out of him if we bring him in, but I don't see the point. It was a put-up job to get Halliwell off the charge, all right, but what's it got to do with his being killed? This was a straight gang killing; one of the Claber lot did it. And they did Gladson, too. It stands to reason."

Devenish nodded, not necessarily in agreement. "What about the first one—Mole?"

"My idea is they read about that in the paper, Harry Claber remembered that one of his boys was a karate expert, and thought he'd use the old karate chop to get rid of Gladson. Then the same man was used for Halliwell, and the same method."

"A bit obvious, wouldn't you say—using the same method twice? Advertising it."

"Crooks have got obvious minds." Brewster grinned. "Like me."

"You could be right, and Harry Claber managed to kid me. But there are car accidents in two of these cases; that's what sticks in my mind."

"So what? Do you mean Jarvis killed Halliwell? You wouldn't

say so if you talked to him. And you said yourself that those two old people thought the sun shone out of Gladson's backside."

Devenish nodded again. "I'll tell you what else sticks in my mind. That bit of conversation Reynolds heard on the phone."

"What about it?"

"Halliwell opened up the shop after it was shut. And yet according to the conversation, it wasn't to anyone he knew. Who's the most likely person he'd have opened up to when the shop was shut?"

"I don't know. I'll buy it."

"A policeman."

ON THE STUDIO FLOOR

"Bless you all, my loves, and good luck," Richard Spain said through the mike. He settled down in his seat in the control room, looking down on the studio, four screens, each showing a different camera's view, in front of him, together with the master screen. Willie, in the chair beside him, lighted a cigar. The floor manager said, "Absolutely quiet now, please," the opening titles were shown over the familiar room in Baker Street, with the camera panning from the *Pall Mall Gazette* to the Persian slipper, and then to Holmes and Watson eating breakfast, with Watson reading the letter from Percy Phelps.

"Listen to this, Holmes," Watson said. The taping of the forty-ninth Holmes episode, "The Naval Treaty," had begun.

It went badly from the start. In the middle of the second scene some of the lights burned out, so that there was a half hour delay. Then the actor playing the foreign minister, Lord Holdhurst, who had a sore throat, lost his voice almost completely. His throat was sprayed, and then all the scenes in which he appeared were taped so that he could go home to bed. This meant taking several scenes out of order, and that in turn meant long conferences between Richard, the floor manager and the technicians on the floor. By the time Lord Holdhurst had been sent home and they broke for a quick meal, tempers were fraying.

Sher sat with Willie, Richard and Basil Wainwright at one of the plastic-topped tables, eating what seemed to be plastic chicken and salad. Willie was making his usual jokes, and laughing at the stories Basil told in the camp style that was his customary way of talking, but Sher barely heard them. The taping of an episode always excited him, so that the images occupying his mind were much more vivid than the scenes in which he was actually taking part. Now the rather inadequate actor who had been playing Joseph Harrison was replaced by Conan Doyle's Joseph, a man so slimy with deceit that treachery could almost be detected in the touch of his damp hand. He saw also the drawing room not as a mere studio mock-up, but as part of that large detached house among the fir woods and the heather of Woking. Words came to him, although he could not have said who had written them. "Out of these shadow shapes, these flummeries of paint and patchwork, we body forth a real world. That is the actor's art." It was the real world he saw, a reality so palpable that an outstretched finger could have touched it.

He became aware that they were all looking at him. Richard smiled.

"I was saying, Sher, we'll go straight ahead now as it's scripted. There shouldn't be any more problems."

"Sher's being Sherlock, didn't you know?" Basil said in his fluted voice. "He's solving the Karate Killings, isn't that right, Sher?" The little eyes in the misleadingly square, solid face twinkled at him mischievously.

"No."

Basil took no notice. "I mean, they're getting rather too close to home for comfort. This last boy who's been killed, Sonny Halliwell—I knew him. He used my club, the Carrousel. I mean, we've actually had a *drink* together at the bar. They're saying he had something to do with gangsters, but he was so *nice* I don't believe it."

"Why do they make so much fuss?" Willie asked. "One gangster kills another, so there's one less."

"Ah, but *was* it gangsters? On the Carrousel grapevine they say it might have been something *personal.* Of course, we know Sherlock could solve it in an hour if he put his mind to it, isn't that so?" He peered at Sher and repeated on a higher note, "Isn't that so, Sherlock?"

"I don't know what you've been talking about."

"Well, I mean, in that interview we all read with such *fascination* you said Sherlock could solve the Karate Killings, so why not do it? And confide the answer to your poor old puzzled Watty."

"Time to get back." Richard started to get up.

Sher was still partly in that real world of the past, but the images had gone, replaced by that appalling voice whose chief offense was that it inhabited the wrong body. His own voice when he answered was not quite his own; it had the ringing cold austerity of the master.

"I said that if Sherlock Holmes put his logical mind to them, he could solve these killings. That is true. And if you were really Watson it would be possible to confide in you. But how is it possible even to speak reasonably to somebody like you? To give such a person the name of Watson is absurd."

"Charming, I must say. Really charming," Basil said, but Sher did not hear this. He had got up and walked away, out of the plastic restaurant toward the studio, where there was at least a colorable imitation of reality. He was in the covered way between the two when he felt a hand on his arm. Willie was by his side. The little Pole's tubby body was vibrant with excitement and anger. The accenting of his English was stronger than usual.

"Sher, you will please come back and apologize. Immediately."

"Don't be ridiculous. You heard him jeering at me."

"He was simply joking, that's all." Willie's voice became cajoling. "You are a professional, Sher. You know as well as I do that when you are working with somebody you must be on good terms. You have to work with Basil, and not just once but to work with him closely, over and over again. Whatever you feel, you must remember that he is a wonderful Watson to your Sherlock, a perfect foil for you." Spacing out the words so that their importance should be recognized, Willie said, "We could not make a change now, we could not give Sherlock Holmes another Watson, any more than we could give Watson another Sherlock Holmes. Do you understand?"

He did understand. He knew that he had been wrong, and when Willie said again that he must apologize he did not resist. Willie said something about tension, and the unfortunate trouble that had meant taking scenes out of order. He went through the apology, speaking with studied Holmesian formality. Basil heard it with what was surely a malicious glint in his piglike eyes, Willie put an arm around each of them and, with a worried-looking Richard Spain behind them, they went back to the studio.

"Cut," Richard said. There was some sort of altercation on the studio floor. He asked the floor manager, "Jerry, what's the trouble?" When he heard the reply he smacked hand to forehead. "More problems with Sherlock," he said to Willie before going out of the room and down the iron stairs. Willie took the band off another cigar.

"Would it help if you came in on a wider angle?" Jerry was saying to camera two.

"It will bleeding well not help, Jerry, my old love," camera two responded cheerfully. "If I go any further I lose half the bleeding room, and Sher with it. And if I only move a couple of feet—"

"Okay, okay, you've made your point." Under the lights Jerry was sweating in his shirt sleeves.

"I don't quite get it. What's the problem?" Richard asked.

"The problem is that in this scene we've got Sher in the bedroom, waiting for Joseph to open the window. Well, from where he is he can't see the window. If I keep him in shot he's got to be here." He indicated a place in the bedroom. "We could move a foot or so either way, but it doesn't help. And if we get Sher to where he wants to be, which is across in the corner so that he can see the window being opened, we've got to shift camera two and camera three and then bring 'em back again, which means a break and a lot of rearrangement."

"Why does Sher have to *see* the window opening?"

"Ask him." Jerry rolled his eyes up to heaven.

Sher and Sarah were both on the set. Sher was sitting on a sofa with an expression of martyrdom on his face, Sarah in an armchair looking bored. Richard bent down and whispered to her that they'd get this straightened out in a couple of minutes. Then he sat beside Sher, and asked him what the trouble was.

"Richard, I just cannot create the required impression of tension when in fact I'm unable to see a glimpse of the window."

"But, Sher, why do you have to see it? We've got you on camera three, showing you ready and waiting. You know just what's going to happen, and that Harrison's going to come in the window. Then we cut to camera two, showing him come in. I don't see the problem."

The deep-set eyes looking at him had an uncomfortable intensity of feeling in them. "Richard, you'll forgive me for saying I've been around longer than you. This is a crucial scene, and you expect me to get the right feeling into it when I can't even see Harrison's entrance, the point of the whole scene."

"Other people do it. All the time."

Sher said nothing.

Richard kept his patience with an effort. "If we change the script the whole scene's got to be rearranged; we're going to waste an hour setting it all up. I've got time trouble as it is. I'd like to go straight through it as it stands. Can we do that, please, Sher." He managed to make the last sentence something between an order and a request. Then he went back to the control room, where Willie asked if he had ironed everything out.

"I hope so. It's Sher; he's being ridiculous." He gave a murmured explanation to Willie while the room below was got ready for action again. The clapper boy said, "Scene 103, take two," and Sher came into the room, spoke to Annie Harrison, sent her out of the room, made up a dummy to look like her, and settled down in his corner, hidden from the sight of anybody at the window. They played the scene through successfully enough, though without a lot of life, until the moment when Holmes looked across the room. At this point Sher moved out of camera range.

"Cut," Richard said, then to Jerry: "Ask Sher what he's doing. He's not supposed to move; he knows that. If he moves we can't hold him in camera."

Jerry spoke to Sher, then spoke into his mike. "He says he moved so that he can see the window."

"Just ask him to play the scene as we rehearsed it, without moving across the floor—okay, Jerry?"

"Right." Jerry had a long conversation with Sher, then came back. "He doesn't think it will work, but he'll do it."

"Good of him. When you're ready."

Beside Richard, Willie put down his cigar, leaned forward.

"Scene 103, take three," the clapper boy said.

They watched the screens in front of them. The scene got to the point where Holmes looked across the room. They cut to the other camera, with Joseph entering the room.

"Thank the Lord," Richard said, and then, "What the hell's happening?"

Sherlock Holmes had walked off the screen, off the set.

"Jerry, Jerry," Richard called. "What's happened to Sher, where is he?"

The floor manager's voice was carefully neutral. "On his way up to you, I think."

Richard said to Willie incredulously, "Jerry says he's coming up here."

There are some unwritten laws in television, and one of them is that the control room is sacred to producer, director and editorial staff, and is never visited by actors. Although the law is unwritten, it is strictly observed. When steps sounded on the iron stairs, and the door opened to reveal Sher, it was an act that challenged the authority of the producer and director.

Sher took two steps inside and began to speak. "Richard, I'm sorry, but it's impossible. Willie, you must see—"

Willie got up. His voice was not loud but the words fell hard as sleet.

"You have no business here. Get back onto the floor and play that scene."

Sher put out a hand. "But, Willie—"

"Listen to me. I will have no more nonsense. If you do not go down there and play the scene the way it was written and rehearsed, I will cancel this whole production." Richard started to speak. "Be quiet, Richard. I mean this."

Sher looked at Willie as though he had been stabbed in the heart. Then he murmured something that might have included the word "sorry" and went down the stairs again.

"Preposterous," Willie said. "He's mad."

"Scene 103, take four."

The scene went through without a hitch, cut away to Joseph and then back to Sher springing out when the hiding place of the treaty had been revealed. The rest of the action went smoothly enough, and although Sher played a little in the manner of a sleepwalker, that might have been considered merely the deep thoughtfulness of Sherlock Holmes. The last exchanges between Sherlock and Irene were reasonably convincing, and they rolled the final credits over a shot of Sarah Peters.

Afterward, Willie briefly congratulated Richard and then left, without speaking to anyone else. When the director went to make peace with Sher, he found that the actor also had gone.

12

SHERLOCK
FINDS HIS WATSON

"The Naval Treaty" was taped on a Thursday. On Friday just after midday, Willie Lowinsky called at the Baker Street flat. He wore a sheepskin coat and a Russian-style fur hat, and carried chrysanthemums and a bottle of Mumm, which he gave to Val. Sher was looking at some press clippings, and greeted him by raising a hand. In the living room, Willie stood with his back to the mantelpiece, hands behind him warming before an imaginary fire, and beamed at them both.

"This weather is coming straight from my own Russian steppes. I shall take to hand muffs if it goes on."

"I thought you were a Pole, Willie," Val said.

"Russia, Poland—the weather's all the same. Val, I don't think that bottle of pop wants to be too cold on a day like this. Just two minutes in your freezer will be enough." He followed her out to the kitchen. "How is Sher?"

"Much as usual. Why?"

"We had some trouble at the studio last night. He didn't tell you?" She shook her head. "I thought perhaps he was under some special strain."

"Not so far as I know. You know what he's like. When he's doing one of these Holmes things he thinks about nothing else. What do you mean, trouble?"

"Never mind. Let's drink the pop." He smiled and patted her bottom. She thought, not for the first time, that he was an insufferably patronizing little man. Back in the living room he popped the cork, and Sher dragged himself away from his press clippings.

"Willie. This is very kind." He sipped. "Glass of Mumm. Delicious."

Willie looked at the bottle, which he had wrapped in a cloth. "I shouldn't have thought you could have seen the name."

"Only the corner of the label. The Mumm label is distinctive. Willie, what would you say to the idea of my playing Sherlock Holmes? In real life, I mean."

Willie stared. He had come ready for recrimination and argument, but Sher seemed to have forgotten about the trouble at the studio. "What do you mean?"

The thin, keen features looked eagerly toward him: "I said to an interviewer that Sherlock Holmes could have solved the Karate Killings. Suppose I took on the case?" He touched the pile of clippings. "I got these from an agency. They're all about the killings."

Willie glanced at Val, who sat composed as usual on a sofa, and then back at Sher. "Are you serious?"

"Perfectly serious."

"I don't know what you have in mind."

Sher looked slightly irritated. "What I have in mind, obviously, is that Sherlock Holmes will solve the mystery of the Karate Killings."

Willie wondered if Sher was altogether sane. At almost the same moment it occurred to him that there could be enormous publicity in the idea. Would the publicity be self-defeating, was it worth risking the chance that Sher would make a fool of himself, did it matter anyway? "Interesting," he said. "But how would you go about it? What resources would you have that aren't open to the police?"

"I have my public." He tapped his knee. "You know how many letters I get, sent here to Sherlock Holmes. Imagine the response if it is made known in the press that I am investigating the Karate Killings in person, and that I am actually asking for information about the cases to be sent to Mr. Sherlock Holmes at this address."

Willie refilled the champagne glasses. The more he thought about the idea, the better the publicity prospects seemed. Perhaps it would be possible to plant a few clues for Sher to follow up? "It might work—it just might work."

"I knew you'd see it." Sher rose and walked up and down, talking excitedly. "It will be Sherlock Holmes versus Scotland Yard all over again. The genius of an individual against the ponderous movement of a machine, the inductive method of one man against a state bureaucracy. Except, of course, that the one man will be helped by the people of Britain because they have faith in him, have an instinctive understanding that he is working for them."

"Do stop talking such bloody rubbish." There was a flush on Val's cheek. It occurred to Willie that he had never seen her so animated, not even when they were making love. "Don't you see all Willie's thinking about is a publicity gimmick. And that's all it is anyway. You don't imagine you're really going to solve these crimes, do you? You know nothing about police work; you wouldn't know where to start. And stop looking at me in that pitying way. Just ask Willie, that's all. Ask him if he's taking it seriously."

Willie began to say something, but stopped when Sher put up a hand. "It isn't a question of what you think, or of what Willie hopes to get out of it. I realize that he's thinking about publicity for the series. But the important thing is this: can Sherlock Holmes, using the methods that were so successful in the past when Scotland Yard failed, solve crimes that are taking place today? That, my love, is the question."

"I think you're round the bend." She turned to Willie. "And you must be out of your mind to encourage him. I'm going down to Greenwich. I hope you'll have forgotten this rubbish by the time I get back."

After she had gone Willie didn't, as he had intended, read the riot act to Sher about his behavior. He talked instead about the possibilities in the quest for the Karate Killer, and only at the end mentioned what had happened on the previous day.

"If I blew my top, Sher, I'm sorry." Willie always savored phrases like "blew my top" because they made him feel particularly English. "But what you did was very naughty. It mustn't happen again, I tell you that."

Sher looked as though he didn't know what Willie was talking about and then said, "Yes, of course. I'm sorry."

"And so you should be, my lad. A series like this is a strain, I know that. We now have two weeks before undertaking our next masterpiece, and I want you to have a complete rest in your mind from the series. Then when we start again, if there are little problems you will see that they are little and not big."

"But Sherlock Holmes will look for the Karate Killer."

Willie put an arm around Sher's sloping shoulders. "Of course he will. But no more tantrums. No more, or daddy spank."

It is always said that bad news travels fast. When Willie got to his office he found a note asking him to speak to Mr. Dryne urgently. J. O. Dryne was the new assistant director of programs. His predecessor, who had favored "drama in the image of the modern," had left after putting on a trilogy interpreting an unborn child's attitudes toward its mother, its father and its sister, seen through a series of unconnected and often undecipherable images which were meant to be a view of life from the womb, intercut with gruelingly realistic passages between father, mother and sister. Dryne had been trained as a statistician.

He wore conservative pin-stripe suits, plain ties, and had lips like two razor blades stitched together. He had one joke, which he repeated often with only slight variation. "I don't know what's good and I don't know what I like, but I do know what other people like. The ratings tell me."

"I hear there was trouble with Sheridan Haynes yesterday," Dryne said. They were in his office, not at the Connaught, and the director was not present. The signs in the tea leaves were ominous, and the fact that Dryne knew about the row so quickly tended to confirm the belief held by many that his spies were everywhere. "Tell me about it."

Computer men like Dryne made Willie feel uneasy, and even afraid. He began on a modified, carefully edited account of what had happened, but was cut short.

"That's not what I heard, but it doesn't matter. Have a look at these." Dryne passed over sheets that gave details of the viewing figures for the new Sherlock Holmes series. Willie had already seen the figures for the first three episodes, and they had not been good. Episodes four and five showed that the decline was continuing, and more steeply. "I daresay Haynes's behavior has been a contributory factor, but the figures speak for themselves."

"Sher isn't a difficult person. He's been under strain."

"I understand he's been a problem all along, but as I say, it's not important. These figures are what matter. Do you have any comments?"

"Only that figures aren't always an accurate guide, especially when they're just for part of a series. Interest in Sherlock Holmes is permanent. Perhaps we have to shift the formula a little more—"

"Those arguments were used at the end of the last series, to justify starting this one. They can't be used again. Clearly the appeal held by Sherlock Holmes is now exhausted." Dryne's eyebrows were thin razor lines like his lips. Between them were two vertical lines of anxiety or ambition. "Obviously the series has been under discussion. Its prestige value, and the success you mention, have been taken into consideration. If these considerations had not existed, it would have been off the box by now. As it is, we shall have to pay for our mistakes. There are three more episodes to be taped. These will be completed, and the present intention is to show them all. Even that cannot be guaranteed, although there must presumably be a level below which the figures will not sink." An adjustment of the lines in his mouth made it clear that this was a sort of joke. "And that will be the end. Perhaps I should say that you are the first person to be told. Until the last three episodes have been taped, this should be regarded as confidential information."

Something about Dryne cowed Willie's usually volatile personality. In any case, there was not much he could say. He made a formal protest about not being consulted, which Dryne brushed aside by saying that he could talk to the director of programs if he wished. Willie knew that this would be like talking to the Sphinx. In the circumstances, there seemed no point in trying to sell the Sherlock Holmes publicity gimmick, to Dryne or to anybody else.

Out into the street, a right turn. The wind keen, so that the body bent into it, hands warmly gloved, a weighted stick in one of them. A raglan overcoat, a wide-brimmed hat above the lean features and the piercing eyes (a deerstalker would have been a little too much, faintly ridiculous), and Sherlock walked again in his London.

But unhappily that was not true. It was not Sherlock's London that Sheridan Haynes walked in, but this modern ragbag of a city, a city destroying itself through the destruction of its stock of worthwhile buildings, its subservience to the combustion engine. Yet it was still worth walking in cities; the magic had not altogether gone from the streets. A walk for Sheridan Haynes, like the one he started on now from Baker Street to take tea with Mr. Johnson in Shepherd's Bush, lifted and depressed his spirits in turn. Even in Baker Street there were decent buildings left, an elegant late-Victorian block here, a glimpse of something agreeable in a street across the road. Though as for crossing the road to look at it, *that* was impossible. In this one-way Baker Street, the shiny monsters stretched endlessly, all snorting from their backsides.

Turn again then, into George Street, cross the road. On the right something appalling, a concrete block like a low prison. On the left, though, a shop at which he always stopped, Mr. Sunley's Music Box. In the barred windows musical Toby jugs, pirates, and of course cuckoo clocks and cigarette cases. But the treasures were within, behind the door that was always kept locked. There were musical chairs, mechanical minstrels, leather-bound books. And stranger things, too: figures making up a complete orchestra operated by a musical box, grandfather clocks with a metal recording sheet instead of a clock face. He had bought from Mr. Sunley four volumes in handsome leather bindings that said on their spines: *Sherlock Holmes's Table Talk, Unrecorded Cases of Sherlock Holmes, The Secret Diary of Sherlock Holmes*, and *A Discussion of Newspaper Types by Sherlock Holmes.* Each volume when opened played a selection of Victorian tunes.

But today the temptation of Mr. Sunley must be resisted, if he was to be in time for tea. At the Gloucester Place crossing he held the monsters at bay with his stick while he walked over the road. Then Montagu Street and New Quebec Street, acceptably Holmesian in fragments, with agreeable small shops, but for the most part given over to hideous or nondescript modernity. And among the small shops proper to the area he was suddenly pulled up short. Where six or twelve months ago there had been a tobacconist's, a sign now read "Launderette." Inside it pig-faced women stared dumbly at the faces of machines that showed nothing but their wash whirling endlessly around. He stared at the disgusting invented word, "Launderette," then at the slaves of the machine. A small boy sitting on a chair saw him, stuck out his tongue, made a face. Sher was seized with anger, raised his stick. The boy fled to his mother, who was watching her machine intently, cigarette stuck to lip. He lowered the stick and walked on.

He was distressed by the disappearance of the shop, shocked by his own anger. Brooding on vanishing London, he was less upset than usual by the totally clogged Marble Arch. It was, as always, impossible to cross the road without risking your life. You were forced into the dismally lighted underground passage, which contained a young man with hair down to his waist, screaming unintelligible words to a guitar. Sher put money into the hat that lay on the ground, then half shouted: "This music is offensive. Why not play something with a tune?" The young man looked at him with mouth open, then shouted back words as unintelligible as his song. Off and away from him, a left turn down another passage, up a steep ramp, and at last he was in Hyde Park.

Had Holmes and Watson ever walked through the park? They must have, but he could not remember it being recorded. But now, even though there was still a traffic hum from Bayswater Road that varied in its swell but never faded to silence, he felt at peace as he crossed the frosty grass. Toward the Serpentine two borzois galloped elegantly while their owner called to them in a birdlike chirp, a boxer trotted beside a long-legged girl, a clutch of Pekingese moved on their leads around a pug-faced woman; in the distance children could be seen on horses. It was England as it had been and should be, and he felt his spirits lifting. Had he behaved badly in the studio? Perhaps, although he could really not remember what it was that he had done or said. What he did recall, although again the details had gone, was that Watson had sneered at Sherlock Holmes. Plainly, if Holmes was to solve the case, he would need another Watson.

At Shepherd's Bush the traffic roars along Westway, London's most recent motorway. Some streets have been obliterated by it, others exist in truncated form, a fragment of street dying slowly like a chopped worm, with windows rattling, ceilings falling, the brick and mortar shaking loose like teeth with pyorrhea. Some of these bits of streets are under sentence of death anyway, the occupants living in houses that will be knocked down when the Greater London or some other council gets around to it. Johnson was in one of these, an end house with a wasteland of junk extending beyond it, and the thunder of traffic above. It was a little Victorian terrace house of no particular style, but it had the distinction among its decaying neighbors that the tiny front garden was neatly kept, the paintwork decent, the brass knocker polished.

"Mr. Haynes, sir. Emmy and I are honored." Johnson, wearing slippers and with a pipe in his mouth, took Sher along to a cozy front room. A fire burned in the small grate, there were ships in bottles on the mantelpiece and tapestrywork pictures on the walls. Two shabby armchairs were drawn up beside the fire. Johnson pointed to one of them. "You sit down there, Mr. Haynes, and Emmy will be in with tea directly. Before it comes, though, I've got one or two little items you might like to see."

The things he had to show were unusual rather than exciting —a complete set of the stories in Russian and another in Chinese were among them, together with some of the early English and American editions, and (a real rarity in the form of an association piece, this) a menu card from the hotel at which the editor from *Lippincott's Weekly* had entertained both Conan Doyle and Oscar Wilde at dinner, and made the arrangement that brought to the magazine both *The Sign of the Four* and *The Picture of Dorian Gray.* It was a printed menu card, with the date of the dinner on it. Johnson had picked it up with a lot of old postcards and Christmas cards. When Sher expressed his interest, the warden immediately said that he must have it as a gift.

"Mr. Haynes, I won't take no for an answer. What did it cost me, after all? No more than a few pence, and anyway it belongs by rights to you. I know what I've got doesn't amount to much, and never will, but I'll be proud to think that a piece of mine is in your collection. Ah, now, here's Emmy with tea. Mr. Haynes, this is my niece Emmy Turner."

"Pleased to meet you, Mr. Haynes. Of course, I don't have to be introduced; I know you already." Emmy looked very much like a smaller version of her uncle, a rosy-cheeked, shining-faced, bouncy little woman perhaps thirty years old. The tray she set down included a fruit cake, bread and butter with two kinds of jam, little sandwiches, and something under a silver lid that turned out to be toasted tea cakes.

"Now don't hold back, please, because it's all homemade, and you've no need to worry about your figure, Mr. Haynes, have you? The bread I baked this morning and the cake, too, and even the tea cakes don't come from a shop."

She turned her head in putting down the tray, and Sher saw that her apple-dumpling prettiness was shockingly marred on the right side of her face by a scar that ran from ear to jaw. The deep weal was purplish in places and unpleasant to look at, but he saw Johnson's gaze on him and did not obey his natural instinct to look away.

"The truth is Emmy spoils me, has done so ever since she gave up work six years ago so that she could look after me."

"And who looked after you before that?" He realized the tactlessness of the question in the moment after asking it.

"My wife. She died of leukemia."

"I'm sorry." There was an awkward silence. Emmy filled it.

"Uncle Joe keeps on at me to take a job again, but I don't think it's right, do you, Mr. Haynes? I think if you're a housewife it should be a full-time job. I know it is for me, even in a little place like this. You might not think it, but he's a very untidy man. And then there's"—her words were drowned by the sound of a particularly loud lorry—"the traffic. It makes so much dirt, I'm forever cleaning and dusting."

He said truthfully that, except for the noise, their house was as he had always thought an English home should be, comfortable and welcoming. He ate the tea cake, a slice of fruit cake, two egg sandwiches and two pieces of bread and butter and jam. With it he drank two cups of strong tea. It was months since he had eaten such a large tea, or enjoyed it so much. Afterward, Emmy took the things away, and Johnson and he sat on opposite sides of the fireplace, chatting about Sherlock Holmes in general and his TV appearances in particular. When the traffic warden said it was a pity they were changing the original stories so much in the new series, Sher's heart warmed to him. Looking at the figure opposite, rosy-cheeked and round-faced, puffing away contentedly at a pipe, it struck him that here was a possible Watson. It was true that he did not look the part, but he had those qualities of tranquillity and solid sense that Holmes had appreciated in Watson, and he was a man who might understand the need to take up the challenge on behalf of Sherlock Holmes.

He began to talk about the killings, and Johnson listened patiently and carefully, intervening only once or twice to ask a question. It might really have been Watson sitting there. When Sher had finished, he puffed away thoughtfully. "So as far as you're concerned, Mr. Haynes—"

"Call me Sher. My friends do. And I shall call you Joe, if I may."

"I'll be honored."

"And, Joe, you ought to regard what I've said about taking on the case as confidential."

"I worked in the docks and then as a security guard, and nobody ever said I opened my mouth too wide. But as I was saying, you're going to investigate this case the way Sherlock Holmes would have done— Why are you laughing?"

"People keep saying I should remember I'm not Sherlock Holmes, but do they really think I'd forget? Holmes was a detective genius. I'm just an actor. I don't have Holmes's brain or his knowledge. But what I do believe, Joe, is this: Holmes was an amateur up against professionals, and everybody says the day of the amateur is over. The professionals have got all the laboratory details; they can distinguish types of blood, individual hairs, one grain of sand from another, very likely. But when it comes to deductions, there must be an individual brain, and an amateur brain may be better than a professional one. The plodding professional gathers the facts, but it needs the inspired amateur to draw the conclusions." He had leaned forward in his chair during this peroration, finger raised, an image of Sherlock. "For example, one point stands out to me in relation to these Karate Killings. You've read about them, as I have. Can you tell me what it is?"

Johnson puffed away. Smoke rose above his head. "The method's the same in each case."

"Yes, but something more than that."

"So the man's a karate expert, or at least knows what he's doing."

"Something more." The warden shook his head. "The victims must all have known the killer, known him well enough that when he approached they didn't feel any fear of him. At least, that's true of the last two. Consider Gladson's case. He was sitting in his car when someone came up, and it's obvious he wasn't afraid of whoever it was. And in the last killing Halliwell actually opened the door to his killer."

"Do you mean the murderer's very daring, takes chances?"

"That's what it sounds like. Suppose somebody had seen the person beside Gladson's car, or outside the door of that place in Soho. He seems to have been taking a tremendous risk. Now, my idea is that this isn't true."

"I don't follow you."

"I mean that in some way this was a sort of invisible man." He dropped his bombshell. "Or a woman."

Johnson took his pipe out of his mouth. "Come now, Mr. Haynes, that's surely very far-fetched."

"Is it? Supposing you're Gladson, in your car in the early hours of the morning. Somebody comes up, and you obligingly wind down your car window so that they can attack you. You're Halliwell, and you open the locked door of a shop. What sort of person would you not feel any fear of at all? A woman, especially if it were an attractive woman."

"And you think a woman would be able to commit these murders—she'd have the strength?"

"It's not great strength you need for a karate punch or chop so much as perfect accuracy. But of course in cases like these nobody would think of a woman. She is, to use an Irishism, a perfect invisible man."

Johnson-Watson knocked out his pipe. He was plainly not convinced. "It might have been a friend of Gladson's."

"And of Halliwell? And of the first man—Mole? I don't think so; not exactly. What I believe is that the killer knew them all, although that doesn't mean they knew him. Or her."

"That's too hard for me, I'm afraid."

"Suppose at some time all three of them had sat on a jury, and they'd sent the husband or son of our invisible man to prison? So that the motive is revenge."

"I seem to have read something like that in a detective story. More than once."

Sher leaned forward, his eager profile sharpened by the firelight. "This may *be* a crime like one in a book, don't you see? I'm not saying that's the answer, but what we have to look for is a common factor joining the victims."

"I should suppose the police have been doing that. Is there any immediate clue you've got, something you can follow up?"

"No. But I place high hopes on the public response when it's known that I am working on the case."

"I might be able to help there. Rather like the Baker Street Irregulars, sir, if I may say so. Keeping an eye open, and then letting you know."

"How do you mean?"

"I'm in charge of a wardens' center, just over forty people working under me. My job is to organize their work, supervise it and handle inquiries from the public. People have got the wrong idea about traffic wardens, you know. They call them snoopers, think they're out to give parking tickets all the time, but that isn't true. The wardens are there to make things go smoothly. When there's a traffic jam, if a policeman isn't there to control it, then a warden stands in. We're not the enemy of the motorist; we're doing a public service."

"You may not be the enemy of the motorist, Johnson, but I am. I believe the car is the greatest evil of our so-called civilization."

"That's talking silly, sir—"

"Sher."

"Sher. If I may say so. We'd all just come to a full stop without cars and lorries. We've got to have them." A crescendo of noise from the motorway drowned out his next words. Sherlock and Watson looked at each other and both began to laugh. "Of course, I've read that you'd like to live in Sherlock Holmes's time, and I don't say *I* wouldn't, but we can't do it, can we? Now, what I was going to suggest was this: The wardens I control, men and women both, they're all sorts and both sexes. All ages, too; anybody between eighteen and sixty is eligible. Some of them are young, twenty or twenty-one. They're used to keeping a sharp eye open; it's their job. Suppose you come along to our wardens' center and talk to the ones on duty, tell them what you are after. I'm sure there'd be some who'd be pleased and proud to work with you. If it suits you, I'd suggest tomorrow morning."

Sher was on fire with the suggestion. "Splendid. They'd be my eyes and ears."

"Exactly. We work shifts: one week seven in the morning till three-thirty in the afternoon, the next ten to seven at night. If there was anyone particular you wanted watched when they were off duty, I know there are some who'd be glad to earn a bit extra, if Sherlock Holmes could run to it."

"You're a man after my own heart." He was especially

pleased that Johnson had kept the spirit of the chase by saying Sherlock Holmes and not Sheridan Haynes. "And I know how I'd like to use them first. There's one person involved in the case, linked with it in some way, I'm sure, whose activities I'd like checked." Johnson looked inquiring. "A woman. Irene Adler."

He returned to Baker Street as bouncy as a man on an air cushion, but within minutes Willie called to say that the company did not want him to investigate the Karate Killings. The producer tried to soften the blow by saying that they thought the publicity would be counterproductive, unless he solved the case. Sher listened without interruption. Then he said, "Very well, I shall announce the investigation myself," and put down the receiver. He phoned the press. Two of the morning papers wanted to run features about the way in which he would pursue his inquiries, but he refused to say anything further.

Val returned in the middle of all this. When he had put down the telephone after talking to the *Daily Express*, she said, "What does that stupid little bastard think he's playing at?"

"Willie? He's got nothing to do with it." His face assumed a long-suffering look that had always irritated her. "The company thinks the publicity will be counterproductive." He emphasized the last word to convey that it was a modern cliché.

"But you're going on? When they don't want you to do it? You must be—" She had been about to say "mad," but the intent stare she got from the deep-set eyes was so irrational that she did not use the word. Instead she went across and put her arms around him. His body remained stiff within her embrace.

"Don't you see that you've let this get out of proportion? You'll get shoals of letters, people calling here—"

"Of course. There may be clues."

"They're going to be total nuts, busybodies, people confessing things, sick people. Don't you *see?*"

He got up, walked across to the mantelpiece, put his arms

behind him. "Do you mean that only sick people are interested in Sherlock Holmes?"

"I just think this idea's insane." There, the word was out, and she did not care. The drive back from Greenwich had been done in heavy traffic that had reduced her speed to a crawl, and then there had been parking trouble because there was a new assistant at the garage where she put the car, and her usual space was occupied. The habitual composure with which she spoke did not reflect the angry turmoil within her mind. "What I mean is that I wish we'd stayed in Weybridge, I wish you'd never started all this TV. I've had enough of this Sherlock Holmes game. I can't put up with it, and I don't see why I should. If you go on with this I shall leave you."

She stopped. He was dialing another number. When she heard him say, "The *Guardian?* This is Sheridan Haynes. I have a message of some importance about the Karate Killings," she walked out of the room, packed an overnight bag and drove to Battersea, where she stayed with an old friend from Weybridge named Marjorie Billings, who had divorced her adman husband and gone off to live with a black actor who called himself Seamus O'Toole. Seamus had recently left her for what he called a mare of another color, and the two women sat up half the night drinking whisky and talking about men. Val woke in the morning with a bad headache, which was not improved by reading two newspaper stories headed respectively: "TV'S SHERLOCK ON TRAIL OF KARATE KILLER" and "THERE'S METHOD IN THESE MURDERS, SAYS TV'S SHERLOCK HOLMES." One story was facetious, the other disapproving. She found it hard to do more than nibble at her toast.

HOW AND WHY

Devenish also breakfasted badly. Sue, in the pursuit of something more interesting than eggs and bacon, had bought some
croissants from a delicatessen, and they proved to be stale. He
was plowing through one when she asked, "But can he do that,
this Sheridan Haynes? He says he's going to investigate the
case."

"Publicity gimmick."

"But I mean, if he came to you for information . . ."

"He wouldn't get it. But it's a free country; people can investigate what they like." He swallowed the last of the croissant
with a gulp. "Got to go now. Back about seven with luck. I'll
ring if I'm going to be late."

He held her tightly, kissed her and then was gone. As she got
the children ready for school, she reflected that a policeman's
wife's lot is not entirely a happy one.

Three-quarters of an hour later, Devenish watched while
they conducted an experiment. A detective constable named
Stark walked over to a Lamborghini, unlocked it, opened the
door, sat in it. Brewster approached, waving to him. Stark
wound down his window, looked inquiring. Brewster, close to

the window, made a punching motion at Stark's gullet. Stark's head went back, he put hand to throat. Brewster leaned inside, pulled the head forward, made two chopping gestures at the back of the neck. Stark was left slumped over the steering wheel.

"It can be done," Brewster said. "Gladson was four inches shorter than Stark, which would have made it easier."

"You couldn't defend yourself?" Devenish asked Stark.

"Not really. Inside a car you're kind of helpless. Confined like, being so low down."

"I saw." Devenish scratched his nose. Stark gazed at one of the great thumbs he had heard about, thumbs that looked as though they could squeeze the life out of anything. "But only if you open the window. Why did you do that?"

"I don't know really. The sergeant waved at me."

"Yes." Afterward, he said to Brewster, "Two things. Gladson knew whoever it was well enough to wind down the window. And the killer was right-handed. To punch and then chop left-handed with Gladson so low down in the car would be pretty well impossible."

"So where does that leave us?"

"With a lot of right-handed men." Back at the Yard, he spent an hour in a time-wasting conference about the case with the top brass. He agreed that a gang war must not be allowed to break out, and said that he was pursuing half a dozen promising lines. At the end of the conference the A.C.'s red-faced deputy made a joke. "Don't want to run any risk of Sherlock Holmes finding the chappie before we do, eh, Thumbs?"

Devenish looked at him with a straight face. "The day a TV Sherlock beats the Yard, I'll write out my resignation."

Back in his office again, he learned the result of two hunches. It turned out that thirty-seven police officers admitted taking courses in karate. Half of them could be ruled out at once, because on the relevant dates they had been on duty in the vicinity of their stations, a long way from where the murders took place. Fourteen men were left, and he told Brewster to put somebody on to checking them out. Brewster looked as though he regarded this as a total waste of time, and Devenish knew he was probably right.

The other hunch related to the Moles' Ford Escort car. It had been sold to a dealer and had not yet been resprayed. The car had suffered damage to the front right fender. The damage was slight, the fender had been only dented and scratched, but it was fairly recent. He read this with interest, and went to see Mrs. Mole.

Devenish did not gamble, but he believed that if a hunch looked promising you should go on playing it. He sat opposite Mrs. Mole in the living room watched over by the TV's blank but somehow seeing eye, and said, "Why didn't you tell me your husband had been in a car accident?"

Her expression did not change but she gave a single gasp, like somebody doused with cold water. "It couldn't have had anything to do with what happened. And besides . . ."

"What?"

"Nobody was there. I don't see how you can know. Afterwards, I was so ashamed. It was the worst thing we ever did in our lives." She dabbed angrily at her eyes with a handkerchief.

He waited, and she told him. It had happened two months ago, in early November. They had been to dinner with her brother and his wife, out at West Hampstead in North London. Charles had had some beer at dinner and then a small glass of port, but she was insistent that he had not been the least drunk. When they set out to go home it was misty, so that the street lights were shrouded. They were driving up a side street named Purefoy Road, which led to the Finchley Road, when she saw something shadowy ahead, and then was aware of a bump. She asked Charles what it was, but he did not reply. Mrs. Mole, looking back, saw that they had passed a zebra crossing, its flashing beacon only faintly visible. She also thought she saw, lying on the white-striped road, a small figure that might have been a child. She had asked her husband to stop, but he took no notice and continued.

Later, he said to her that he had seen absolutely nothing, although he had felt the bump. There was nothing he could have done. She did not feel at all sure that he was telling the truth. When she said again that he should have stopped, he asked whether she understood what she was asking. It was a zebra crossing, in which the pedestrian always has the right of way, and if he had hit somebody he would certainly have lost his license and been fined, perhaps even gone to prison.

"We did try afterwards," she said. "I made Charles buy the local paper for two weeks, but there was no report in it. It was an awful thing to have done, though. I should have made Charles stop. I've never forgiven myself. He said it must have been a mistake, and that the damage to the fender had happened before, but I knew that wasn't true. It's strange that there was nothing in the paper. It can't have been serious, can it?"

"I've heard worse." He was not given to judging other people. He knew that there are a lot of hit-and-run drivers, and that there would be more if they thought they could escape detection. "But you think you did hit somebody?"

"Of course, it was misty and we couldn't see, but I'm afraid we must have done. I don't see why . . ."

"Yes?"

"Why you want to know this. Has somebody come forward and complained? There couldn't be a charge now, could there? I don't think I could stand that."

It was typical of somebody like Mrs. Mole, he thought, that she stoically accepted the death of a husband but could not endure the thought of being brought into court on a motoring charge. "Nobody's complained. And there'll be no charge."

Later, he talked about it with Brewster, whose philistine common sense remained unmoved. "It's very far-fetched, Chief, isn't it? She says herself nobody saw the accident. So all right, maybe she was wrong, but it has to be somebody who spotted the car number and was prepared to kill as a punishment. Then in the Gladson case, the Pages are out as suspects. And in this Halliwell business, too—"

"I know all that. But the fact remains: three people have been killed, and every one has been involved in a car accident. *And* in each case the driver was at fault and got away with it. You're telling me that's coincidence?"

"Of course it is. Why you worry with it, when the Clabers had the best of reasons for knocking off that little queer, I don't know."

"I don't like coincidences." Roger Devenish sat for a moment or two at his desk, his face heavy and brooding. "I want a man to go to Purefoy Road and the streets around. He'll be looking for an accident, perhaps involving a child, last November. Needn't be serious; any sort of accident. I'll want all the details —family and so on." Brewster made a note. "And we'll have the Clabers in. Both of them. Though we shan't get anything out of them."

He was right, of course. They came and sat in his office, Harry with his comical look and Jack with his air of finding it hard to follow what was going on, and said they didn't know what he was talking about. Harry was voluble, almost eloquent.

"Now look, Thumbs— Don't mind my calling you that, do you? You must know it's what all the boys call you when your back's turned." Devenish nodded. Harry spread out his hands. "You're brainy; you must know if we were going to do somebody over it wouldn't be like that. That's even if I had a boy who could do it, which I haven't. Right, Jack?"

"Right."

It was true that a good deal of asking around among people who knew the Claber gang had not turned up a whisper about a karate expert inside it. You can't prove a negative, but still this was the kind of news that never remains secret for long. Harry went on about running a straight business in spite of a lot of police interference and suspicion. Jack looked worshipfully at his brother. Devenish felt it was time to say something.

"You're up to your neck in this, Harry, and you know it. Gladson gets it after he's had a row with your bird, and Sonny Halliwell is knocked off to show Freddy Williams he can't muscle in on your territory."

"I tell you there isn't a boy of mine—"

The chief superintendent raised his voice, and slapped the table in front of him. An inkstand rattled. "I don't care what you tell me or where your boy's stowed away. You've got a reason for having these two jobs done, and I want the right story."

"Thumbs, Thumbs," Harry said, with the smile made more comic by his crooked nose.

"And you can stop calling me that. I want the right story, and I want it quick. If I don't get it I'll slap those clubs of yours down so hard there won't be one left open inside a week. Don't tell me I can't do it because I will."

That's the way to talk to them, Brewster thought. Jack Claber's mouth fell open and he looked at his brother in alarm. Even Harry's cultivated ease was ruffled. He uncrossed his legs, put his hands on his knees. "You've no cause to talk to me like that."

"Harry, if this job belongs to you I'll stick it on you, however hard I have to work to do it. Now, you just give me the story, and tell your idiot brother there to shut his mouth."

How much his anger was real and how much simulated, Devenish could not have said himself. He might prefer the Clabers to Freddy Williams, but really he hated all professional crooks. Their existence represented a threat to all he valued most—the house in Wimbledon and its small green lawns front and rear, the peaceful life there with Sue and the children. He did not often think about such contrasts—he was on the genial terms with most villains that a detective had to be—but there were times when he would have liked to see the Clabers and their hangers-on put inside forever, and this was one of them. Or at least that was part of what he felt. Another part of himself noted Harry's uneasiness with detached interest.

"There's nothing to say. Honest. I don't know what you want."

Brewster spoke. "Williams is moving in on you and you're doing nothing about it—is that what you want us to believe?"

There was a quick exchange of glances between the brothers, expressing perhaps amusement, perhaps a shared secret. Then Harry said solemnly, "On my word of honor as a Catholic—and I wouldn't go against it, you know that, Chief Superintendent —I don't know a thing about what happened to Sonny Halliwell. And that goes for Jack, too, isn't that so?"

Jack raised one hand as though he were in a witness box. "Word of honor," he said.

When they had gone, Devenish said, "Do you know, I'm inclined to believe them?"

"Not a bit of it, Chief. Did you see the way they looked at each other? They're up to something."

Whatever they were up to, however, it seemed that Devenish's warnings might have had some effect. The Clabers opened up no more shops, Freddy Williams attempted no reprisals. On the other hand, the trail leading to the policemen who had learned karate seemed to be petering out. Only two of them, D.C. Morgan and Detective Sergeant Edwards, seemed to be possibilities. They would both have had opportunity in all three cases, and they were known to have talked about the ease with which a karate chop could kill a man. It was all pretty thin, but Devenish ordered a further check run on them to find out if either man had connections with the Clabers, and whether they hated cars.

THE CARROUSEL

In the street it was trying to snow but getting no further than a thin, hard rain. The wardens' center was hot and steamy. A smell of well-brewed tea blended with a smell of drying overcoats. Wardens sat at plastic-topped tables drinking mugs of tea, eating buns and talking. From the general concerto, single threads of sound came through to Sher as he moved among the tables, looking for Johnson.

"—said to me, 'I should think you could find something better to do.' "

"—meter's out of order. I said, 'It's not, you know.' "

"—smashing film at the Odeon—"

"—tragic really. I mean, since it happened he just isn't the same."

"What did you say after that?"

"—wouldn't demean myself to speak; just gave him the ticket."

" 'You've stuck a dud coin in the meter,' I said, 'that's what you've done.' "

"Jack Nicholson turns me on in anything. I mean, he could—"

"—face up to things. It was an accident, after all, not as if it was his wife; no use being morbid."

"—quite agree; got to keep a sense of proportion."

"Just what I say. I mean, an animal's an animal, after all. Got to keep a sense—"

"He could recite the alphabet and it would turn me on."

At the other end of the room there was a raised platform in front of a big wall map showing the Baker Street–Oxford Street area, through to Hyde Park on one side, Regent's Park on another. Colored pins were stuck in at traffic junctions, like acupuncture needles in vital spots. A woman in uniform sat on the platform, listening to a radio receiver and then talking earnestly into a microphone. In a cubbyhole beyond the platform he found Johnson. He was on the telephone.

"I'm sorry, madam, I really am, but there's nothing I can do. Yes, I am the controller, but I don't have the authority to cancel a notice. I appreciate that you'd only stopped for a few minutes, but it was on a yellow line, and that's a traffic offense. If—"

He put the receiver down, grinned at Sher. "She hung up. They often do. Now come along and let me introduce you to Betty." Here in the center Johnson was more assured, less deferential. He steered the way to a table occupied by a large woman who was drinking tea. "This is Betty Brade. Betty, you'll remember I was talking about Mr. Sheridan Haynes."

" 'TV's Sherlock on Trail of Karate Killer,' " Betty Brade said. Her bulk strained against the confines of the uniform; the hand in which she held the teacup made it look like a toy. Small eyes were merry in the unleavened dough of her face. When she smiled, her wide mouth showed gold teeth. "Joe says you want help. I'm not surprised."

"She's a tough nut," Johnson said with a kind of rueful admiration. "I've tried to convince her that it's a serious idea, but she's a tough nut."

It was a situation of a kind that Holmes had never been obliged to face, one in which he had to persuade somebody by sheer eloquence, but Sher felt himself equal to it. He fixed Betty Brade with what he knew from many TV appearances to be a compelling gaze, and gave his voice a level of deep seriousness that he knew to be convincing.

"I can only tell you that the company producing my series have told me that my investigation will be counterproductive unless I solve the case, and they are opposed to it because they don't think I shall solve it. Personally, I believe in the genius of Sherlock Holmes, and I hope I can reflect some of that genius in myself. But I shall need helpers to act as my eyes and ears. The question is, are you prepared to help me?"

Betty Brade laughed raucously, with a flash of gold.

"It sounds so dotty I just have to go along with it. Sherlock, you've got yourself a helper."

Johnson was pleased. "Don't think Betty won't be useful. She was—"

Sher held up a hand. "Before you say anything, let me tell you one or two things I've noticed. First of all, it's probable that Miss Brade is not of British origin. Her parents may well have been Central European—"

Betty intervened. "My mother and father were Hungarian. I was a teen-ager when I came over after the fifty-six revolution. Is it the accent? I thought I'd lost it."

"You have. It was the gold teeth. Not at all British."

"And what did I do before I took this job—can you tell me that?"

"Perhaps I can. You aren't fat; that's tremendous muscle development in your arms. Your hands are big but well kept, no manual work, but they've obviously been used in what you were doing. You might have been a chucker-out in a pub, but I'd think some sort of athlete is more likely, a weight lifter or a shot putter. They wouldn't be jobs, though." Something in her attitude gave him inspiration. "A wrestler, a woman wrestler."

"I used to be an all-in wrestler till I got musclebound. Full marks, Sherlock."

Johnson was looking around. "Jim's not here?"

"He's knocked off. Said he'd be in the Bear and Staff."

"That's our local. Jim Cassidy I'm talking about; you know him. Why don't we adjourn, Betty?"

"I was waiting to be asked. This tea was made with bilge water. You can't drink the stuff, only pour it back."

The Bear and Staff was a couple of minutes' walk away. They found Cassidy there, ruminating over a glass of beer.

"You remember Jim Cassidy," Johnson said. "He's ready to be the second of your Baker Street Irregulars. I'm the third." Betty looked mystified. "They helped Sherlock Holmes."

Cassidy's lugubrious look changed to something near a smile. "Glad to help, Mr. Haynes. Any way I can."

"The thing is," Betty Brade asked, "what do you actually want us to do?"

It was a question to which he had given thought, without finding a fully satisfactory answer. "If you've a phone at home I'll take the number, so that I can get in touch if it's urgent. I'd like you to ring me each morning, so that I can tell you if there's anything special I want you to check. There is one particular woman whose movements I'd like to know about, an actress named Sarah Peters."

"She's in your series," Betty Brade said.

"That's right." He wrote down the address. "She lives in this area, but of course I realize you can't keep a check on her movements while you're doing your job. If you can do it when you're off duty, follow her and let me know where she goes. I particularly want to know what contact she has with Harry Claber, the gambler, if that's the right thing to call him."

Betty popped a piece of gum into her mouth and began chewing. "Jim and I are on at the same times. We're not going to be able to make any proper check." Johnson said that they could alternate shifts, and that he would do some checking himself. She shrugged. "Seems to me you'd do better with a good private detective. What else?"

"I shall want you to follow up any leads I get from letters and telephone calls. And then, two of these crimes have taken place in the street. I'd like you to tell me anything out of the way that happens, or that you notice, when you're on duty."

"You mean that?" Betty asked. "We're always getting in trouble; a lot of people hate the sight of us. Couple of days ago a man took a punch at me for giving him a ticket. I had to lay him flat on his back. You want to hear about things like that? It was the biggest thing in the day for me."

"Or the ones who try to slip a pound in your pocket and say, 'You didn't notice my car here, did you, officer?'" Cassidy said. "I tell them, 'If you're going to try to bribe me you should make it worth my while.' They turn quite nasty then."

Johnson intervened. "Use your own discretion, and your intelligence, is what Sher means. He wants things to do with the case, not bits of autobiography, isn't that so?"

Sher nodded.

"Okay," Betty said heartily. "Then the only thing to be settled is the lolly, the moola. The green stuff. In short, folding money."

It was hardly the attitude of the Baker Street Irregulars, but these were different, degraded days. It was evident that his helpers were going to cost a lot more than those hired by Sherlock Holmes.

The telephone rang. Cassidy's solemn voice sounded over the line.

"I followed Miss Peters from her home as you suggested, sir. In a taxi. She is now in the Carrousel, which is a gaming club in Shepherd Market, on the corner of—"

"I know it. I'll be with you in half an hour. Can you wait until I come, and let me know if she leaves in the meantime?"

Cassidy said he could, and Sher returned to contemplation of the papers and magazines piled on the floor, and the note that had been pushed through the letter box that morning. It consisted of letters cut from papers in the classic manner, and it said:

ITS UNDER YOUR NOSE MR. HOLMES WHY IS SARAH PETERS SO THICK WITH THE CLABERS SHE DID GLADSON AND THEY COVERED UP THEN THEY KNOCKED OFF SONNY COME TO THE CARROUSEL SIT IN BAR AT NINE TONIGHT I WILL CONTACT.

Most of the message was cut from the *Daily Mail* and the *Daily Telegraph*, judging by the type faces, but the names had been cut out in single letters, and for some time he had been unable to identify their source. He had eventually found them in the women's magazine *Cosmopolitan*. Did this mean that the message was a piece of malice on the part of a fellow actress? Possibly, but it had seemed worth pursuing the possibility of Sarah's involvement. In any case, it was the only thing of potential interest in a flood of ridiculous or obscene material. The communications that came through the post had varied in absurdity from a letter that said the Karate Killer was obviously a member of the royal family ("Did you know that Prince Charles practices karate in *secret?* Remember Jack the Ripper and the Duke of Clarence") to one that suggested the killer was the son of the Boston Strangler. He had been reading these letters when Val telephoned, said that she had seen the papers and asked if he was giving up this ridiculous idea. When he said no, she repeated quietly that she had meant what she said yesterday, and rang off. It occurred to him afterward that he had not expressed surprise or regret at her absence, and had not asked where she spent the night. He had been so totally absorbed by the letters that he had not even thought seriously about her absence. In the past after a row—and they had had very few rows in their twenty-five years of marriage—she had twice gone to stay with her sister, who was a doctor's wife in Sanderstead. He phoned the sister now, but she had heard nothing of Val, and he drew a blank at the Greenwich shop, which she had not visited that morning.

At that point he gave up. He found it impossible to concentrate on these personal problems (if they were problems, for he had no doubt that Val would be back in a few hours, when her tantrum was over) while the question of the Karate Killer remained unsolved. He had a feeling that some thread was in his hands which, if he pulled it in the right direction, would lead to a solution based on reason and logic. So strong did this feeling become that, as he wandered around the room putting straight the poker from "The Speckled Band," lifting the plastic top that covered the five orange pips and running his fingers over their faintly glutinous surface, some magnetism seemed to be transferred from them to him. His fingertips tingled, as though a message was being relayed to him which he lacked sufficient wit to interpret. If he could enter into the secrets of those past cases, he might solve this one. He felt like a medium straining to receive a message from the other world that is not quite intelligible.

Cassidy was outside the Carrousel, looking leaner and more hangdog now that he was off duty and out of uniform. He said that Sarah Peters was there, and asked if he was still needed.

Sher hesitated. "If your wife's waiting for you—"

"Nobody waiting, Mr. Haynes. I live on my own."

"Then you may as well wait. I'm expecting to meet somebody here. If you see me come out with someone else, follow us."

The Carrousel was discreet, or as some would have said, funereal. The hatcheck girls wore Victorian black top hats and might perhaps have been hatcheck boys; the bar was done in swirling art nouveau bands of black and gold. The lamps were buried in black shades designed to eliminate as much light as possible. A small fountain poured out two streams of water, one black and one gold. The waiters were pretty boys who could not possibly have been girls. They wore black bell bottoms and gold shirts. The seats were black armchairs, set in groups of two or three. He sat down and ordered a lager from one of the waiters. There were very few people in the bar, and none of them showed any interest in him. The time was three minutes to nine.

Ten minutes later nobody had approached him. People passed through the bar on the way to what was presumably the gaming room. One of them was a medium-sized broad-shouldered man with his nose a little askew, who stopped and spoke to one of the waiters before going inside. Sher recognized him from photographs as Harry Claber. He got up and followed Claber into the gaming room.

Here the black-and-gold motif was modified, and the total effect less dim. There were pools of light over a dozen tables, and the devotees who sat at them were grave as any other worshipers as they watched the decisive cards or ball. Dealers and croupiers presided, acolytes of the power that they also dispensed, going through the ritualistic moves of distribution and collection. Claber stopped at a roulette table and bent down beside one of the players. It was Sarah Peters. She had a pile of chips in front of her, and barely looked up from them. He said something to her and then walked away, through a gold door that said in black letters, "Private."

Sher returned to the bar, sat looking at the black and gold streams of water and wondered what Sherlock Holmes would have done. In fact, this was a question not too difficult to answer. Disguised as an Arab sheik rich with oil profits, he would have been playing roulette. A few of the Baker Street Irregulars would have raised a fire scare, Claber would have rushed out of his private office and made for the door. In a moment the sheik would have been in the office, and out again with the vital information. But what was the information? And did that job lot of traffic wardens measure up at all to the Baker Street Irregulars? He feared not.

His watch said nine-twenty. It looked as if the message was a bad joke. He ordered another lager from the waiter, who tossed his head skittishly and walked away without a word of thanks as Sher gave what he regarded as a reasonable tip. He decided to wait ten minutes more and then give up.

A thin, angular girl with long hair came in from the entrance hall. She wore jeans and a thick pullover, and looked as much in place as a miner at a garden party. What might have been the headwaiter hurried over and blocked her entrance to the gaming room. She spoke to him, and he talked earnestly to a telephone hanging on the wall. She waited, dipping into a bowl of nuts on a table where a man dressed trendily enough to be a salesman was sitting with a well-enameled girl in a peacock-blue dress, the top of which seemed to have disappeared. The thin girl took nuts by the handful and pushed them into her mouth. The bare-shouldered girl—her breasts had no visible support but just stayed under cover—spoke to her escort. The girl stopped chewing and stared at them as though they were an unknown species. The headwaiter put back the telephone and returned to her. She nodded, took some more nuts and went through the door to the gaming room.

"If it's not my old partner and colleague." He looked up into the beaming foolish face of Basil Wainwright. "And what are *you* doing here, my old duck, in these haunts of wickedness?"

Sher said truthfully that he had been waiting for somebody who apparently wasn't going to turn up, and added that Sarah was inside playing roulette.

"Oh, my dear, she's here *every* night just now." Basil lowered himself into the neighboring chair. "I mean, they say Harry Claber's taken over where Gladson left off. He stakes her to some chips, and anything she wins she takes away. Of course, he demands his pound of flesh." He giggled briefly. "But Sarah's got the gambling bug. She lives for it."

"What about you?"

"Me? Oh, my dear, not my bag."

"So why are you here?"

One of the bell-bottomed boys glided past with a tray of drinks. Basil giggled again. "Isn't it ravishing? You really are an old goose. I say, what's that when it's at home?"

The doors from the gaming room opened and Claber came through them, together with the girl in the pullover. They were talking as they passed. Claber said, "Of course I want to see it; what do you think. . . ."

Sher drained his glass and got up. This was the only faintly interesting thing that had happened in the club, and he decided not to lose it. "My dear, you're positively taking off," Basil said, watching his progress with amusement. Then he turned to greet a young man who had just come up to him, smirking delightedly. *"Basil."* Sher left them together.

When he reached the street Claber and the girl were crossing the road to a Mercedes coupe, parked on a double yellow line. Its license plate had the letters "HC," presumably for Harry Claber. They stood talking while Claber leisurely unlocked the door. To follow them Sher would need a taxi, and at that moment one drew up, letting out a man and woman who went into the Carrousel. Sher was about to get in when a voice said, "Mr. Haynes."

He had forgotten about Cassidy, who now emerged from the shadows. "Do you want me?"

"What? No, I don't think so." Claber had got in and was about to start the car. Sher leaned out of the taxi. "I may be on the track of something."

"Shall I come with you?" Cassidy asked hopefully.

"No, I don't think so. Ring me tomorrow."

"Or follow Miss Peters?"

The Mercedes was pulling away. He opened the sliding glass panel and said, "Follow that car." Then to Cassidy, "Yes, wait for her and follow her."

"Shall I—" Cassidy called something else after him, but he did not hear what it was. They pulled out into Curzon Street. "Follow him, cabby, don't lose him," he cried.

The driver, young, curly-haired, looked around.

"Don't lose a Merc? Me, in this old banger? You've got to be joking."

He played a Holmesian card. "Double fare if you can keep him in sight."

"I'll do me best, guv, but no guarantee."

They were going up toward Park Lane. What part of London were they bound for? One of those vile alleys where Watson had once found Holmes in an opium den, on the track of the man with the twisted lip? Or what Watson called the maritime area, where tenement houses reeked with the outcasts of Europe? Or a large dark house like The Myrtles at Beckenham, where the mystery of the Greek interpreter had been finally unraveled? As they crawled down Park Lane, moving forward in quick rushes when the light was green, they stayed just a couple of cars behind the Mercedes. "Traffic keeps like this we can't lose," the driver said. "Any idea where he's making for? No? Pity. I'll just have to stay on his tail."

From Park Lane they went into Knightsbridge, along the Brompton Road to South Kensington station, and then down the Fulham Road. The Mercedes was evidently in no hurry, and it was easy enough to stay behind him. All the way down Fulham Road with its newish semi-smart restaurants, past Chelsea football ground, up North End Road, where the rubbish from the stalls that line the road during daylight was still in the gutters. Then left and right. It was in these dingy streets that they might be noticed by the car in front. Sher leaned forward.

"If he stops, go straight on and stop in the next street."

Another left turn and the Mercedes stopped. As the taxi cruised past slowly with a headlight illuminating the name, Dingwall Street, Claber and the girl could be seen about to enter a house. On the fanlight was a number: 24. The taxi stopped around the next corner. Sher paid the double fare and got out.

"I don't suppose you often have an assignment like that."

"You'd be surprised. Geezer the other day told me to follow a bird. She meets another bird and they go off together. He's bloody purple in the face when he sees 'em. You know why?

The first bird's his tart, the other's his wife, and they're having it off together. And his wife won't sleep with him, says she's frigid. He tells me all this, mind you; I never ask a question." He looked with some curiosity at Sher, then started his engine. "Cheerio then, guv. Good hunting."

As the taxi moved away, Sher reflected that every aspect of modern life had about it something jarring. A cab driver in Holmes's time would not have shown this unseemly familiarity with lesbian practices, and Holmes himself would surely have spoken of them only as an awful moral evil. The reflections brought him to number 24. It was similar to its neighbors, a workman's cottage that had come up in the world, but not very far. No light showed upstairs, but there was a gleam behind the curtains lining the ground floor bay window. Holmes might have crept up and listened outside, or have found a handy adjacent ladder and made an entry up above with Watson's connivance, but that was not a practical possibility today. No ladder was visible, and people were passing. Fortunately there was a pub opposite called The Jolly Burglar. With any luck he would be able to watch the house from inside the pub.

And indeed the house, with the car outside it, was clearly visible when standing at the bar. He downed almost half of his pint of bitter, and said to the girl who had served him, "You don't often see a Mercedes parked in a road like this. Does it belong to the people there, do you know?"

He had noticed before that his mastery of the common touch was not complete, and now the girl gave him a blank look for answer. From a little way down the bar, however, somebody spoke. "Oh, no, that'll not be their car. The Drummonds have got no money."

The speaker was a tall, thin young man, with fair hair cut unfashionably short, and very bright blue eyes. He wore an old tweed jacket and dirty gray flannel trousers. "Did you want the Drummonds?"

It is usually a good idea to go as near the truth as possible when you are telling lies. "I don't think so. That car looks like one owned by a friend of mine named Claber. He's got a number plate with his initials on it, and the number's very much like that one."

The young man moved up the bar. The girl behind the bar, polishing glasses, watched them warily. "That wouldn't be the Drummonds; the idea's a joke. He's a kind of a journalist, they say, calls himself a writer, but he can't make a living at it. I don't know what he does make a living at. Often in here, though." He moved his empty glass about on the counter in an experimental way, and Sher took the hint. "Isn't he, darling?" the young man said to the barmaid. She looked at him and made no reply.

"He's married?"

"Indeed he is. And got a son."

"Is his wife a dark girl who's usually rather untidily dressed?"

"That's her. You've got her perfectly. Chrissie, his better half. She's an artist, and very clever, they say. Commercial, of course. Whatever bread comes in that house, she brings it home."

"You called her Chrissie. You know her?"

"Ah, everybody round here knows Chrissie. They feel sorry for her with a husband like that. I mean, Hugh Drummond is no good, he's a bad character."

"Hugh Drummond?"

"You recognize the name, you're a reading man yourself. Yes, he's got the same name as Bulldog Drummond." The young man's smile was wolfish, showing sharp white teeth. "Did his parents give him the name or did he take it for himself? Who can tell? You haven't said how it is you know Chrissie Drummond."

"I don't know her by name. My friend Claber knows a girl who looks like that."

The young man did not seem to notice the yawning gap in credibility here, which Sher realized as soon as he had spoken: why should the fact that Claber knew a girl who looked like Chrissie have made him imagine that it was this girl? The young man drummed with his fingers on the counter and looked at Sher, still with the wolfish smile. A man came out of the house opposite. It was Claber. He got into the Mercedes and drove away. Sher was uncertain what to do. Should he call at the house?

"Well?" the young man said. He was off the bar stool and in front of Sher.

"What do you mean?"

"Was it your friend Claber? You were looking hard enough."

"I think it was; yes."

The barmaid spoke for the first time. "We don't want any trouble in here, Mr. Drummond."

At that the young man relaxed and made a mock bow. "Hugh Drummond at your service. Come and meet Chrissie."

A couple of minutes later Sher was in the front room with the bay window. It was a living and dining room, and it was extremely untidy. Two ashtrays overflowed with cigarette butts and a third had been knocked onto the floor. There was an old sofa and a couple of shabby chairs with empty coffee cups on them. A toy garage stood under a table, and toy cars were scattered around the floor. A plate was on the table with a half-eaten piece of bread and butter on it. Beside it were crumbs of fruit cake. Around the walls were half a dozen paintings that looked to Sher like splurges of color running into each other. He disliked them, he disliked the sluttishness of the house, he disliked Drummond.

And no doubt Drummond disliked him. He had shouted "Chrissie" at the bottom of the stairs, and now stood in the doorway. A switchblade had appeared in his right hand. He tapped the point of it gently into the palm of his left.

"So what's the story?" Sher did not know what to say. "Come on, buster. You go in that pub and you ask a lot of questions about me and my family. I'm entitled to know what it's about. If you ask me, I've been too damn nice already." He threw up the knife and caught it. "You like Bulldog Drummond?"

116

"It's a long time since I've read about him."

"English, are you?"

"Of course. Why do you ask?"

"Not so much 'of course.' This country's getting crowded out with foreigners, friend—Pakis, blacks, yids. Some you can tell, but the worst are the ones you can't, the ones that look just like you and me." He opened the door, shouted, "Chrissie, I called you," closed it again and went on talking. There was something uncertain about him, a geyser of malice bubbling up that never quite boiled. "That's why I'm proud of my name. Bulldog Drummond—what a character. A real Englishman. He knew what to do with the reds and the yids, and he'd have known what to do with the coons. They're all around, you know, it's not just Brixton and Battersea; they're here in Fulham, too, just a couple of doors down the street. They even use the boozer over the road. I tell you, I sometimes don't fancy drinking there; I'm not sure how well they wash the glasses. How about you?"

"What do you mean?"

"Drink out of a glass after a coon, would you? A bloody nigger-lover. What are you doing here? Come on—I want to know." He was pressing the button on the knife almost automatically, in out, in out, as he came nearer. Sher was conscious of danger, and his own movement was almost involuntary. He took one step forward, kicked hard at Drummond's instep and at the same time grasped the other's wrist and twisted. Drummond cried out. The knife dropped to the floor. Sher picked it up and put it in his pocket.

There was handclapping at the door. The girl with long hair stood there. "Clever Hugh," she said. "Next time you should take on a blind old-age pensioner; it would be more of a match."

Drummond sat down in one of the shabby chairs and looked as if he was going to cry. "He was in the pub. Asking questions about you, who you were. He said he knew Harry, he was a friend of Harry's. He's a spy. And what's Tony doing here, for God's sake?"

A small boy in pajamas had sidled into the room. He at once settled down on the floor and started pushing the toy cars about, muttering to himself as he did so.

"If he's a spy it's more than you'll ever be. Do you know what he did a few months back?" she said to Sher. "Put one of those ads in the *Times*, saying 'go anywhere, do anything.' And he got some answers."

"Ah, they weren't serious; they were—"

"There was a man came here, said he was a colonel, getting together a commando group to fight in Angola, but would he go? His teeth were chattering so loud the colonel couldn't hear himself speak. Piss and wind, that's what he's made of, piss and wind and pot. Half the time he's stoned out of his mind."

"I never trusted the man; he was a crook. If it's the way you say, why is Harry pleased to use my services?"

"As an errand boy. You were frightened even to speak to him tonight; I had to do it myself." She took a cigarette from a pocket in the stained smock she was wearing and stared at Sher from under thick brows. "I know you. Do you know who this is, Hugh? It's the actor who plays Sherlock Holmes on the telly. Sherlock was on drugs, too, they tell me, a mainliner, only he had the guts to kick the habit. Isn't that so?"

"Main line," said the boy on the floor. "Main line goes along motorway zoom zoom, here comes drugs zoom zoom, and they go—crash." He turned over both cars.

"Sherlock Holmes meets Bulldog Drummond." Drummond's laugh was thin, nervous. He moved between Sher and the door. "But what's he doing here, what does he want?"

"Don't make yourself more ridiculous than you are." She said to Sher, "You can give him his toy back. He wouldn't hurt you with it, not unless you turned your back on him. But I think I know what you're doing, Mr. Sherlock Holmes. Something to do with what I read in the paper this morning, isn't that right?"

When lies are no longer possible, then truth is the only resort.

"That's right. I saw you leave the Carrousel with Claber this evening and followed you."

"And you let him in here," she said to her husband. "You're clever. Yes, you're a smart boy, you are."

Drummond said defensively, rhetorically, "And isn't that just where we'd want to have him? Wasn't it a good move? He leaves when we say so, and not before."

The little boy was using Sher's shoes as traffic islands around which his cars moved. Sometimes the cars cannoned into the islands, sometimes they whizzed past them. All the time he kept up a muttering, in which words ran indistinguishably into each other.

"What are you after?" The girl tapped her cigarette on the edge of the table and the ash dropped to the carpet.

"Anything to do with the killings, nothing else. I had a note to meet someone in the Carrousel, but he didn't turn up. You looked the wrong sort of person to be there, so I followed you."

"And?"

"And your husband says you're a commercial artist. I suppose those paintings on the wall are yours."

"You like them?"

"I can't say I do; no."

"More fool you. They're bloody good, and someday some stinking gallery owner's going to realize it." Drummond, beside the door, began to whistle "I'm a Dreamer, Aren't We All?" She said without heat, "Do you suppose the reason I stay with him is he's such a clown?"

"So you really are a painter. You've got paint marks on that smock. But still, I imagine it was something else that Claber wanted."

He felt something cold and hard inside his trouser leg, and looked down. The little boy said, "Main line gone to bed." When he shook his leg the toy car dropped to the floor. Tony yelped in protest. As Sher looked up again it seemed to him that he had missed some look that was passing between the Drummonds.

A telephone began to ring. Chrissie Drummond said, "Good night. If you want a bit of advice, don't play around with Harry Claber."

Drummond showed his wolfish teeth. "It could be dangerous. I'm a friendly man myself, but Harry . . ." He shook his head. "Are you not going to answer that telephone, Chrissie? And could I have my knife back?"

The telephone was in a corner of the room. The girl crossed to it, said, "Just a minute," and put her hand over the receiver, waiting for Sher to go. He handed back the knife and Drummond immediately pushed the button so that the blade flicked out. Sher stepped back and something crunched under his foot. There was a wail of anguish. Fists pummeled his leg.

"Main line, you broken main line." Tony held up the squashed car.

"Be your age," Chrissie said to Drummond, and to Sher, "He's like a kid playing with those things. They make him excited." Her hand was still over the receiver.

As Sher moved past Drummond into the hall, the fair man made a playful gesture with the knife, stopping it three inches short of Sher's stomach. Tony followed him, crying, "You broken main line, you spy, you broken main line," and battering away with punches below knee height. A pound note quietened him only momentarily. At the door Drummond said, "I'll remember you," and made another playful thrust. It was a disorderly retreat.

SHERLOCK IN TROUBLE

On the following evening Sheridan Haynes and Joe Johnson sat opposite each other in the Baker Street rooms. Smoke curled up from Johnson's pipe. It was a Sherlockian scene, except that Johnson had come straight from work and was still in his uniform. And there were other differences, when you came to think of it. The smokeless fuel was warm enough, but it did not contain those flickering blue-gold flames into which both Holmes and Watson had often broodingly looked. There was, of course, no Mrs. Hudson. And more important, coming back to actuality, there was no Val.

She had returned that morning, to find Sher in the middle of what turned out to be a very long telephone conversation with a man who said that he was the Karate Killer, and wanted both to confess and to give details of his next crime. He sounded so convincing, and seemed to know so much about the killings, that Sher did not put down the telephone until he had heard the man's account of his next victim, and the place of execution. The victim was to be the prime minister, and the place 10 Downing Street.

He found Val packing clothes in the bedroom. It seemed that

two people within him watched her as she put in the clothes with her usual neat efficiency. One was Sheridan Haynes, who had lived with Val for more than a quarter of a century, had slept in her bed and given her a child, and yet perhaps had never fully understood what lay beneath her surface practicality. This man would miss Val; her absence would leave a gap in his life that would ache forever like a missing limb. But another man within him felt that women at best were an indulgence, that they interfered with those logical processes of the mind that were man's chief claim to be distinguished from the animals. This second man, who was not Sherlock Holmes but who regarded Holmes as a figure to whose genius one should aspire, saw what was happening almost with indifference. With one part of his mind he felt that the great detective would at last be free. Both the grieved husband and the indifferent detective found it equally difficult to say anything, and it was Val who spoke.

"I told you I should. And you know why." There was something unusually defensive in her tone.

"Because of the investigation; yes." Was it Sheridan or Sherlock who had the upper hand? He could not be sure.

"*Investigation.* You can't think how ridiculous you make yourself. You don't understand that, do you?"

For a moment as she looked at him, he saw the woman who had been contented as the wife of a moderately successful actor, who had brought up their son and had been delighted by the occasional finds she made in the antique market. "Val," he said questioningly, almost as if he were groping for her, unsure that she was there. Then the moment had gone, and whatever spark of emotion flashed between them had gone, too.

"I'll leave you with the collected works; you don't need me." She made a gesture toward the side of his bed, where the individual volumes stood, each of them specially bound. He had said something then, something about her return when this was over, and she had commented that he didn't even want to know where she was going. This was true, or at least it was true that part of him simply wanted her to go away. He said that he had supposed she would be going to her sister.

"I shall go to Willie." Even then he did not understand until she spelled it out for him. "He's been asking me to live with him for a long time. Since we started going to bed together. You didn't know that."

"No, I didn't know that."

"Anyone else would have. The awful thing is that what I loved always was the fact that you didn't notice things—oh, *some* things, I know, but not that kind—and now . . ." She did not finish the sentence, but began another. "Why did I tell you that? To hurt you, I suppose. I'm sorry."

"Are you in love with him?" Again, part of him was hardly interested in the answer.

She laughed. "With Willie? He's just a fat little Pole out for everything he can get. But I can talk to him, and he answers. Half the time you don't even know I'm there. That's why I'm off." She touched two fingers with her lips, pressed the fingers to his cheek and was gone.

Afterward, he tried to discover what he felt. The act of physical unfaithfulness had never meant much to him, and there had been times in the first years of their marriage when both of them had been to bed with somebody else, and both had understood that these affairs were not to be taken seriously. Why did he feel this to be something different? Partly perhaps because those other beddings had been long ago, and it was years since he had wanted to sleep with another woman; but there was a special feeling of betrayal that she had slept with Willie. It was Willie who had been the inspiration of the Holmes series, and it seemed to him that she had deliberately set out to spoil his pleasure in the Sherlock Holmes association. Or was all that an illusion, an obsession? The thought was still worrying him when he went in the afternoon to the Anglo-American Fitness and Athletic Club, which he had used for some years, and had a

123

workout with Riverboat Jackson. Usually they had three minutes of what was mostly shadow boxing, but today he found pleasure in landing punches to the head and body, and in avoiding Riverboat's half-power returns.

For his white clients Riverboat often played the role of American Negro, Mark I, in action and speech. He allowed himself to be used as a punching bag as long as he didn't get hurt, and then camped it up afterward.

"You sure in fine condition," he said now. "You ain't even raised a sweat, and just look at old Riverboat puffing. And that right hand—I thought you got lead in that glove."

"You could lay me flat in thirty seconds," Sher said, but he was still pleased.

In the changing room Riverboat said, "I was reading in the papers about that investigation of yours, and you know what I thought? I thought you ought to take lessons in karate or judo, Mr. Haynes."

"What for? Would it help to find the killer?"

"You ain't going to find no killer; that's all publicity." He saw from Sher's face that he had not said the right thing, and changed course effortlessly. "Just that my opinion is these ain't no karate killings. I had a big man walk in here from Scotland Yard, man working on the case; told him the very same thing. I reckon this is some amateur riding his luck. Course I could be wrong; it's just what old Riverboat thinks. But what I was going to say, why don't Sherlock Holmes take a few lessons in karate, then you tell those studio bosses you discovered he's a black belt, and you bring it in in one of the stories?"

Riverboat grinned happily, a simple nigger easy to please, and Sher responded as he always did to discussions of Sherlock. He knew very well that Riverboat was stringing him along, but he took the question seriously.

"As a matter of fact, Holmes did spend some time in Tibet, but there's nothing in the stories to say that he knew karate or judo. He was a baritsu expert, though. Do you know what that

124

is?" Riverboat shook his head, grinning. "Neither does anyone else."

"But how about that now, Mr. Haynes? You take a half dozen karate lessons—quick like you are, it's all you need—and then—"

"No. I had an unlucky experience once. I don't want to take karate lessons. Or judo." The way the words were spoken told Riverboat not to go on.

He had told Johnson about the visit to Dingwall Street. True to his Watsonic persona, the traffic warden expressed himself totally puzzled by the connection between Claber and Chrissie Drummond. It was less in character that Sher was baffled, too, but at least he had an idea for solving the puzzle that seemed to him properly Holmesian in its approach. He was explaining it to Johnson when the telephone rang. Betty Brade's voice said, "Any orders for this evening, sir?"

He said to Johnson, "Shall I ask her?" An upturned pipe stem signified approval. He explained what he wanted. "Joe's here, and says he'll cover you, but I ought to warn you that there might be some trouble, though I don't expect it."

Her laugh boomed down the line. "Never found the trouble I can't deal with. Okay, Sherlock, see you in an hour."

"Betty's reliable," Johnson said after Sher had hung up. "And it's right what she told you: she used to be a wrestler. Gave it up when she married. Her husband's a shrimp of a man. She does everything he tells her; perfectly happy with him."

"What's Cassidy's background?"

"In the army when he was young; I believe he served in Cyprus. Then he was a copper till he was in an accident—piece of timber fell on him when he was getting a kid out of a burning house, left him with a limp. You'd hardly notice it, but it meant he wasn't up to police standard. They're three good men I picked you, myself included, even if one is a woman."

Claber's Mercedes was at the Carrousel, parked on double yellow lines, in almost the same spot as on the previous night. As Sher approached the entrance he saw Betty.

"Hi, Sherlock."

He pointed out the car.

"Right, then; going into action now."

"Good luck."

"You've got it wrong. I don't need luck." A gleam of gold showed in her smile.

He went in the club, walked straight through to the gaming room and bought ten pounds' worth of chips. There were only a few people in the room, and Sarah was not among them. He felt his heart throbbing as it had when he was a young man playing a big part. The idea was worthy of the Baker Street Irregulars, but would it work?

In the street Betty walked once, twice around the Mercedes, then took out her notebook. With head bent over it, she still saw the doorman lumbering across the road.

"What's up?" He had a squashed boxer's face, pale worried eyes. His black-and-gold uniform made her traffic warden's outfit look shabby.

"Parked on a double yellow. Have to give you a ticket. And get it moved."

"You what?" The words came out as a croak. "We got an arrangement."

"Not with me you haven't, not for leaving it on a double yellow. You the owner?"

There was a kind of wheeze that might have been interpreted as laughter. The owner's Mr. Claber, Mr. Harry Claber."

"If he's in the club, tell him to come out and move his car."

The battered face came close. "You're making a mistake. You don't want trouble; nobody does. Just forget it, eh?" A hand clasped Betty's, a piece of paper in it. She broke the grip and held up the pound note.

"Naughty." She tucked the note in his breast pocket. "Don't

126

you know a good girl when you see one? Another move like that and *you'll* be in trouble."

"Dunno what you mean." The pale eyes were bemused. "I tell you it's Mr. Claber. He's got—"

"An arrangement. I heard you the first time. Now you be a good boy and go and tell Mr. Claber to move this car. Now."

"I dunno why you're doing this. It ain't right." He shook his head like a boxer after a punch, and was gone.

Harry Claber came out, wearing his smile. "Jack here says you want me to move my Merc."

"That's right. You're on a double yellow; got to be moved."

"I'm busy right now; it's not convenient. If you'd just like to give me the ticket."

He held out his hand. Betty presented her golden smile. "I think you didn't hear. I said it had to be moved."

Claber looked her up and down. "You're a big hard bitch."

"Flattery will get you nowhere."

"And ugly. But you could be uglier."

"What does that mean?"

The smile was back in place. "Take it how you like. Look now, be reasonable. It's hard to park around Shepherd Market. I always leave my car here. *And* the police know about it. *And* they don't interfere. I'm Harry Claber."

"Your sheepdog told me." The doorman looked from one to the other of them, baffled. "It means nothing in my life. Will you move the car?"

"Jack, take the number this cow's got on her jacket." He turned back to her. "What are you in uniform for? You must be off duty this late at night."

"I'm going out with my boyfriend. He's a Guardsman. We both fancy uniforms."

Claber stared at her, got into the car, slammed the door and drove away. The doorman was fumbling in his pocket.

"You got a bit of pencil I can borrow? And paper?" As he wrote down her number he croaked, "You didn't ought to er done that. You've upset 'im, and it takes a lot to upset Mr. Harry."

Sher was standing at the table nearest to the gold door when Claber went out. He was in Claber's office within seconds. If there had been anyone inside he would have apologized and gone out again, but the room was empty. The black-and-gold motif had been abandoned here. This was an office like a thousand others. There was a large desk with a swivel chair behind it, a couple of filing cabinets and a wall safe. The safe was locked, and so were the filing cabinets. The drawers of the desk were locked, too. If he had been Sherlock Holmes he might have been able to open the safe, and could certainly have forced the desk drawers, but he lacked even a chisel.

There were papers on the desk and he looked at them quickly. Bills, a couple of applications for a croupier's vacancy, a report detailing the takings of five other Claber clubs over the past month, a letter offering special terms for the supply of wine with a label saying "Carrousel Club Special Reserve."

The telephone rang. He picked it up without thinking what he would say if the door opened and Claber came in.

"That Mr. Claber?" The voice was Cockney working class, the tone respectful.

What did Claber sound like? He tried a general London voice, as neutral as he could make it. "This is Harry Claber."

"Joey—Joey Lines. Sorry to bovver you, Mr. C., but I oughter tell yer I'm goin' ter be a bit late. I been kept later than I expected unloadin', see. Shan't get there before half nine."

"Half past nine. Right." It occurred to him that he might have said "Half nine," but the voice at the other end went on.

"You'll let Shorty know. He'll be expectin' me before nine, see, and—"

"He's not here now. You'd better give me the details."

"I'll be in a jack-tar vey call the parade ground in the old ball of chalk, East India Dock Road."

128

"He'll recognize you?"

"Course 'e will. 'Ere, that is you, Mr. C., ain't it?"

"Who the hell d'you think it is?"

"Just you sounded funny like, as if you—"

"I'll tell him." He put down the telephone. It took an effort of nerve to open the door again, but when he stepped out into the gaming room nobody took any notice. In the entrance hall, he passed Claber returning. Another minute and he would have been caught. When he got outside Betty was not to be seen. He asked the doorman whether he had seen a traffic warden.

"You mean the one made the guvnor move his car? She's made 'erself scarce, and I don't blame 'er. The guvnor don't never lose control, but 'e was wild. 'E'll 'ave something to say to 'er boss in the morning. What's up—you got a car parked, sir?"

"Just round the corner. On a double yellow."

"Lucky if you're still there, then."

He spent the next couple of minutes looking without success for Betty. He was beginning to be worried when she appeared out of an alley.

"It worked," she said.

"Splendidly. But the doorman says Claber's angry. I hope I haven't got you into trouble."

"So he reports me, but who does the report go to? Joe. Anyway, they're used to complaints at the center. Did you have any luck?"

"No useful papers, but I took a phone call for Claber. Someone called Joey Lines is going to meet a man of Claber's named Shorty, in a jack-tar named the parade ground, at the ball of chalk in the East India Dock Road."

"What does all that mean?"

"It's Cockney rhyming slang. A jack-tar is a bar, and ball of chalk means Duke of York, the name of the pub."

"Sherlock, you're wonderful. Going down there, are you?"

"Yes." He anticipated her next question. "Alone. If I were with you I'd look conspicuous."

"Look after yourself. It strikes me that Harry Claber's friends might play a bit rough. Sure you wouldn't like a woman to take care of you?"

He said he wouldn't. On the way down to the dock area in a taxi, he was aware that he was enjoying himself enormously.

"But how did you *discover* it? I mean, the *docks?*"

"I read this *Observer* color-supp piece, you see, and it said all the obvious places are finished, a house in Battersea even costs a fortune, but around the East India Dock area there were still some of these perfect little squares—"

"Lived in by the peasants, no doubt, with a loo out at the back—"

"Exactly, and there was this perfectly dreamy little house, just a cottage, and Fabrina said it had terrific possibilities—"

"Possibilities. I should think so."

He listened gloomily to the exchange taking place between a couple with long flowing hair, both wearing bell bottoms and bright turtlenecks. Did the absence of makeup indicate their masculinity or the opposite; were their voices male or female? He found it impossible to say. The pub depressed him. It had been done up by the brewers, and in honor of its name they had turned it into a kind of military encampment. Reproductions of battle scenes were around the walls, regimental flags and scrolls took up other bits of vacant space, what had once been public and private bars were now called Sergeants' Mess and Officers' Mess. It was certainly not what it had been in Holmes's time, and he would infinitely have preferred a few villainous Lascars to the trendy young creatures who mixed with the tough-looking dockers. Not that the dockers seemed to mind either the desecration of their pub or its part occupation by these aliens. From the large central bar, which was actually called the Parade Ground, Sher pondered on the superiority of past to present. He was jerked out of this reverie by the words: "That's Joey, just come in."

The barman had been speaking to a tall, very thin man who wore a mustard-colored suit. He had been eating veal-and-ham pie, and now he turned with his mouth full. The barman nodded. The man raised a pale, fleshless hand, and Joey came over. He was red-faced and red-haired, in his twenties, and he had on a lorry driver's dirty overalls. The man who must be Shorty sprayed pie crumbs at him. "You're bleedin' late."

"I was kept. And I been parking the lorry."

Shorty ordered pints of bitter for them both, gave Sher a long stare, and led the way to a table in a corner. Joey followed with a plate containing three ham sandwiches. Shorty fell on them like a starving man, talking between mouthfuls. Joey listened, chewing thoughtfully like a red-faced bull. Shorty had started on a second sandwich while Joey was still munching on his first. The tables next to them on either side were occupied, and there was no way of hearing what they were saying, except by standing nearby in a way that would have made Sher look conspicuous. It was such humdrum obstacles that posed problems to an investigator. With this awareness of inadequacy went a feeling that he had missed something significant in the fragment of conversation he had heard. After five minutes he finished his beer and went out.

The night was bleakly cold. Traffic rumbled past, vans and lorries and great articulated monsters. He remembered what Joey had said about parking. If he waited, he might at least find out who Joey was working for. He stood in a dark doorway just down the street, stamping occasionally to keep his feet warm. He had to wait ten minutes before the two men came out, crossed the road and went down a side street. He followed twenty yards behind. Warehouses and an office block or two lined the street; large lorries were parked all the way down it. Joey and Shorty stopped beside one of these. In the silence their words floated back.

"You won't need no bleeder this size."

"Course not. We use an ordinary van for jobs like the one for this geezer Williams. Nothing particular about it, except he often uses us, so it's got racks inside, see, been specially put in. Thing is this, though, Shorty: I don't want to get in no bleedin' trouble."

"Who said there'd be trouble? Anyway, it's a hundred nicker."

"That's what you say, but—"

"Shut up."

To avoid coming up with them, Sher had started to cross the road. The name of the van, East London Transport Company, was clearly visible. As he crossed, Shorty's face was turned toward him, the head thrust forward. Now the tall man came over to intercept him. Joey followed, cutting off the chance of retreat.

Sher ran. He ran on down the street, looking for a turning that would lead him back to the safety of the East India Dock Road. Feet pounded after him and he did not dare to turn around. There were no turnings to the right, and at last he went to the left in the hope of finding an alley in which he could lose the men. His heart beat strongly, and to sustain himself he counted the paces he was taking, something he had not done since his youth. Another hundred and he would have thrown them off. Ninety, eighty, seventy . . . His heart seemed to be moving up into his throat, something he had read about in books.

He was running beside a long, long warehouse with several separate sheds that had words painted on them. He told himself that when the wording ended there would be a gap. The sheds went by. J. Hampton—Cellulose—Acetate—and Paint—Manufacturers. Sure enough, there was a dark gap to the left. He ran into it and fell over, among a clatter of paint drums. Another moment, and they were up to him. The two of them stood staring at him in the dismal light of a street lamp a few yards away. He moved a couple of yards back, kicked against another drum, looked around and realized that he had trapped himself in a small courtyard where empty paint drums were kept. He was not afraid, and his mind was working clearly. He remembered the significant thing that he had missed in the conversation. It was when the barman had pointed out Joey. On the telephone, Joey had said that Shorty knew him, so the mention of Joey's name had been a deliberate trap. And he had fallen into it by revealing his interest.

Shorty advanced toward him with hands raised, not threateningly, as it seemed, but in a gesture that might have been one of greeting. For a moment the light shone on his face, and Sher saw that his jaws were still moving. As the thin figure came in his direction, Sher stepped sideways to avoid him, and Joey at the rear moved in counterpart. Light gleamed briefly on the brass knuckles in Shorty's hand. Sher felt a paint drum shift as he moved away. It occurred to him—his thoughts were of an icy Holmesian clarity—that if he could move a drum with his hand, it could not be heavy. He picked up the last one over which he had stumbled and clumsily threw it at Shorty. It struck the tall man without force, but he staggered. In a moment Sher was past him and approaching Joey, who blocked his way rather half-heartedly. He was aware of a door opening, a dog barking. Then he bumped into Joey with fists flailing. At the moment of punching Joey in the stomach, he felt the absurdity of what he was doing. Then he had the impression that in the dark he had run into some invisible obstacle. He put out a hand to push it away and felt himself slowly sinking to the ground.

Somebody, presumably a nurse, was washing his face, using a washcloth made of spongy material. A man's voice expostulated with her. The washing stopped, then started again. He opened his eyes to see the head and shoulders of a large dog. It bent down, tongue lolling.

"I said get away, Whisky. A fine guard dog you are. Trouble

133

with him is he loves humanity. You okay?" A young man with a straggly beard was bending over him.

Sher got up slowly. "He hit me on the back of the head, but no serious damage. I don't know what might have happened if you'd not been there. What are you, a night watchman?"

"Right you are. For Hampton's. Not that there's much to watch—who wants to steal paint? Down, Whisky. See, he just loves people."

The dog, now on its hind legs, was trying to clamber over Sher in pure friendliness. Would it look like the Hound of the Baskervilles if its muzzle and dewlaps had been covered with luminous paint?

"I'll just see you down the road. What were they after—your wallet?"

At this gentle hint Sher extended a pound note. The young man slipped it into his pocket in a matter-of-fact manner. As they turned into the next street, Sher saw that the van had gone. "This can't be a full-time job, surely?" he asked.

The young man laughed. "I'm on social security. This is just a bit extra; doesn't get passed through the books, see—no tax."

"You mean you don't do any regular work?"

"Right you are. What's the point? Girl I'm shacked up with works at a toy factory, brings home a nice little packet. I do the housework and the cooking. I make a beautiful beef Stroganoff, though I says it as shouldn't."

"And you draw social security?"

"You got to try and make ends meet with the cost of living what it is," the young man said seriously. "You got no idea what Whisky costs. Sometimes I worry that I'll have to go out to work. I mean, my girl can't boil an egg. Here we are at the East India Dock Road. Sure you're all right now, squire? Then I'd better get back to guarding all that paint."

As he walked along looking for a taxi, Sher reflected that even night watchmen were not what they had been.

A TRAP UNSPRUNG

"You're a fool," Harry Claber said.

"I could have carved him there in the house. Can you imagine, he gave the shiv back to me."

"He took it away from you first. Chrissie told me."

"Ah, it wasn't like that. He caught me unexpected, that's all."

"He walked into this office last night, picked up that phone and answered a call for me. Then he saw Shorty with Joey."

"Who's Joey?"

"Driving the van for the job," Harry said impatiently. "Knows nothing. So Shorty just put a scare in him. He showed a bit of sense. There'll be another time."

"Why don't you let me get after him? No reason for anybody else to be around. I'm just passing him in the street and—" Drummond made an upward gesture, accompanied by his theatrical laugh.

"You think I want that kind of trouble with a man like him? So that it's plastered all over the papers? You want to grow up, sonny boy."

"Chrissie thought you might want to call the deal off."

"It isn't a deal; it's a little job of work she's done for me. She's been paid for it."

"The thing is, I wouldn't want her to get in any trouble over it. With this Sherlock Holmes poking his nose in—"

"She'll be in no trouble, and neither will you. Not unless somebody's gabby."

"You know me, Harry."

"I know you."

"What is it then, this—some sort of joke?"

"I'll be laughing. I don't know about other people. I've got a sense of humor."

"So what about this Sherlock Holmes?"

"You think I like him coming in here, sitting in my chair, using my phone? That's a liberty; I don't like someone to take a liberty."

"So I might have a chance at him? Sherlock Holmes versus Bulldog Drummond—I fancy that."

"You get after him when I tell you. Till then you leave him alone." Claber rose, patted Drummond on the head. "He won't do anybody any harm."

At just about the time Claber was speaking those words, Sher was on the telephone, trying to prove him wrong.

"East London Transport Company? I'm calling for Mr. Williams. He wants to know when the job you have in hand for him is going to be carried out." His voice had the slightly pettish note often heard in the tones of personal assistants to well-known men when they are speaking to those they regard as inferiors.

The girl said, "What's the job, please, and where's it going?"

"I can't tell you that. Mr. Williams is out now, and that's all the information he gave me. Oh, one other thing. He mentioned the name of the driver. Joey Lines."

"Joey, yes; that's a help. I'll check on his jobs." He waited half a minute. "Four o'clock this afternoon, Mr. Williams, Ryder Street Gallery, that right?"

He said it was right and rang off. Then he called the wardens' center and talked to Joe Johnson. Betty Brade was on the ten-to-seven shift, and so was Johnson himself, but Cassidy would be free, and owned a car. He would be in Ryder Street with it at a quarter to four.

Sher was there at half past three. He walked briskly past the Ryder Street Gallery, which appeared to be an art gallery much like any other, and was staring into the window of a snuff and tobacco shop when a van marked "East London Transport Company" drove up and red-haired Joey got out and went into the gallery. There was no sign of Cassidy. Five minutes later Joey came out again, with a gallery attendant. They were carrying what from its size and shape was a fairly large picture.

Joey got into the back of the van and Sher, free from observation, saw the picture lifted in. It was wrapped in canvas and protected by a wooden frame battened down at the edges, with a blue label stuck on the left-hand top edge. The gallery assistant jumped up into the van after the picture, and then down again. Sher turned away as Joey got out and signed a piece of paper, presumably a receipt.

Where was Cassidy?

A small maroon car, high-bodied and square-topped, looking like an entry in the London to Brighton race for vintage cars, turned the corner into Ryder Street and came shakily up to it, followed by a trail of blue smoke from its exhaust. With dismay, Sher saw Cassidy's long horseface behind the wheel. He moved to open the door, but Cassidy did it from the inside.

"Sorry to be late; had a bit of bother starting. Better not switch off now." The car shook slightly under them. "Have to slam that door."

The door shrieked protestingly as Sher pulled it shut. "That van's what we want, the one pulling away. Can you follow it?"

"Nothing easier." The vehicle leaped forward in a series of jerks, like a horse trying to buck its rider. Sher banged his kneecap against a projecting bit of dashboard. "The clutch is a bit fierce; should have warned you."

As they went along Piccadilly, Sher found himself shaken from side to side like a man using a slimming belt. "How old is—"

"Nineteen thirty-eight. She's a good girl, Miranda. Tends to boil going up steep hills, that's all."

"Do you think we'll be able to keep that van in sight?"

"You'd be surprised. Shouldn't have any trouble. Not unless there's a big hill."

The door and roof interiors, and the dashboard, were covered with photographs. Sher looked upward and sideways to inspect them and saw that they were all of Cassidy. Miranda also often appeared. There was Cassidy sitting in Miranda, standing by her, inspecting her engine, Cassidy with large collie dog and Miranda, Cassidy with large collie dog on hillside, Cassidy in police uniform with the rest of his squad. Three or four pictures had been taken at what were presumably police sports, with Cassidy, gawky but athletic, in the long jump and fighting at singlestick. The dashboard showed Cassidy with a girl standing by Miranda, both man and car looking a good deal younger. There were half a dozen other photographs, mostly of Cassidy and the dog. The girl was in one of them. He looked up to see that they were keeping within comfortable distance of the van.

"Pretty girl," he said, although she wasn't.

"Just a girl I played tennis with. I only keep it to show what Miranda was like when she was young. I'm not married. Never felt the need for it; always got on perfectly well on my own. People think that's strange, but I ask them why. Seems to me the strange thing is a man and a woman living in the same house forever, sharing the same room."

The remark echoed some of what he had been feeling about Val. "I know what you mean."

"All you need is a friend, just a friend. But if you lose him . . ."

Sher feared that he might be about to receive some homosexual confidences but Cassidy said nothing more, perhaps because they were going up a slope and Miranda showed signs of disliking it. The engine thudded like an exhausted runner's heartbeat, and the whole car shuddered as though about to come apart. Cassidy bent forward over the wheel, crooning unintelligible words. When they had reached the top he straightened up. "We made it. Good girl, Miranda." Fortunately, the van also had crawled up the incline, and was not much more than a hundred yards ahead.

"You like cars?"

"I like Miranda. She's been a good and faithful servant, and I've looked after her. That's the way it should be. There's nothing wrong with cars, only with the way people drive them."

"I hate the thing itself, the internal combustion engine. If I could, I'd sweep it away. It's destroying everything I know and love about England." The words put him in mind of a poem by Philip Larkin that he had read in a BBC radio program. Afterward, he had learned the poem by heart, and now he recited one verse:

> And that will be England gone,
> The shadows, the meadows, the lanes,
> The guildhalls, the carved choirs.
> There'll be books; it will linger on
> In galleries; but all that remains
> For us will be concrete and tires.

Cassidy was silent for a few moments. Then he said, "I don't agree. You've got to have machines, otherwise everything would run down. But you've got to have order, too, and rules. That's what they taught me in the police, and I've never forgotten. Obedience to rules, that's what counts."

"You won't like Sherlock Holmes, then. He often broke the rules."

"But he was doing it for the rest of us, isn't that right? That's the way it seems to be, watching your programs. And that's not what I mean at all. Some people break the rules for nothing."

"Watch it, Cassidy, he's pulling in."

They were in North London. The road was wide and tree-lined, the houses elegant early Victorian structures, each with its semicircular front drive. The van had pulled into one of these.

"What do you want me to do?"

"Drive past half a dozen houses, then stop." He felt in his pocket for paper, found none, took an old envelope addressed to Cassidy from the dashboard shelf and wrote the house number on it, and the van's number as well. Cassidy pulled up sharply, with the aplomb of a rider stopping a runaway horse.

"What happens now?" His slightly curled lip showed, in the friendliest possible way, the professional's doubts about the amateur.

And what did happen now? What was he expecting to find? It was heartening to have an ex-policeman with him.

"I'm going along to that house. If I'm not back in ten minutes, come and ask at the front door."

"I'll do that. And I'll bring the policeman's friend." On his side of the dashboard shelf he showed a miniature police truncheon. "Less than half standard size, but it can be useful."

When he walked up the drive, Joey was talking to a middle-aged woman at the door. The picture stood beside him.

"I told you Mr. Rochester is expecting it," the woman said. "I can take it in for him. He's busy; he can't see you now."

"They said it was for personal delivery, but I suppose that's all right."

Sher's steps sounded on the frosty gravel. The woman looked beyond Joey. "Did you want Mr. Rochester? I'm afraid he's busy. Can I help you?"

Joey turned and saw Sher. The red left his cheeks as though the blood had been drained away. Sher was almost at the door. He bent to look at the wrapped picture, then straightened up.

"I don't think you can." He nodded to them both and turned. It was his first successful exit during the investigation.

On the way back to central London he was monosyllabic in answer to Cassidy's questions as to what it was all about. By the time he had reached Baker Street he had decided that he ought to report what he had discovered to the police.

He saw Devenish on the following morning, and found him in a bad temper. The detective chief superintendent had just finished talking to D.C. Morgan and Detective Sergeant Edwards, the two karate experts. Morgan was a cocky young man who had a theory that the killer was Japanese, and thought that he was being asked to join the Flying Squad when he was asked questions about cars. Edwards, by contrast, was a family man with three children, a good solid policeman, so law-abiding that it was hard to imagine him having a drink after hours. Morgan had no car, Edwards owned a Hillman. No connection with the Clabers had been turned up. They were both ruled out, and Devenish thought that only a lack of elementary good sense by Brewster had ever let them in. But Brewster's view was that the idea had been a crackpot one to start with, and it was possible that he had been demonstrating the fact. Devenish tucked away the thought of somebody who had been taking lessons in karate, rather than discarding it. After all, it was hardly the kind of thing you would advertise.

He saw the man Haynes chiefly because Sue, who was devoted to the TV series, had irritated him by saying that it would be extraordinary if Sheridan Haynes turned up something, and then asking whether he thought that it was really possible to use Sherlock Holmes's methods. One night she had even made a dish called eggs Sherlock Holmes, in which perfectly good eggs were ruined by being turned into a sweet-tasting mess with the help of Tokay, which she said was mentioned in the Holmes stories. So he saw Haynes, and listened to his story. The man seemed to him less impressive in appearance than he looked on the screen, rather actorish, as though he were playing a part, and he told the story in a dramatic manner that added an edge to Devenish's annoyance.

Sher on his side was disconcerted that Devenish was younger than he had expected, perhaps ten years younger than himself, and he noticed the gigantic thumbs, which made him a little uncomfortable. He found the detective a silent but not particularly receptive listener. No Lestrade, obviously; more intelligent than that. Perhaps he would be on a level with young Stanley Hopkins, that promising detective for whose future Holmes had at one time had high hopes.

When Sher had finished, Devenish said, "You're certain there was no blue label on the picture this man was delivering?"

"Yes. I was close enough to see the other side as well."

"The label might have come off in the van. Or it might have been on the bottom of the frame so that you couldn't see it." Sher shook his head. "You're saying it was a different picture."

"That seems the only logical conclusion."

"And what do you expect me to do about it?"

Sher was taken aback. "I thought you would be interested. It's said the Clabers are connected with the killings."

God preserve me from amateur detectives, Devenish thought. "Who's said that? Not the police. You come here and tell me a story about entering Claber's office illegally, getting into a punch-up, following a van which was delivering a picture from an art gallery to somebody who'd no doubt bought it. You say the van driver was shaken when he saw you, and no doubt he was if he was the man you'd been fighting the night before. And you say the picture was different, which may or may not be true. So I'm asking what you expect me to do about it. Are you telling me a crime's been committed?"

Sher could only shake his head. He had expected praise and was meeting hostility.

"You don't know. Neither do I. I'll tell you what I will do, and that's give you some free advice." Devenish's blue eyes stared directly into Sher's brown ones; his voice was hard and level. "I've read some of the things you've said about what people call the Karate Killings. They may be good publicity for you, but they don't make my job any easier. You're entitled to make any investigations you like—it's a free country—but if I find you're getting in my hair you'll wish you'd never started playing Sherlock Holmes."

That, he thought afterward with some satisfaction, had seen Sherlock off with a flea in his ear. At the same time it was an odd story, and he talked about it to Brewster. The sergeant was modestly triumphant.

"I said Claber was up to something."

"Obviously, but what? Williams sells a picture to this man Rochester. He runs his art gallery perfectly straight—it's his pride and joy—so what's in it for our Harry?"

"Why don't we talk to Williams, find out what the deal is?"

Devenish twiddled his thumbs while he considered. It was a fearful sight. "No. I think we take it from the other end. Find out who Rochester is, what he does, whether he's got a record."

"He's just bought a picture, that's all. What makes you think—"

"I don't think anything. Harry Claber takes a hand in seeing a picture is delivered to this man Rochester, and our Sherlock says it wasn't the same picture taken from the gallery, because of the label. Maybe he's mistaken, but then again, perhaps he isn't."

"Could be this actor's just a nut, out for the publicity."

"Perhaps, though he didn't impress me that way. If he's right, Harry's playing some trick on Williams."

"Should we care?"

"There's nothing I'd like more than to see Freddy Williams get his comeuppance, but not if it means a gang war. I'd like the intelligence on Rochester quick as you can."

Just after lunch Brewster put on his desk a memo about Sammy Rochester's career. "It smells," he said. "You could say it stinks."

"Yes, but what does it stink of?"

Half an hour later he knew what the stink was, when the afternoon edition of the *Evening Standard* was put on his desk and he read the headlines:

"HE SOLD ME FAKE COROT,"
BUSINESSMAN ACCUSES ART DEALER

Now that he knew what the game was, he went to see Freddy Williams. The art dealer was quite shaken out of his usual complacency. Devenish had never known a crook so pleased to see a policeman.

"Mr. Devenish, you've seen the paper? I shall sue, of course, but something like this is devastating. My good name will be destroyed, utterly destroyed." He ran a hand over his egg head; his little feet beat a tattoo on the carpet. A girl brought in tea. Devenish felt the thinness of fine china against his lips.

"I can see you'd be concerned about your good name."

"You may find it hard to believe, but I am. I value the paintings I sell here more than anything else in my life. I would no more sell a painting I knew wasn't genuine than . . ." He waved his hand to indicate the impossibility of finding an adequate comparison.

"I'm crying for you. This man Rochester says you sold him a fake, right?"

"He telephoned not two hours after the picture had been delivered, to tell me that Dudley Kirk was with him, and that Kirk had said the Corot delivered to him was a forgery."

"Kirk's an expert?"

"He's a professor of fine arts, yes, but how does he just happen to be staying with this man Rochester? So this morning I went down to look at the picture."

"And you found it was a fake, not the one you'd sold him."

"How do you know?"

"The interesting thing is how you hope to prove what you say." Devenish was enjoying himself. "It looks to me as though that's going to be difficult."

Williams put back his cup noisily on the saucer. "I've been framed. The picture he has is a crude forgery, painted recently, and by recently I mean in the last few days. Nobody in his senses could possibly believe it to be genuine."

"But Rochester says it's the one you sold him? And I expect he's got some way of proving it?"

"He says he put a cross in red ink on the back of the canvas, and there's a red cross on the back of the fake. Of course, it proves nothing, but he was totally unreasonable. At the same time, I didn't suppose he would call the newspapers. It's absolutely outrageous behavior."

"Oh, outrageous," Devenish said blandly.

A spot of color showed in Williams's cheeks. "If you've come here to laugh at me—"

"I said I might be able to help. Tell me what happened."

"This man Rochester came into the gallery one day, three or four weeks ago, and said he was interested in Corot. I soon saw that he didn't know much about pictures, and I gathered he was buying as an investment. Many businessmen do. It struck me that he'd been badly advised if he wanted to buy a Corot as an investment, because there have always been a great many Corot forgeries about. I tried to steer him toward something else, but he'd seen a very pretty silvery Corot I had, a landscape, and liked it more than anything else I'd shown him, even though I told him the provenance wasn't absolutely certain. He came to see the picture twice before making up his mind."

"The provenance? That means you couldn't guarantee it was authentic?"

"In this case it means that it couldn't be traced back exactly, step by step, to the time it was painted and the first purchaser."

"If he wanted to say afterward that you'd sold him a fake, that would be an advantage. The second time he came, did he bring somebody with him?"

"Yes; a tall, thin girl with long hair, not much to look at."

"And she took a photograph of the picture?"

"Yes." Williams got up. He looked ridiculous, a plump egg among the egg-shaped furniture. "You know all about it, you know what happened."

"I'm just making educated guesses. Tell me the rest."

"Rochester said he'd be buying the picture and he gave me a check for it, but he said he didn't want to take delivery for ten days. His girl wanted to take a photograph, and I saw no harm in that. He called the girl something, some vulgar abbreviation."

"Chrissie."

"That's right, Chrissie. You know her?"

"I've heard of her. Go on."

"There's nothing more to say. Yesterday the people who do most of my van delivery work collected the picture and took it to him. I don't understand when the fraud can have been substituted. Are you telling me that the girl was the forger?"

"Right. She worked from the photograph."

Devenish could see the wheels turning in Williams's mind. Agitation disappeared, he looked at home again among his furniture, his odious poise had returned. "My dear Devenish, you are so clever. We must drink to your skill, this time in something stronger than Madeira." With precise old-maidishness, he took a small key from his watch chain, unlocked a cupboard, took out glasses and a bottle, which he held between reverent plump hands. "This is not just a malt whisky, but a malt highly refined. A few hundred bottles is all that the distiller produces, and I count myself lucky to have got some of them." He poured a careful measure into each glass. "I drink to your sources of information. And to your acuity." He sipped at the whisky like a bird. "I may assume, I'm sure, that you will deal with Mr. Rochester, and that I shan't hear anything more of him."

"I don't see why you should assume anything of the sort. If Rochester brings an action, the press will have a field day, whether he wins or loses."

"You wouldn't let that happen," Williams said, but he sounded uncertain.

Devenish looked at his empty glass. "I'm not like you, I don't know much about whisky, but I should call this a nice drop of stuff." He pushed the glass toward Williams, who refilled it, less carefully this time. "Let's say we both know who was responsible for this. The point is, what are you going to do about it?"

Williams took another bird sip. "You can leave that to me."

"That's just what I'm not doing. You're up shit creek, Williams, and you want me to give you a paddle. All right, I can do it, but I want something in return. I don't mind what you think about who was responsible; you can think what you like as long as you don't do anything about it."

"I believe that's called liberal philosophy."

"I'm not an educated man. I wouldn't know."

"You are asking something impossible." The rosebud mouth was pursed. "Other people can make educated guesses, too. If I let this happen to me and do nothing about it, they'll say Freddy Williams is losing his grip."

"If it's impossible, okay." Devenish drained his glass. "I thought you valued your reputation. As an art dealer, I mean."

"Whatever I might be willing to do personally, I have associates who wouldn't be satisfied if I merely kept quiet."

"Don't give me that. Your associates do what they're told. And anyway, this is a private grudge match; they don't come into it. It's you that's being got at. Now, I might be able to get you in the clear. And if you ask me what guarantee is there that the other side will keep the bargain, I'll see they do."

"You mean that charges will be dropped?" Devenish nodded.

"And that there'll be no question of my returning any money?"

"I don't guarantee that. But you'll either keep the money or get your picture back."

The pursed mouth relaxed. "Then, my dear Devenish, honor will be satisfied and I shall be happy to accede to your request. I shall also acclaim you as a miracle man. There's just one thing. We have established that you are not interested in money. I don't quite understand your position."

"I've told you already, but I'll spell it out. If it was just a question of you and the Clabers, I'd leave you to get on with it, and let the worst man win. But it isn't. In a gang war other people get hurt, ordinary harmless b and e men start carrying shooters. Trouble escalates. I won't have it. If it was me I'd tie the lot of you in a sack, hang a big weight on and sling it in the Thames, but my bosses won't let me do that. They're the liberal philosophers, not me."

"I take the point." Devenish got up to go. "It's been a most valuable discussion. I look forward to hearing from you later, when you've had a chance to talk to the other side. One more question, though I think I know how you'll answer it. Suppose I should hear from you that this little affair has been settled. I am basically a gentle person, but perhaps I might feel impelled after all to attempt some—should I call them reprisals? What would be your attitude then?"

The policeman stood a head taller than Williams. The black-and-white walls and the black ceiling seemed to be closing in on him as he spoke.

"If that happened, we'd discover something. Like a false back behind one of these pictures you import, and some packets of H tucked away inside it. Don't tell me it couldn't happen; a policeman has to do a lot of things he doesn't like. And I'll tell you something: what we found would be connected with your gallery here. Don't ask me how I know that; I just do."

"Very good." The gold-rimmed spectacles gleamed up at him benevolently. "Very good indeed. Just the answer I expected.

You are a man after my own heart, Devenish. Not a liberal philosopher, as you say."

He could not get in touch with Harry Claber until early evening. Then Devenish ran him to earth in the Carrousel. The club had no restaurant, but there was a room adjoining the bar that served thirty different kinds of sandwich, including smoked salmon and corned beef. Harry was drinking milk and eating a corned beef sandwich. They sat in one of the high-backed compartments where the punters came to stoke up after their losses, and gather strength to lose some more.

"Join me, Thumbs. Best salt beef in London." Harry's manner was as jokey as his twisted nose. Devenish ordered the sandwich, but with lemon tea instead of milk. "To what do we owe the honor, I might ask, but I don't need to, do I? You've come to see if I'm running a straight game, isn't that so? Just look around. If you find a table out of true or a dealer who's cheating, tell me."

"We check it every month. Sometimes I put a man in as croupier." This was not true, but it stopped Harry's smile for a moment, and Devenish's next words wiped it away for good. "Where is it?"

"Where's what?"

"What do you think? The picture." Claber stared at him. "The picture, Harry boy. Come on, give—where is it?"

"I don't know what you're talking about. You're a bloody mystery-maker."

"You read the evening paper? Doesn't matter, you don't have to. Harry, I didn't think you'd waste my time like this. I thought you were too smart." His sandwich and tea came. He squeezed the lemon against the glass, and said to the waiter, "I want a straw."

"A straw?"

"To drink it through."

The waiter looked as if he might protest. "Bring him a straw,"

Claber said. The waiter brought two straws and backed away to see what Devenish did with them. He drank through one of them, making a bubbling noise. The waiter retreated.

"I don't know about a picture." He added with emphasis, "I don't know why you should know about a picture either. Is it anything to do with you?"

Devenish put mustard on the sandwich and bit into it. The corned beef was just as he liked it, moist without being gluey, and with a vein of fat running through it. "It has to be something to do with me. I wish it weren't. You want to show Freddy Williams that he's got to stop standing on your feet. First you give him a lesson by knocking off one of his boys—"

"I've told you I had nothing to do with Halliwell. From what I hear, it was another poof who did it."

"Who says that? All right, I hear you say it, but what have you got to back it up? I don't want to talk about that, though, not now. You had another idea, one that would really hit Freddy where it hurt; you decided to get at him through his art gallery. You know where the soft spots are, Harry, I'll give you that. And you're smart. Only you're too ignorant to be really smart; you're half smart."

Claber put aside the remains of his sandwich. "Don't push too hard, copper."

"You think you were really smart? I'll tell you what happened, and you can judge for yourself. You talk to an old chum of yours, a con man named Rochester. He's in the money now and living it up, but he's got a record long as your arm. Fraud charge in 1965 and sent up for three years with a friend of yours named Snuffy Craven—remember Snuffy? It wasn't too bright to use someone like Rochester, but he must owe you something, and you think it doesn't matter; all you want is to hurt Williams. So Rochester arranges to buy a picture from Williams, and pays for it to show his good faith. Who wouldn't trust a client who pays in advance, after all? The picture's a Corot, and whether it's absolutely authentic is just a little bit doubtful. You get a copy of it made by a girl who's married some thug who works for you. The copy she makes is such an obvious fake it wouldn't deceive a short-sighted man on a dark night, but again you think that doesn't matter, because the fraud's meant to be discovered. The picture switch is made by the van driver. He collects the original from Williams and delivers the copy to Rochester, who just happens to be entertaining an art expert at the time. Expert denounces it, Rochester tells press. And now you've got Williams by the short and curlies. Either he gets off your patch or he finds his reputation as an art dealer ruined. You expect him to play ball; in fact, you're certain of it. If he does, then the charges are mysteriously dropped. Maybe he even gets his picture back. How am I doing?"

He sucked up more tea and took another quarter of the sandwich.

"I'll tell you what, Thumbs—you ought to apply for a job telling stories on the 'Children's Hour.'" But Claber had relaxed; there was no malice in the words.

"You're with me so far? You think it's clever?"

"I don't know anything about it. But if someone did something like that, it sounds as though Freddy's in trouble. Poor old Freddy. I know how he loves his gallery—thinks he's a cut above the rest of us. But whoever did that, if they did—yes, I'd say it was pretty smart."

"Wrong. It was half smart. I'll tell you why." Devenish spoke thickly through corned beef, and marked off points on his fingers. "One, it was stupid to use Rochester. I know you didn't expect the case to go to court, but if it had, any decent counsel would have slaughtered him in the box. Two, from what I've heard, the fake was too crude. I know you meant it to be discovered, but you should have got a better copyist. If an art dealer sells a fake, it has to be halfway decent. I daresay it looked all right to you, but then what do you know about art?" Claber made an angry gesture, quickly suppressed. "So a court case wouldn't have worked out the way you expected. But then there's point three, almost the most important. The story in the press has hurt Williams's reputation anyway; he's got nothing much left to lose by fighting it out."

"You mean, even supposing the case was dropped, Freddy would still be in trouble." Claber looked thoughtful.

"You've got it. Dropping the case would help him, but not much. I reckon the only thing that would put it right for him would be if the genuine picture was found and it turned out some bit of rubbish that ought to have been slung out had been delivered by mistake. Then Rochester would have his picture, Freddy's in the clear, everyone's happy."

"He wouldn't bloody want—" Claber recovered himself. Devenish looked at him blandly. "Nothing doing. I don't know why you come to me. I told you I know nothing, it's nothing in my life."

"You don't think you can help?"

"With Sammy Rochester, you mean? I used to know him, you're right, but I haven't seen him in years."

Devenish had finished the sandwich. Glutinous bits of beef had lodged between his teeth. He took a toothpick from the container on the table and probed meditatively.

"That's it, then, Thumbs. Sorry I can't help. And now I got a club to run. You'll have to excuse me."

"You think you can just let it ride, you think I'd let you do that? You're not even half smart, Harry, you're stupid. Let it ride, and I'll tell you what I'll do. I'll bring in the girl who did the job—Chrissie. I'll bring in the driver who got paid a hundred nicker for doing the switch and delivering the picture. They're not pros; how long do you think they'll stand up under questioning? Then it'll be Rochester, and I don't know what you've got on him, but it'll have to be very good if he's not going to talk to save his skin. And then we'll take you, Harry, and that'll be a pleasure."

"I know where this comes from. That snooper, the actor."

"What does it matter where it came from?"

"So Freddy's got a copper in his pocket. I'd never have thought you were that way, Thumbs."

Devenish stood up. "If that's what you want, okay. I came here to offer you a deal, but you're too stupid to take it, you'd sooner go inside, do that."

He was pushing his way out when Claber said, "All right." Devenish took no notice. He was clear of the booth as Claber repeated, "I said all right. What do you want me to do, go on my knees? Sit down again, for God's sake."

The waiter moved toward them, but stopped when he saw Devenish's face. It would have been hard to tell whether the anger on it was real or simulated. The detective sat down, pushed his head forward and said in a voice as thick as if he had still been chewing the corned beef, "To me you're shit and Williams is shit, too. You understand that? You don't say things like that to me."

"You can't take a joke."

"Not from you."

"About this picture. Tell me what you want."

"Sorrel soup. Do you like it?"

"Delicious." He would have settled for another corned beef sandwich, but the soup was followed by what Sue called *paupiettes de porc*, pancakes with some sort of minced pork filling. While he ate them, Sue asked him to explain.

"I don't see what you were trying to do."

"Make sure they didn't start a gang war. It could have been nasty all round, and the A.C. would have blamed me for letting it happen."

"But you don't *know* that Claber will return the picture. You can't be sure. He might destroy it."

"Of course he won't. What would be the point? He set a trap and it's come unsprung. He has to accept that. The only thing he stuck at was keeping the picture, and Williams keeping the money that had been paid by his dummy, Rochester. So Williams will get his picture delivered back to him tomorrow, and when he gets it he'll hand the messenger a check. That leaves it straight."

"And can you be sure Williams will do that?"

"Why not?"

"It's fascinating. You make them all sound so honest, keeping their word."

"Only because it suits them. Williams values his reputation as an art dealer more than anything else, and Claber doesn't want to find himself inside. So it suits them to do what they've promised."

"I don't think it's right for you to do deals with crooks like them." He belched, and she frowned. "Roger, please."

"Just expressing my opinion of your ethics. A copper does deals with crooks every week; it's part of the job. You don't have to like the people you're dealing with."

"It's a kind of game."

"If you like. Only sometimes a copper is killed or injured, and more often we put the crooks away. So it's a rough game, you might say. It just so happens I can't put either of these two away this time, but I will."

"I suppose it's all right. Can I say something?"

"Why not?"

"Does all this have anything to do with the killings?"

"As far as I can see, not a thing."

"That's what I thought. And something else?"

"Yes."

"It was that actor Sheridan Haynes who put you on to this. Won't he be in danger now; won't Claber try to hurt him?"

"Could be. If he doesn't want to be boiled in oil he shouldn't play with cannibals."

"But that's awful," she cried. "That's disgusting. Roger Devenish, I think you're a filthy, nasty man."

When Sue became indignant, as she was now, he found her so desirable that he could hardly wait to get her to bed. He picked her up and carried her upstairs. After they had made love, he weakened so far as to say that he would ring Haynes in the morning, thank him and tell him to watch out for himself.

"And *you* give *him* a bit of information. You owe it to him. After all, he helped you."

"All right. I'll tell him something. Mind you, it won't be any use to him."

"And apologize," Sue said sleepily. "From what you've told me about what you said to him, I think you should apologize."

"Policemen never apologize."

DEBACLE IN HYDE PARK

Val spent a restless night. When she opened her eyes she found herself looking at a chamber pot hanging on the wall, with a design of roses on the outside. She averted her gaze, closed her eyes, opened them again and saw another chamber pot, this one with "Forget Me Not" lettered on the outside. These were two of a dozen. Marjorie Billings had had a brief love affair with Victorian chamber pots. In the course of it she had collected nearly fifty of them, and had hung a number in the two spare bedrooms of her flat. Her friends agreed that this was an immensely amusing thing to do.

Val decided that she would smoke a cigarette before she got up. After lighting one, she sat back and tried to decide what to do. In spite of what she had said to Sher, she had not yet gone to Willie. Perhaps Sher had gone half out of his mind, but would living with Willie be any better? He was a charmer, no doubt about it, but he was also fat, lazy and a liar. Was there any point in setting up house with such a man? At the same time, it was clear to her that she could not possibly stay with Marjorie for long. Marjorie's whole character seemed to have changed. In Weybridge she had given carefully devised little dinner parties for her husband's friends, at which Sher and Val had represented the bohemian arts. Now she was a hard drinker, lived in something approaching squalor and seemed to have developed a passion for blacks. Seamus O'Toole had been replaced by a huge black singer who called himself simply The Thing. He had said to Marjorie two or three times in Val's hearing, "Little girl, you look so good, tonight I eat you up every bit." He looked quite capable of this. Val became aware that the flat was unusually quiet. Had The Thing eaten Marjorie?

Marjorie, however, was in the kitchen, surrounded by a litter of dirty cups and plates and an extraordinary quantity of burned toast.

"Coffee." She waved a hand. "The Thing made the toaster go wrong. You'll have to do some under the grill. And he burnt the milk saucepan. *He* made breakfast."

"I'll manage."

"What a night." Marjorie was a once neatly preserved but now rapidly decaying blonde. In Weybridge she had been reticent about her sex life. Now she was eager to tell all, and all turned out to be a great deal. The Thing had done so many other things to Marjorie that it could only be a short time before he ate her up, Val thought. She was still reticent herself, and as she listened to the long recital and looked at the offending chaos, she knew that she could not stay with Marjorie another night. It would have to be Willie.

Sher woke at six. Where was Val? he wondered as his eye met the untouched counterpane of her bed. The realization that she had gone and that the telephone was ringing came at the same moment. A vital clue? He lifted the receiver. A whisky-laden voice said, "Potts here, Harry Potts. You the Sherlock Holmes chappie?" Sher said he was and the voice took on a richer tone, as though a further injection of whisky had been pumped into it. "Live near Colyton, little place in Devon, d'you see. Got this feller living down the road, named Thrale. Funny sort of feller altogether, but the point is he cuts up logs of wood and d'you know how he does it? By *karate strokes . . .*"

By the time he had got rid of Potts, who seemed unaware that he was telephoning in the early hours of the morning, further sleep was impossible. He washed, shaved and thought with indignation about the way in which the Scotland Yard man had brushed aside his suggestions. He thought also about Val, and realized that he was missing the pleasure of having somebody to talk to. And, he reflected as he ate an egg that he had thoughtlessly left boiling for twelve minutes, somebody to cook his meals. He could advertise for a Mrs. Hudson, but he sadly knew that she would be nothing like the original. Although, he reflected, Mrs. Hudson herself seemed to have cooked very little except bacon and eggs.

By nine o'clock he had read the papers and received three more telephone calls. The first was from a man who suggested that a Japanese gang was operating in London and that the three victims had been killed by karate chops when they refused to submit to blackmail; the second from a housewife in Penge who said that a man in her street had half throttled a number of people in the course of arguments; and the third from a Black Panther who said that whitey was trying to fix these killings on the blacks, and described in detail what this particular black would come around and do one evening. In between two of these calls came the post, which brought a letter from a member of an Occult Circle, who suggested that the problem of the killings could easily be solved through séances. When the telephone rang again he considered leaving it unanswered, but curiosity was too strong.

He found himself speaking to quite a different Devenish, urbane and friendly, a man who talked to him as an equal and acknowledged that his information had been helpful.

"I thought I'd tell you, since you're working on the case, that this whole thing about the picture doesn't seem to have any connection with the murders. It appears to be something quite separate."

"Do you mean that the Clabers have nothing to do with the killings?"

"Ah, now, Mr. Haynes, I didn't say that." Devenish's laugh was mellow and genial. "Have to be careful, you know, we policemen. What I said was something different. I can't go into details, but you seem to have stumbled across a plan by one gang to put the skids under another. I think we've put a stop to what might have been a load of trouble."

"Stumbled across," Sher thought indignantly, but he said nothing.

Devenish went on. "Now, there are two things I'd like to say. The first is that although of course I didn't mention your name, it's possible that somebody guessed where my information came from. I'm not expecting any trouble, but if you'd like me to put a man on to keep an eye out for the next couple of days—"

"Good heavens, no." The idea of Sherlock Holmes being guarded by a policeman outraged him. "I can look after my-self."

"I'm sure you can. Just don't walk down too many dark alleys alone at night." Again a comfortable laugh. "And the other thing is this. I'm grateful for your help, and I thought you might like a piece of information which could be connected with the murders. You remember the first case, Charles Mole. Well, now, I had an idea myself about the possibility of a car being connected with all the murders—can't let you have all the bright ideas—and I talked to Mrs. Mole again." He went on to tell Sher the result of that conversation. "So you see it's a bit of a baffler. Did they knock down somebody on the crossing in Purefoy Road, or not? And if so, why wasn't it reported? I've had a man working in the area, and no accident was notified to the police, and there was nothing in the local paper. In case you come up with a brain wave about it, Mr. Haynes, this is my extension. . . ."

When Devenish put down the receiver he felt that he had done his duty by Haynes, and by Sue as well. The Mole lead seemed to be a dead end, but if this amateur Sherlock could make it come alive, nobody would be more pleased than Roger Devenish.

Sher also was delighted. To be consulted by Scotland Yard was altogether in the spirit of the stories, and the change in Devenish's approach was right, too. The information he had given carried with it some sort of link which he could not identify. He was trying to do so when the doorbell rang. The young man standing outside was vaguely familiar.

"Mr. Haynes. We did meet, just, at the Carrousel the other night, but you won't remember." He did remember, though. This was the young man who had come up to Basil with a shriek of delight. In a light, high voice, slightly strangled as though somebody were gripping his vocal chords, the young man said now, "My name's Jimmy Quade. Could I talk to you, just for five minutes?"

In the hall he removed a dark short coat with a red silk lining, and revealed a white turtleneck, tight black trousers that flared at the bottom, and well-polished, expensive, high-heeled shoes. In the sitting room he looked around appreciatively. "Freezing cold outside, but very cozy here. And you've got it all exactly the way it was in the magazine I saw, a color-supp feature. I do think Victoriana is such fun, don't you?"

"You were with Basil Wainwright."

"That's right, you do remember. I'm an actor. I was in that series 'In My Lady's Parlor,' but I don't suppose you saw it. And I'm kind of a friend of Basil's."

A muscle twitched in Quade's left cheek. Sher summed him up. Middle twenties, queer, of course, the kind of hanger-on who likes to think of himself as an actor but never gets more than occasional small TV parts, and drifts out of the profession after a few years. Not hard up for money, from his general appearance. Perhaps Basil's current boyfriend. For some reason distinctly nervous. And his voice, in spite of the incipient strangulation, bore what used to be thought of as a public school hallmark.

"You're investigating, doing a kind of Sherlock act over these murders, aren't you? That's fun, I do think, but is it—I mean—" He looked down at his highly polished shoes. "Are you serious?"

"Of course. About anything connected with Sherlock Holmes I'm absolutely serious."

"Because I've got some information, but it's kind of, you see, difficult. To talk about, I mean."

"It's something you overheard or saw when you weren't meant to be there?"

"Something like that. And it may be nothing, not important at all."

"I think you've decided already to tell me about it, or you wouldn't be here. So you'd better do it."

Looking down at his shoes, Jimmy Quade said, "It means sort of betraying Basil's confidence. But I think he's in trouble—I mean, I know he is. He keeps getting phone calls from a man who's—well, I should say threatening him. Not an English voice, perhaps West Indian or Pakistani, rather singsong. And it's not one person who rings up; it's different people. I've answered the telephone and spoken to a couple of them. They always say, 'I want to speak to Basil Wainwright,' in a tone that really, you know, made me shiver. And they frightened poor Basil, they truly did. The last couple of times they called, he wouldn't speak. And then he rang Sarah, Sarah Peters, and said he wanted to talk to her alone, would I mind? And I'm supposed to be his friend."

"And that's it—that's all?"

"No, it isn't." Quade hesitated. "I suppose I may as well tell you—it's what I've come to do. Basil had a letter yesterday morning, and it upset him. I asked what it was about, but he wouldn't say. Then he tore it up, and the cleaning woman must have thrown it away. But she dropped a bit of it, and I found it." From his pocket Quade took a piece of paper, which he handed to Sher.

It was of a stock writing paper size, blue in color, the kind of paper commonly sold in packets by any large stationer. It had obviously been torn almost in half, and what remained was the right-hand half of the sheet. The writing was scrawling and wavery. Sher read:

enough playing about
don't care which, either
settle for this consign—
do a karate job on
Ten o'clock Thursday. Sarah
Hyde Park past refresh—
by clump of bushes you know
must know what to expect

san
atel

He read the fragment over and over with rising excitement. "There's no hope of finding the rest of the letter?"

"No; I've searched. What do you think? I feel truly awful about it—I mean, snooping like that—but I'm afraid for Basil. Was I right to bring it to you?"

"Absolutely right." He could not resist adding, "I've been working with Chief Superintendent Devenish on another aspect of the case. He's just rung to thank me for clearing it up. But this is more important."

Quade looked alarmed. "But you won't tell the police about this, will you? Please. The first thing they'd do would be to talk to Basil and to Sarah, and Basil would be furious. He'd never speak to me again. So if you thought of doing that, I'd sooner you gave me the letter back."

"Don't worry. I'll be keeping this to myself."

When Quade had gone he telephoned Joe Johnson. The warden was not free until the afternoon, and by the time he came around Sher had thought of an explanation for the way in which the letter was written. He asked the warden to write the words with his left hand. The result was very similar in appearance to the letter fragment. Johnson was disconcerted, as Watson might have been.

"You don't think I had anything to do with this?"

"Of course not. The point is that the letter was written left-handed by a naturally right-handed person. Most left-handed writing by somebody who's right-handed looks alike because the person loses his natural writing characteristics. It's one way of concealing your writing identity."

"What does your left-handed writing look like, then?" Johnson was still a little ruffled.

Sher smiled. "No good my doing it; I'm very nearly ambidextrous. Do you notice anything else? About the writing, I mean?" Johnson looked at the fragment again, shook his head. "It's hard to be sure because we don't have the whole letter, but look at the way the line "settle for this consign—" differs from the next, "do a karate job on," in the spacing. All writing with the weaker hand tends to be thin and spidery, but it can differ in the amount of space you leave between words. I think two people wrote this letter, each doing alternate lines. When you consider that the last two word fragments could be signatures, the possibility becomes almost a certainty."

Johnson looked at it again, then said excitedly, "I believe you're right. That's a fine piece of deduction. It's like that case —you remember the one—"

" 'The Reigate Puzzle,' you mean, where the letter was written by old Cunningham and his son."

"Right. I call this a real Holmesian deduction."

"Not quite, because Holmes deduced that there were two writers from only six written words and we had half a page. What else do we get from the letter, Joe?"

"It looks as though Wainwright and Miss Peters know something about the murders. Of course, you were on to her from the start, weren't you?"

"Not so fast. It's true I thought she must have a link with the case, but so far there's nothing to prove it."

"Would it be the Clabers threatening them, do you think?"

"No. Criminal gangs don't write threatening letters of this sort. And anyway, why would the Clabers write to Basil Wainwright, when he goes to the Carrousel and they can talk to him there? What about those signatures? If they are parts of names, they're suggestive."

"Are they?" Johnson seemed completely puzzled. "They're rather unusual names, that's all I can think of."

"What about them being Egyptian or Indian names? Like Hassan and Patel."

"My word, I believe you've got it. I call that really brilliant."

"As the master said, we mustn't rush to conclusions on insufficient evidence. But the question is, Joe, are you game for an expedition to Hyde Park tonight? You are? Splendid. I have no Mrs. Hudson here, and no niece to bake a cake, but there are crumpets in the kitchen, and although the crumpet is only a humble cousin of the old English muffin, it is not to be despised when toasted and buttered. And while they are toasting and the tea is brewing, I will tell you about the reaction of Chief Superintendent Roger Devenish in relation to the curious case of the wrong picture. He says that he feels sure it has nothing to do with the killings, but I'm not certain that he is right."

The fringes of Hyde Park along the Bayswater Road and Park Lane are well lighted at night, but in the center, only an occasional lamp makes a pool of light in the surrounding darkness. On summer evenings this part of the park contains a number of figures going about solitary business: voyeurs who pad along the paths and then veer off suddenly across grass and go as near as they dare to couples clasped together; women walking alone who cannot safely be accosted as prostitutes; couples who meet for a few moments and then quickly separate; and other couples who meet apparently for the first time, and go off arm in arm. But all that is in the summer. Tonight, as Sheridan Haynes and Joe Johnson leaned into the east wind and felt hail sting their faces, they met only a couple of people as they came to the closed refreshment house. The illuminated dial on Sher's watch said seven minutes to ten.

What did "past refreshment house" mean? Sher had walked across this part of the park in the early afternoon, and there was no clump of bushes very near. The most promising thing seemed to be some bushes three or four hundred yards away, in the direction of the Serpentine. They walked this way over the grass. Just before they left the path a man passed them, wearing hat and overcoat, and a muffler over his face. Something about him seemed familiar, but he had gone by in a moment.

Thirty yards from the bushes there was a small storage hut used by the park attendants. Standing beside it, they could see anybody who approached the bushes from this side. The disadvantage of the position was that a man coming from the Park Lane direction was likely to be concealed, but still it seemed the best place in which to stand. Sher felt in his hip pocket, took out a flask and handed it to Johnson. The warden put it to his lips, gave a sigh of satisfaction and handed it back. Sher felt the whisky sting his throat and then glow through his body, and he experienced an accompanying emotional glow, a feeling of pure joy. The icy night, the sense of being on the track of a

165

mystery in the heart of a great city, the possible nearness of danger among the bushes—all this, surely, was what Holmes had meant when he said to Watson, "The game's afoot."

"That really hit the spot," Johnson murmured. "What are we going to do?"

"Wait to see if Sarah keeps the appointment, and what happens when she does. If she doesn't come, then we may get cold outside but we shall stay warm within."

"You haven't brought a camera?"

"Holmes never took photographs." He spoke sharply, and Johnson looked at him in surprise. Sher laughed. "That isn't a good reason, I know. I do have a camera with a flash, but I forgot to bring it."

"How about a revolver?"

"I have no license."

"What happens if we see somebody?"

"We do whatever seems right at the time. We shall have to improvise."

Johnson subsided, although he was evidently not satisfied. Minutes, or what seemed like minutes, passed. The hut protected them from the sleet, but not from the wind. The traffic warden stamped his feet, then said, "I think I can see people moving. Through the bushes. We ought to be on the other side of them."

Sher saw them, too, what looked like three or four figures grouped together. Then some of them moved away. "We can't be on the other side; we shall be seen."

"Doing no good here, though, are we? Shall I start to work my way round?"

Before Sher could reply, a thin scream sounded on the air, and was repeated. Both men broke from their cover and ran across the grass.

As soon as they reached the bushes, Sher saw the body. It lay on the grass face down, the body of a woman lying sideways in an awkward posture. She was wearing a coat, and the clothing was not disarranged. An open handbag was by her side, with the contents scattered on the grass.

Johnson looked around. "I don't see anybody." Sher was on his knees beside the body. "You shouldn't move her."

"She may still be alive." Sher turned the body over gently, to make sure that it was Sarah. The fine profile and the arrogant look were unmistakable. A gout of blood had run down from her mouth.

He looked up to tell Johnson that it was indeed Sarah Peters and that he thought she was dead, when a flash bulb went off. Three people were standing a few yards away, one of them the photographer. "Thank *you,*" he said, taking a shot of the bewildered Sher beside the body, a shot from above, a double shot of Sher and Johnson. "Thank you, thank you." Then the other two were with them, Basil Wainwright and the mufflered and hatted man, who revealed himself as Jimmy Quade. Sarah sat up, peeled the plastic blood from her face and said, "I'm bloody cold."

"Darling, you were superb. Just superb, wasn't she, Jimmy?" That was Basil.

Sher stood up, dusting his knees, turning his head slowly from side to side to look at them. "It was a trick."

"Your face. If you could have seen your face." Basil let his jaw drop, wagged his hands like an idiot.

"If he could see it now," Sarah said.

Johnson's Pickwickian features were unusually solemn. "I suppose the photographer was from a paper." The man was already fifty yards away. "Shall we try to stop him?" He spoke to Sher, who stood like a statue, apparently unhearing. The traffic warden transferred his attention back to the others. "A nasty trick."

"Who are you—his Watson?" Basil giggled. "That ought to be me. We simply *had* to do it. You've no idea how we've suffered, has he, Sarah darling? All those tantrums in rehearsal. And then saying to me, 'I'm investigating the case.' I mean, really. Too much."

"I don't mind somebody being stupid, but I do object to them thinking they're so bloody clever," Sarah said.

"So we thought we'd play this little charade, and see if he fell for it. And dear Jimmy helped. First the anonymous letter saying meet me at the Carrousel, to see if he bit, then the sinister letter fragment. We thought you'd like that, Sher."

Sarah sneezed. "I'm simply freezing. I shouldn't be surprised if I've got pneumonia."

"Darling, you're made of tougher stuff than that." They looked, now a little nervously, at Sher, standing apart and staring across the park.

"You've upset Mr. Haynes," Johnson said. "You shouldn't have done it. He was just playing at Sherlock Holmes, not doing any harm. Now it'll all be in the papers."

"It was your idea to tell the press," Sarah said defensively to Basil. "What paper did he come from?"

"He's an agency man. I gave him a *scoop*. I tell you what: why don't we all go and have a drink together and get hold of that photographer, Dickie whatever his name is, and he can take a picture of us all together, all good friends."

"Sher's gone." The tall figure was striding away across the grass. Johnson hesitantly followed him. "Oh, balls to Sherlock Holmes," Sarah Peters said. "Let's go and have a drink."

It was one in the morning. The residential street was empty except for some parked cars. Sarah stopped the car, got out, picked up the cat and took it to the pavement. It miaowed in faint protest, arched its back. A spurt of blood came from its mouth as she laid it gently down, and then it stiffened. "Christ," she said. "Bloody bloody bloody hell." The cat, a handsome large black-and-white cat, was dead.

She stood looking down at it, wondering what to do. She had

not seen the animal at all, just felt the smack as she hit something. She had been driving over the speed limit, but then who doesn't at one in the morning? And she had had a good deal to drink, although she was far from drunk. It was a bad end to an evening she regretted, although she had gone along with Basil's idea happily enough at the time. But what was she going to do about the cat? Ring the bells of these darkened houses, wake the occupants to ask if they owned a black-and-white cat and then say that she had killed it? In the end she picked up the cat carefully and placed it just inside the front gate of the nearest house, so that it would not be kicked accidentally by somebody passing. Then she drove slowly and carefully to her Paddington flat.

18

LAST DAY
IN THE LIFE OF

Val had, after all, stayed another night with Marjorie Billings. She had been unable to reach Willie. His secretary said that he was casting a new play, not TV but live theater, and had gone up to Manchester to see an actress playing in rep up there, a girl totally unknown outside Lancashire, who was said to be a new Vanessa Redgrave. He was staying overnight. And who with? Val wondered. Would the totally unknown actress be able to resist the charm of *Mitteleuropa?* So she telephoned Marjorie, who was always delighted to have somebody to talk to about her nightly problems and achievements.

It was not about The Thing that she spoke, however, when she burst into Val's bedroom waving the *Enquirer,* which was the newest of the tabloids.

"Sherlock in the news," she cried. "Really in the news. Did you know about it?"

The headline said: "SHERLOCK FINDS A BODY," and then beneath: "ONLY THE BLOOD WAS PLASTIC." There was a picture of Sher leaning over Sarah Peters, another of the recumbent body, and a third of Sher looking up into the camera. She read the story, which was written in a vein of unrelentingly heavy humor, and handed it back.

"Did you know about this?" Marjorie asked eagerly.

"I told you he was investigating. I didn't know he'd fall for anything like this. Basil Wainwright must hate him."

"So what are you going to *do?*" New woman Marjorie loved drama. She was obviously disappointed by Val's response.

"Nothing. I've left Sher because he was making a fool of himself. Why should I worry if he proves to be a bigger fool than I expected?"

Nevertheless, when she left Marjorie an hour later, she thought about Sher on the drive down to Greenwich. It was a foggy morning when she left Battersea, and by the time she reached the shop the fog was quite thick. After her arrival she had to restrain herself from making a sympathetic telephone call to him. What would have been the point?

Sher had asked for incoming telephone calls to be cut off after he reached home the previous night, but the papers—the *Times*, the *Telegraph* and the *Enquirer*—were on the floor, pushed through the letter box. He read the *Enquirer* story and then turned to the others. The *Telegraph* had a picture, and a paragraph that included a short interview with Basil, who said the whole thing was a joke. The *Times* ignored it. In a couple of days, Sher thought, it would be forgotten. Had he been foolishly credulous in believing the evidence of the letter fragment? Perhaps he had, and the remembrance of Basil's red gloating face made him angry. But how many other people who laughed at him would have been deceived as well?

In the kitchen, making coffee and toast, he looked out of the window and exclaimed aloud, "There's a fog!" True London fogs were rare nowadays, and this was hardly a fog as yet but only a yellowish swirling mist that dulled sounds and softened outlines, making the buildings on the other side of Baker Street look mellow and gentle, giving a mysterious delicacy to the shop fronts below.

As he stood looking out, he saw through the mist a vision of the past. On such a day, on such a day as this, had Holmes and Watson rattled in a cab through London's opalescent reek toward the adventure of the Abbey Grange. On such a day had the great detective stood at the window, where Sher stood now, and exclaimed about the yellow fog as it drifted across the dun-colored houses opposite. In the mist there were visions of the great man and his friend, sounds of clip-clopping horses. The vague shop lights held an image of the gas illumination in which Sherlock Holmes had read many messages and started on many quests. "You would have made an actor and a rare one," Athelney Jones had said to the great man once. If a detective could be an actor, was it not possible also for an actor to play the detective?

"No more, love."

"They're American," Sue said. "Called dollar pancakes. The children loved them."

"Putting on too much weight, got to cut down." He burst out laughing. "Sherlock's got his comeuppance. Look at that."

It was a center spread in the *Daily Mail.* "What a dirty trick!" Sue exclaimed. "And they're supposed to be his friends."

"With actors it's hard to tell friends from enemies, so they tell me. He deserves anything that comes to him."

"You didn't say that when he was being helpful to you."

"That was luck. Anyway, I thanked him. And gave him some information." He began to pick his teeth, stopped when he saw Sue's reproachful look. "I can't stand bloody amateurs, that's the truth."

"I think he looks sweet here. As if he's lost, somebody from another world. But I suppose that's what he is in a way, isn't it? With what he thinks about cars, and all that."

He stared at her. "Come again."

"He wishes the internal combustion engine had never been invented. Hates cars, he'd like to go back—oh, seventy, eighty years, I suppose. Back to the days of Sherlock Holmes. *Everybody* knows that."

"I didn't," he said meekly. He kissed her good-by with more enthusiasm than usual. "Shall I tell you something? I love you." When he got in he asked for a check to be run on Sheridan Haynes. He also rang a journalist for whom he had done a couple of good turns, and arranged that he should be given access to the newspaper's morgue.

Sarah's flat was in a dead-end mews. It was a neat little place with largish living room, tiny dining room, bedroom and bath. Outside were window boxes, which she looked after carefully. Crocuses were beginning to show through, even in this hard winter. Below was the garage in which she kept her MG.

From time to time she had shared the flat with men she fancied, but always within a few weeks she got bored with them and turned them out. She was eating her grapefruit alone when the telephone rang. It was Willie, spluttering with anger.

"Darling, I have just arrived from Manchester by the train, and I have seen the papers. What can have made you do such a stupid, stupid thing. From Basil, yes, I expect stupidity, but you are intelligent. I can tell you now, the company are simply wild. They have gone through the roof—do you understand?— through the roof."

"Yes, I know what 'through the roof' means."

"As a thing to do it was, I must say, darling, idiotic."

"It seemed like fun at the time."

"I can tell you they are talking about stopping the series. Not completing it." Dryne had been at Willie a week ago and told him in a few ill-chosen words that this was under consideration, and although it was supposed to be confidential information, Willie saw no harm in repeating it.

He wanted Sarah at least to say that she was sorry, but she did not give him the satisfaction. "Good idea. Everyone's sick of it anyway. And as for Sher, he's round the bend."

Why didn't she say she was sorry? He said venomously, "A thing of this kind, it gets to be known. Afterwards, it is not so easy to get work. People say, 'Sarah Peters, a good actress, yes, but she is not reliable.' What you have done is not so clever."

Willie had become tiresome, and she had a standard reply with which she finished a tiresome telephone conversation. "Oh, balls," she said, and put down the receiver.

Johnson went on duty at seven in the morning. Emmy had given him eggs and bacon for breakfast, but the chilly mist penetrated his thick overcoat, and after a couple of hours his feet felt like lumps of ice. Traffic wardens can start booking cars on yellow lines after eight o'clock, but Johnson was indulgent that day and didn't hand out a single ticket until nine. At ten o'clock he knocked off for a tea break at the center, and there he saw the *Enquirer*.

At first Sher's agent, Desmond O'Malley, had approved of the investigation as a good publicity gimmick, but he had changed his mind when he heard that the company was opposed to it. Willie was circuitous as ever in talking about it, but as O'Malley liked to say, he kept his ear to the ground, and what he heard about J. O. Dryne was not reassuring. When he saw the *Enquirer,* he tried to ring Sher without success, and then went to Baker Street.

Sher had just finished dictating to a secretary his answers to the morning's mail. O'Malley, who valued his own power of persuasion highly, found it almost impossible to talk to him. He refused to discuss the effect the publicity might have on the company, or to consider giving up his investigation. At last O'Malley lost patience.

"Look, Sher, if you want to make sure the company don't

renew the contract the end of the series, you're going the right way about it. Viewing figures have dropped, and this sort of thing isn't going to help." He tapped a newspaper. "The least you can do is to agree to give it up. I'll be honest with you: I thought at first it was good publicity, but I was wrong."

Sher had been pacing up and down the room. Now he stopped by the window. "I believe the fog's thickening. Tonight it could be an old-fashioned pea-souper."

"Sher—"

"I heard what you said. Suppose Sherlock Holmes solved the crime: what effect do you suppose that would have on the ratings?"

It was useless to talk to him, and O'Malley said so. He said a few other things about Sher's stubbornness and stupidity, but they had no visible effect. He summed it up to his secretary afterward. "I'll be sorry to say good-by to Sher, but I shall have to give him up." The secretary, who knew how reluctant O'Malley was to give up anything resembling a meal ticket, thought it sounded as if he meant it.

Val had rather a good morning at the shop. She sold the two near-Morlands to an American who had just discovered English painting, and a damaged Pembroke table skillfully repaired by Fritz to a woman who was actually looking for a brass fender. Then she phoned Willie, who was delighted to hear from her.

"Darling, I have just got in from Manchester. I rose at the most impossible hour."

"How was the new Vanessa Redgrave?"

"Unbelievably hopeless. Seven feet tall, and like a wooden puppet. When you pull a string she starts to talk to her leading man as if she cannot see him because her head is in the clouds and he is somewhere down below on earth. And then I come back to find this idiocy that happened last night. What are they doing, I ask you? Do they all want to destroy themselves? I have tried to speak to Sher, but he has cut off his telephone. Darling, where are you speaking from? You must talk to him, make him see sense."

"There wouldn't be much point. I've left him."

Total silence. She could almost hear the wheels turning in Willie's mind. "Wonderful news. That will bring Sher to his senses."

"That wasn't quite what I had in mind."

"Ah."

"Willie, I'm coming to move in with you. That's all right, isn't it? You've been talking about it long enough."

"Wonderful, wonderful. When are you coming?" Evidently the wheels had finished turning. Willie sounded absolutely himself, enthusiastic, happy, unreliable. She said that she would be with him by five o'clock.

At eleven-thirty a friend of Sarah's named Joyce Lane came around. Joyce lived farther down the mews. She was an actress of sorts, but not a very successful one, and for the last couple of years she had been living with an East End pop singer named James James, who enjoyed knocking her about when he was drunk. This morning she was sporting a black eye.

Sarah gave her coffee and they talked about the affair in Hyde Park. Sarah said she didn't care whether or not it was bad for her image. Then they moved on to Joyce's problems. She got no sympathy from Sarah, who said, as she had often said before, that Joyce must like being knocked about as much as James James liked hitting her. If she didn't like it, what stopped her from leaving?

"But, darling, why should I leave? It's my flat. And if I turned him out, God knows what he'd do to me."

"You need someone to look after you."

"What do you think I am, a tart trying to find a ponce?"

"Nothing to do with being a tart. Suppose I asked Harry

Claber to have a word with your East Ender? You'd have no trouble afterwards."

"But James might get hurt."

"Not if he behaved himself. If he didn't, Harry would have him roughed up a little."

"James would never stand for it. He'd leave me."

"I thought that was what you wanted. You just said you didn't dare to turn him out. All right, I'm saying I can get it done for you if you really want it." Joyce gazed at her in a woebegone manner. Her black eye made her look ridiculous. Sarah went on triumphantly. "But you see you don't. Just as I said, you like it. Okay, but don't complain."

"I didn't know you were so close to Claber. I mean, to ask him to do something like that."

"No problem. Harry says do it, and it's done."

"I'd be frightened."

Sarah stretched her long body and curled her legs beneath her. Even in this position the effect she produced was that of hardness and hostility, as though she were a beautiful coiled spring. "It's a change. I get bored with acting."

"Nothing frightens you," Joyce said worshipfully.

"Harry's been asking me to live with him."

"Are you going to?"

"I might try it. He'd want me to stop acting, but I don't know that I'd mind. It's full of queers and nuts. You should have seen Sher's face last night. I almost felt sorry for him." She showed her fine teeth in a smile.

"Of course I can do it."

"I don't know what makes me think so." Harry bent over the table, head low over his cue. He cut a red in, brought his ball around the table for position on the blue. They were in the youth club.

"Lovely shot." Shorty was marking. He was also eating potato chips. A fragment sprayed out as he spoke.

"Keep your food to yourself." Harry took the blue, then yellow, green, brown. "You want three snookers. You'll have Shorty with you. Think the two of you can deal with him?"

"I said yes." Hugh Drummond knew that he was a better player than Harry, so why did he always lose? He played a delicate shot on the blue, leaving it on the edge of a pocket, and putting his white ball behind the black, a perfect snooker.

"Lovely shot," Shorty said again.

"That picture's gone back. You made me look a right fool."

"You said you didn't lose any money." Drummond made one of his indecisive gestures and said, as though it were something original, "It's money makes the wheels go round."

"I don't like it when I'm made to look a fool. That Devenish, he's—" He gave up trying to say what Devenish was, and went on. "In the next couple of days. Any time, any place. Shouldn't be no trouble. If you have trouble, you take what's coming to you." He sighted down his cue, played away from the black off two cushions, hit the blue and knocked it into the pocket.

Drummond racked his cue. "Better to be lucky than clever, they say."

"That wasn't luck," Claber said coldly. He put away his own cue carefully in its case. "I want him cut."

Shorty said, "He's an actor."

"Right. The next part he plays, he can be the monster."

Two-thirty in the afternoon. Down in the street it was possible to see no more than a few feet in front of you. It was extremely cold, and the cold made the fog seem to freeze in the air, so that you felt it might be touched by putting out a hand. It made the eyes smart a little, and dirtied the nostrils. Yet Sher, as he walked the half mile to the athletic club, found pleasure in it. From a few yards' distance people appeared so much softened in outline that it was possible to believe they were

178

figures from the past. Even when they came close, their footsteps were more tentative than usual, and even their appearances seemed to have changed. The cars and buses purred rather than roared through the streets. Many were using dipped headlights, and the fog made these headlights look like orange or yellow flowers.

In the club he tapped away at the punching bag, did some work on the parallel bars and a little skipping, chatted to Riverboat. A feeling of frustration oppressed him, almost a physical ache, and it was not dispelled by the physical activity. Returning to Baker Street and looking around the rooms, he was depressed to see the unmade bed and the unwashed dishes. Val had always refused any help, saying that she could perfectly well manage on her own. He tidied up ineffectually, and thought that he must put up a notice on a news agent's board for a woman to come in and clean, something that seemed to him humiliating. It occurred to him that he was missing Val. Was he also jealous, upset by her affair with Willie? If so, the feeling was unconscious. His chief reaction was a reluctance to speak to Willie, or even to think about him. He was not aware of jealousy. He considered the idea of telephoning Val at Greenwich, but decided against it. What would he have to say?

There was another reason for the ache. In a situation like this, where a case had come to a full stop, Sherlock Holmes often responded by initiating action that brought the criminal out into the open, but how could that be done here? If an advertisement were put into what used to be called the agony column of the papers, how could one be sure that it would be read by the right person, as it invariably was in Holmes's time? He spoke to the telephone supervisor and lifted his ban on calls, but the machine stayed silent. Then he wandered about the rooms, picking up bits of the Holmesian past that seemed to mock his own ineffectiveness. And always in the pit of his stomach there remained an ache which said that he was in possession of some information that would be helpful if he made a proper mental connection. Was it linked with what Devenish had told him about the Moles' mysterious accident? What kind of accident was it in which nobody was reported hurt? He considered this question, without result.

When the telephone rang he snatched at it, hoping for a possible answer. The call was from the features editor of the *Enquirer,* who invited him to make his own comments on the Karate Killings, saying that they were anxious that he should give his side of the case. The journalist's voice, dripping with syrup, angered him, and he broke in on it.

"Two actors, people who are supposed to be my colleagues, set a deliberate trap to make me look foolish, and you have made yourselves part of it. Such behavior is typical of the gutter press in any time—the yellow press, as we used to call it. I never replied to the yellow press, and I shall not write in it now."

The syrup drained away from the voice at the other end. "The yellow press? Do you mean you were around and refusing to write for it back in the nineties? Do you mean you're Sherlock Holmes?"

He put down the receiver without answering. Why had he mentioned the "yellow press"? What had made him use that ancient phrase? When the telephone rang again he picked it up, expecting it to be the *Enquirer.*

A voice as dry as cardboard said, "Sheridan Haynes? J. O. Dryne here."

He had been told about Dryne by O'Malley and by Willie. Perhaps this was a chance to talk about the series? He began to do so, but was cut short.

"I had already told Lowinsky that this would be the last series, but that we would complete the last three episodes in spite of the viewing figures. Did he pass on that information?"

"No, but I'd like the chance of talking to you about this personally."

"There would be no point. I rang to say that in view of your behavior in continuing with what you call your investigation, against the company's wishes, and especially after what happened last night, the last episodes will not be made."

"You can't do that."

"Oh, yes, we can, Mr. Haynes. You will find a clause in your contract which operates if your activities are of such a character as to affect unfavorably any programs in which you may have been contracted to appear. We shall be invoking that clause."

"I shall fight it. I shall talk to my agent. To my lawyer."

"Do so by all means," the voice said, dryly triumphant. "You would have been well advised to talk to them before."

When he put down the telephone he felt dizzy, as though he were about to faint. Willie had tried to prepare him for this being the last series, and so had Val, but he had refused to accept the words he heard. Now he felt as if his life were over. He had thought a few minutes ago that the Sherlockian relics mocked him, but still they had retained their meaning and value as part of a shadow play he brought to life every week on the TV screen. They had been reality for him, rather than studio properties. Now they might as well be thrown away.

At just about this time Devenish was reading about Sher in the *Banner*'s morgue. The New Scotland Yard check had drawn a blank. He had never been in trouble with the police, and his prints were not on file. The material in the morgue was another matter. The morgue is the department where files are kept for everybody who might conceivably be worth an obituary. The *Banner* morgue was unusually comprehensive, and it contained some interesting material about Haynes.

Most of it related to the years since he had become famous as Sherlock Holmes. Devenish skimmed quickly over the stuff about his likeness to Holmes, his ideas about Conan Doyle's character, his opinions on acting. He read with more care the dislike Haynes had often expressed for the car as a symbol of the rush and stress of modern life. Then he came to an account of Haynes's activities in the case of Lisa Hayward.

Lisa Hayward had been six years old, the daughter of one of the Hayneses' neighbors in Weybridge. She had been knocked down one day by a van driven by a local butcher named Pygge, and had died of her injuries. The evidence at the inquest showed that the little girl had run out into the road, and that Pygge had not been able to avoid her, but there was a conflict of opinion about the speed at which he had been driving. He estimated it himself at fifteen miles an hour. Haynes and another witness, who had been in the road a little way from the accident, thought it was over forty, but a third witness gave evidence that Pygge could not possibly have avoided the little girl. The verdict was misadventure, and the coroner stressed that parents should impress on small children the need for care in crossing the road.

That was the end of the case, but it was the beginning of Haynes's activities. He said that the verdict was a scandal, and organized a protest against it, combined with a move to ostracize Pygge. The protest fizzled out, but the ostracism proved very effective. The fact that a butcher, and a butcher named Pygge, had killed a child, even though accidentally, left a feeling in many minds that he was somehow dealing in human flesh. This was encouraged by placards with slogans like "Don't Buy Offal from Pygge" and "Pygge *Is* a Butcher," carried by Haynes and other local residents as they walked past his shop. Pygge threatened legal action, but instead sold his shop and left the district.

All this had happened ten years earlier, long before Sheridan Haynes began to play Sherlock. It was interesting, although you couldn't say more than that. The file was in reverse chronological order, and Devenish skipped quickly through the snippets about plays in which Haynes had played during his early career. Then, right at the end of the file, he found something that surprised him.

It was an account of the court-martial of Sergeant Instructor S. Haynes, of the 8th Blankshires. The accounts were of wartime brevity, but the case had received some attention because of its unusual nature. Haynes had been an instructor in physical training, which included unarmed combat. He took several groups for this, and in one of them, a draft almost ready for overseas, was a man named Macrae. During an unarmed combat session Haynes had thrown Macrae heavily. Macrae fractured his skull in the fall and died in hospital. Haynes was then charged with manslaughter.

At the court-martial, two men gave evidence that Haynes had it in for Macrae and picked on him at every opportunity. On the other hand, Macrae had a bad record, was known as a troublemaker and had been heard saying to Haynes that a good kick in the balls followed by eye gouging would make your ordinary unarmed combat fighter look silly. Accounts of what had actually happened at the training session conflicted. It was said that Macrae had tried to carry out his precepts, going for the instructor's eyes and bringing up his knee at the same time. Others had seen only that Haynes moved quickly behind Macrae, got an arm around his throat in a stranglehold, and then threw him very heavily. There was medical evidence to say that Macrae's skull was unusually thin. Haynes had been acquitted.

Devenish left the *Banner* office in a thoughtful mood. Back at the Yard, he told Brewster what he had found out. The sergeant didn't think much of it. He still favored Harry Claber, or somebody Claber had hired. Devenish agreed that it was all circumstantial, but thought that it would do no harm to put a man on Haynes. It was what he'd suggested to Haynes himself only a day or two ago. Constable Lovesey got the assignment.

A little earlier in the afternoon, Harry Claber had been talking on the telephone to Sarah.

"Hi there. You got any spare time tonight?" She was not deceived by the tone. Harry was casual only when something was important to him. He went on. "Got Lord St. Claremont coming to the club. Going to buy a few chips, then I'm giving a little supper party afterwards. He'll be there. Thought you'd like to come."

Lord St. Claremont was the oldest son of the Duke of Drongan (which people pronounced Drone). He was well known as a playboy and gambler, and his father was an important man in the Tory party.

"Flying high."

"Got one or two interesting people to meet him." He named them: a City financier, a woman who edited a women's magazine, a couple of others. "Want to come? Get to the club around half ten; it'll be in time. Thing is, I can't pick you up; got to go to a meeting of the South London Boys' Clubs committee. They made me chairman, so I can't duck out, and afterwards they expect me to give them a drink, push the boat out a bit."

"Important man."

"You like to take the piss out of me, don't you? I like it, too. You'll come?"

"I'll come."

His voice, always cheerful, became brighter yet. She recognized that brightness as a warning note of trouble. "Your friend's been taking the piss, too, or trying to. Know who I mean —Sherlock Holmes? He's given me some trouble. I didn't like that so much."

"Bad luck." Sarah never sympathized with anybody, not even herself. "Basil and I caused a bit of trouble for him last night."

"I seen it. Good for you, smart girl. But I'm going to do something about it, teach him a lesson." The threatening note in his voice was something she very much enjoyed. "See you half ten then, or round about. And I tell you something." She half expected a declaration of love, but he said, "I got to have a hostess, know what I mean? All right?"

She said yes. Later she reflected that Harry's crudity, which for her was his chief charm, would soon pall. She also, to her surprise, found herself thinking about the cat she had run over, hearing again the faint miaow, feeling the body stiffen in her hands. The image of a helpless thing destroyed stayed with her. But what else could she have done?

At three o'clock the fog was thicker. Traffic slowed down further. Baker Street was a solid mass of cars right up to Portman Square. At the top of Portman Street there was hopeless confusion, as cars going along Oxford Street clashed with those trying to turn right from Portman Street. Johnson gave up booking cars at meters, and lent a hand to Betty Brade, who was trying to create some kind of orderly flow. Their service was not appreciated. It was difficult for cars to see the wardens, and Betty got into a prolonged altercation with one motorist who pulled up just a couple of yards in front of her. Cars behind the motorist hooted, heads were stuck out of windows. Johnson went over to make peace, but as soon as he left his traffic line, the cars moved forward and created another jam.

They were due off at half past three, but worked on until almost four o'clock, when two policemen on motorbikes turned up and took over. Johnson made his way to Marble Arch underground. In three-quarters of an hour he would be home, and Emmy would have tea ready. After tea he would ring up Mr. Haynes. Johnson never thought of Sher as anything but Mr. Haynes.

"My darling." Willie's embrace was as warm as ever. She was enclosed in his atmosphere of masculinity and aftershave. "My darling, come in. Let me take your case. Did you have an incredibly disgusting journey?"

"Incredibly disgusting. It took me more than an hour from Greenwich. The fog's getting thicker."

"Poor Val." She looked at him suspiciously. Willie was most sympathetic when he was preparing you for something unpleasant. This tenderness, as of a doctor being indulgent before breaking the news of a terminal illness, was ominous. She lighted a cigarette and sat on the sofa, where they had often

185

made love. Willie perched himself on the arm of it and looked at her quizzically, indulgently, sorrowfully.

"Well?" Willie continued to look. "Here I am. It's what you've always said you wanted, for us to live together."

"But *of course*. I remember that day in the garden at Weybridge, the first time you came here—everything. I remember everything. This is what I have always wanted. It is as you say."

"Willie, you've got something to tell me."

"You are so clever. It's what I have always loved about you. Such intuition. I can hardly believe you are English. You had a Hungarian grandmother. I think you have already understood."

"I think so, too, perhaps, but I shall understand even better when you tell me."

"The blow has fallen." Rather in the tradition of a Marx brother announcing bad news, but in his case with perfect seriousness, Willie allowed his head to droop. "Sherlock Holmes is finished. Cut off. Like that. The last three scripts for the series are not even to be made."

"I haven't got an ashtray." He got up and brought one over, looking at her penetratingly as he did so, a doctor waiting to see if the patient was seriously affected by the news. Val tapped ash serenely.

"After that affair last night—so ridiculous, so awful—they have operated one of the clauses in, as they say, the small print. And what objection could I raise? *So* ridiculous."

"I agree. Isn't there anything to be done?"

He shook his head. "There is a terrible man named Dryne."

"I've heard of him."

"He talked to me. By now he will have spoken to Sher. I thought it was better if it was Dryne who said it, otherwise Sher might have suspected that I had something to do with it. Under the circumstances, you know." He sighed profoundly. "Poor Sher."

"Poor Sher. Still, this doesn't exactly come as a surprise, does it, Willie?"

186

"But to learn these two things together. Can you imagine?" He smacked one plump fist into the other fat palm. *"Biff*, I have lost the part that has made me famous. *Biff*, I have lost the wife I love to my best friend."

"I wouldn't say you were exactly Sher's best friend. He doesn't have many friends."

Willie disregarded this. "Val, we cannot do this to him. You and I, at such a time—we cannot do it."

He was offended when she burst out laughing. "I'm not laughing at you."

"You are not? I could have been fooled, as they say."

"Dear Willie, you're an original, you really are. Why was I so stupid?" Tears formed in her eyes, and she could not easily have said whether they were of laughter or vexation. "Don't worry. I can take a hint if I'm hit over the head with it. Going to bed is one thing, living with somebody is another. I should have seen it. If I came and lived with you I might even start talking about marriage."

"My darling, you are being unjust." A pout of disappointment was contradicted by his almost evident relief. Arms were flung wide. "You stay here as long as you like. Stay forever. What more can I say?"

"It's not what you say, it's the way that you say it."

"What I say is that we cannot do this to Sher. We must sacrifice ourselves."

"Enough is enough, Willie. You needn't go on. I think you're right really; we're both too old for this sort of thing. So it's over and good-by. No copulation without cohabitation will be my motto in future."

She stubbed out her cigarette, and moved away when he tried to embrace her again. He asked what she would do now.

"Don't worry about me. I'm a survivor."

"But you cannot go now. In the fog."

"Oh, yes, I can. Good-by, Willie."

Then she had gone. He looked out of the window and saw her

get into her car and drive away slowly, merging with the mass of traffic. It was not what he had envisaged as the end of the scene, and he felt slightly cheated.

Sarah would have been leaving the Sherlock Holmes series in the next episode in any case. In that story she escaped from a police trap set for her, and Holmes then let her go on condition that she leave England forever. Accordingly she was looking for a play, and she was reading a script that had been sent by her agent when Basil rang, full of glee about the success of what he called their little prank, and saying that he had been asked to write an article for a Sunday paper on what it was like to work with Sher.

"Of course, this rather nice journalist will be doing it mostly, putting it all down on paper after talking to me. You know the kind of thing, frank revelations, and I really *do* intend to let my hair down. I mean, he really is—let's face it—round the bend."

It was a phrase she had used herself when talking to Willie, yet somehow she did not like it being used back at her. She was becoming less sure every minute that she approved of what she had done the night before.

"The thing is, sweetie, if *you* liked to do something, too, about how we planned it and wrote that note, I think the paper—"

"No, I wouldn't."

"*Oh,*" Basil said expressively. "Of course, if *that's* the way you feel—"

She was suddenly sick of Basil. "The way I feel is that we've had our joke and that's it. The poor bastard may be a little bit round the bend, but if he isn't, you're going the right way to send him there."

"I didn't know you were so *moral.* I mean, somebody who goes to bed with Harry Claber shouldn't be quite so choosy, is what I think."

"Oh, balls."

It was hardly a satisfactory way of ending the conversation, and she was still thinking about Sher when Joyce returned in tears. James James had been back, had called her a stupid slut who was no use even in bed, and said that he was bringing a bird home with him that night, and that if she didn't like it she could get out.

"It's so unfair," Joyce wailed. "I mean, it is my flat. What shall I do?"

"I told you I can get Harry to lean on him. Okay, so you don't want that. Well, then, you can choose between getting out or staying and sharing him with his other bird. I daresay that's what you want anyway."

"Sarah, you are beastly to me."

Sarah ignored this. "I've just had a call from Basil Wainwright. Some paper's asked him to write about what working with Sher is like, and of course he's going to put the boot in. I wish we hadn't done that to Sher last night. Or I wish we hadn't told the press. That was Basil's idea."

"You went along with it."

"I didn't realize they'd make him look such a fool."

"You must have known what papers like the *Enquirer* would say. And you told me yourself that he's round the bend."

"Maybe, but I don't want to feel responsible for putting him in a bin." She crossed to the telephone and began to dial.

"What are you going to do? I mean, what will you say?"

"Tell him I'm sorry. And there's something else." She was thinking of what Harry had said about teaching Sher a lesson. When she got through, Joyce could hear the voice at the other end loud and angry, although she could not hear the words. Twice Sarah tried to interrupt, but the voice evidently overbore her. Joyce saw the ivory of Sarah's complexion turn a dull red. Again she tried to say something without success, and then she put down the receiver.

Joyce had her share of the malice of the weak. "That didn't seem to go too well. What did he say?"

"The company aren't going to make the last three programs

at all. It doesn't matter to me, they'll pay me out, but I don't know what it'll do to Sher."

"He blames you?"

"You could put it like that."

"What did he say?"

"Ruining his life was about what it amounted to. He's apparently in some trouble with his wife, and he seemed to blame me for that, too. I rather liked him. He seemed almost human for the first time, instead of sounding like a third carbon copy of Sherlock Holmes. There's one thing, though."

"What?"

"There was something I meant to tell him, and I never got around to it."

After speaking to Sarah Peters, Sher was utterly exhausted. The ache in his stomach was still there, but with it went a weariness so great that he could hardly keep his eyes open. He sat in the chair beside the telephone, wondering whether he had the energy to get into the bedroom and lie on the bed. To consider this more carefully, he closed his eyes.

He was walking down a street that he knew yet failed to recognize, until he saw "J. Hampton—Cellulose—Acetate," and realized that it was the street down which Shorty and Joey had pursued him. As soon as he understood this he began to run, but although he ran and ran, the street seemed to have lengthened immeasurably, because he never reached the end of it. At the same time he was aware that somebody was running at his side and, turning, saw that it was Lestrade, foxy-faced little Lestrade. What a relief! He tried to say this to Lestrade without ceasing for a moment to run down the street, but the Scotland Yard man did not seem to understand. They turned into another street, and this surprised him because he had not realized that this turning existed. He tried to say as much to Lestrade, but the detective merely grinned, and said as they ran gasping along, "Pure, Mr. Holmes, you have to be pure. That's the answer." What did the man mean? "Pure, you must pass the Pure Fruit Standard if you want to go down there." Now he was pointing a finger downward, and the descent was steep, they were running and slipping and sliding downward. He tried to hold on to the sides of what seemed a grassy slope, but his fingers could get no purchase, and he understood that they were slipping down into danger, and that Lestrade had led him here quite deliberately.

They were very close together, an arm was around his shoulders, and the face pressed to his, the teeth that nibbled at his ear, were not Lestrade's but belonged to Sarah Peters. She whispered something to him, and by a great effort he managed to hear the words. Slowly, as she pulled at his ear lobe, she said, "The karate killer has the naval treaty." That's the answer? he asked incredulously, and she said solemnly, Yes, yes.

The revelation had been made, and he knew the urgency of acting on it, and of moving up, up out of the pit. "You will find it in Hyde Park," she said, as he struggled upward at last, moving away from her and from Lestrade, until he had reached the top of what turned out to be a kind of well. It should have been simple enough to hoist himself out of it, but when he tried, something passed over his fingers with a quick damp movement like that of a sponge. This continual damping of his fingers made it impossible for him to get any hold on the surface above ground. Who was doing this? He hardly dared to look up, knowing as he did what he would find. At last, with infinite effort, he raised his head, to discover the terror he had always known. It was the Hound, the Hound of the Baskervilles, with lolling, licking tongue outstretched, muzzle and dewlap outlined in flickering flame. With that knowledge he heard a terrible cry.

And woke, woke screaming, to find the light on and the telephone ringing, and to know that the cry was his own. He stared at the black instrument, which seemed an extension of his dream, then lifted the receiver and spoke.

Joe Johnson's voice said, "Mr. Haynes, is that you?"

"Yes."

"You don't sound like yourself."

"Perhaps I am not."

"What's that? Mr. Haynes, are you all right?"

He replied that he was all right. Johnson went on to say that it was a nasty night, a real fog like they'd not had for ages, but that the tube lines were running, and if Mr. Haynes would like him to come along, if there was anything they ought to talk about—

He interrupted. "Joe, I've had a dream. I want to think about it."

When Joe Johnson had rung off, he said to Emmy that he hoped Mr. Haynes was all right; he'd sounded very funny.

Sher thought about the dream. It seemed to him that something had been said in it, something holding the answer to the final problem. Some elements of the dream were easily explicable: the run down the street, Sarah's presence, the transformation of the dog that had licked his face into the Hound of the Baskervilles. If one said that Lestrade stood for the unknown killer, what had he been trying to say? Was the killer somebody always at Sher's side? Why had Lestrade talked about being pure? In wondering this, he put a hand in his pocket. The hand touched paper. He drew out the envelope upon which he had written the number of Rochester's house and of the van that had delivered the picture. He looked at it and he knew the answer, the answer to the question he had asked himself the whole afternoon. He knew what the dream had been trying to tell him.

He telephoned Johnson again, and talked to him for five minutes. Then he made another call. The person he wanted was out, so he left a message. Then he turned off the light, put on his thick raglan overcoat and went out.

The Devenishes were giving a dinner party, and Roger had promised to be home by six. He came in an hour after that to find Sue upset, partly because of his lateness and partly because the pâté she had made as a first course had turned out to be so thin that it could almost be poured. She had then tried to thicken it, and mysterious lumps had appeared. When he tasted it and shook his head, she burst into tears.

"Do you know what we shall have for the first course?" she asked between sobs. *"Tinned—soup."*

"Never mind. Maybe they won't come, it's such a filthy night. Or maybe I'll have to go out." To make her forget about the pâté, he told her about the court-martial of Sergeant Instructor Haynes. As therapy it was entirely successful. She stared at him wide-eyed.

"But you can't think he'd have anything to do with the murders. I mean, why?"

"It was you who told me he wished the internal combustion engine had never been invented. All the people killed have been involved in car accidents. He's an expert in unarmed combat, or he was. And he once killed a man."

"I don't believe it."

"I don't say that I do, but it seemed worth putting a man on him. It could be for his own protection, too, just in case Harry Claber tried to be funny. My man might just ring up. So be prepared. And speaking of that—"

"Oh, no, Roger, we haven't got time."

And she was right. On the way up to the bedroom she was saved by the doorbell.

It did not prove easy for Sarah to get rid of Joyce Lane. But in the end Joyce returned to her flat after Sarah had given her a spare key and said that if James James brought back his threatened bird, Joyce could come and stay the night. Left alone, Sarah found herself thinking about the black-and-white cat. In her thoughts the cat assumed a bloodiness it had not possessed in fact, and in recollection it also seemed to have had an enormous head. She could feel this head burrowing away into her hands, and letting out its wretched rusty miaow. Why did such ideas enter her mind when she knew them to be false?

A game of patience was her usual solvent for emotional problems, and she got out the cards. She played all sorts of patience games, from simple single-pack patiences like Miss Milligan and the elegant Windmill to complicated double-pack games like French Blockade and Triple Line. Tonight she played one of the very few triple-pack patiences, the Curse of Scotland. This patience took its name from the fact that the nine of diamonds is known as the Curse of Scotland, and the foundation cards used were the three nines of diamonds in the packs. The game was complicated, with all sorts of possibilities becoming apparent in the first moves, and this intellectual and mathematical quality was one of its attractions for her. Another was that you never completed it, or at least she never had. You could be going along swimmingly for three-quarters of the game and then come to a total block quite suddenly. On the other hand, you could stumble along at the beginning and then have an exhilarating run. The book in which she had found it said that the chances against finishing it were several million to one.

The game took about an hour, and in playing it she became completely absorbed. She had a difficult passage at one point in transferring cards from one column to another. Then the difficulties cleared, and she built rapidly on the foundations. Suddenly there were less than a dozen cards left. She played them hesitantly, unbelievingly. They went into their proper places. She had completed the Curse of Scotland!

While she was looking at the neatly piled cards, the telephone rang. She lifted the receiver, gave her number and then said, "This is Sarah Peters." The receiver at the other end was replaced. She put back her own telephone, poured herself a large vodka gimlet and thought again about the cat. Somehow the conjunction of the three things—the successful game of patience, the telephone call and the image of the cat—made her shudder.

Cassidy signed off at seven in the wardens' center. Then he went out to look at Miranda, who was in the adjacent car park. He unlocked the door, switched on the engine and listened to its rackety coughing. Then he turned it off, relocked the car and patted the hood.

"You're a good old girl," he said to Miranda. "But you're not going home yet; it's too foggy. And anyway I want some nosh. And I've got things to do. See you later, old girl."

In this, however, he was mistaken.

It was another world out here. You could see only a few feet, even in brightly lighted Baker Street, and the people who loomed in front of you moved as though there were a nimbus of mist around them. They did not scurry like modern ants, but moved gently and cautiously, as though they had only recently recovered from an illness and were a little unsure of their legs. And the faces that emerged out of the fog seemed, as they came close and then passed, gentler and more attractive than anything seen in the hard light of day. The women in particular had some quality of mystery about them. Many of them were wearing hats, and beneath the brims their faces took on the quality, at once vague and solidly fleshy, of a painting by Renoir.

Constable Lovesey had seen the light go out in the rooms. He let Haynes get a few yards ahead and then followed him down Baker Street. Haynes was walking slowly, and Lovesey stopped once or twice to look in shopwindows. Tailing somebody was in Lovesey's view almost impossible in daylight if the man you were following had his wits about him, but on a night like this it was a cinch, even though you couldn't call it a pleasure.

Hugh Drummond, who was standing in a pub doorway a few yards from Lovesey, also saw the light go out, and went into the pub to get Shorty. They had agreed to take turns in keeping watch. This meant that Shorty, whose appetite seemed inexhaustible, spent a lot of time in the pub. Drummond found him eating sausages and drinking beer. He gulped down the last of the beer and came out wiping his mouth. "Where is he?"

Drummond looked up and down. "He's gone. If you'd not spent all your time in the pub—"

"Why didn't you wait till he came out, so that you could see the way he was walking? You don't know you're born, do you? If you'd seen the way he was walking, we'd have been with him in a minute. Come on." He began to walk briskly in the direction of Marylebone Road.

Drummond followed, protesting. "How do you know he went this way?"

"I don't. We take a chance—can't do anything else. No point in splitting; we'd never meet up again. Watch where you're going, mate." Shorty shouldered aside a man walking the other way, and jostled a girl in front of him. "You'd better hope I'm right. Harry won't like it if we've lost him."

"There he is." Just a little way ahead, a tall figure in a raglan overcoat walked along, slowly, meditatively. They passed him. It was Haynes.

"Right, then, it's your lucky night," Shorty said. "We stand here trying to cross the road, let him get on a bit. Then we follow on. Can't do it here—too many people."

Crossing Baker Street would have been a daunting enterprise, not because the traffic was moving quickly, but because the people in the cars moving forward at snail pace were ignoring the existence of anything except the machinery that contained them. Traffic lights showed dimly their ruby, amber and green, but many drivers paid no attention to them, going forward in their head-to-tail crawl whenever they saw a space, so that street intersections saw many cars trying to cross simultaneously but at right angles. These near-collisions, however, were strangely unaccompanied by anger. Drivers leaned out of windows, or got out of their cars, and discussed the unsnarling of their particular traffic knot in the calmest of voices. It was rather as though the fog were a disaster, like an earthquake or an air raid, which made the victims indulgent toward each other.

Drummond and Shorty were far from such thoughts. "I tell you what," Drummond said with a giggle. "The fuzz'll be so busy sorting out this lot, they'll have no time to worry about us. It's perfect, just perfect."

Shorty made no reply, but the remark irritated him. Everything about Drummond irritated him. Lovesey, following Sher, passed them standing looking across the road, and just after he had gone by they began to walk in the same direction, two men who had apparently made up their minds not to attempt crossing the road.

Johnson sat in one easy chair, puffing at his pipe and watching the TV. Emmy was in the other, knitting something. When they sat like this the bad side of her face was turned away from him.

"You want this on, Emmy?" It was a quiz program. She shook her head. He turned it off and stood beside the set, his cherubic face puckered. Then he left the room, and came back wearing his good thick overcoat and a scarf.

"Uncle Joe, you're never going out."

"Think I ought to, Emmy. That call from Mr. Haynes . . ."

"Yes?"

"It worries me. I don't know what he's trying to do."

"But how will you find him? Shouldn't you ring up first?"

"I think I know where he'll be."

She pulled aside the curtains. "It's *thick*. You'll get lost."

He kissed her good cheek. "Looks thicker than it is here, because we haven't got street lights this end of the road. Don't worry. I'll go on the tube."

When he was outside he found that the fog had certainly thickened. Just at the end of the road the traffic along Westway purred instead of roared. He lost his way to the underground station, and it took him nearly thirty minutes to cover less than half a mile.

Sher walked along without particular purpose, except to gather his thoughts and decide upon a course of action. If he told Devenish what he had learned, the chief superintendent would laugh at him. He had no proof of what he believed to be the explanation of the killings, and proposed to solve them as Holmes might have done, by direct confrontation. Holmes had never flinched from such encounters, either with real villains or with intangible terrors. What an occasion it had been when, in the affair of the Devil's Foot, he had exposed both Watson and himself to the subtle, nauseous odor of an unknown poison. Well, there was no Watson with him now, and if he was right there was no villain, only a pitiable man who had done villainous things.

While thinking about this, he almost cannoned into a man who was shuffling along head down. The man shouted abuse after him, waving a bottle and then throwing it, so that it crashed on the pavement. The encounter was distasteful, and Sher turned left into York Street. Here there were fewer people, less light. Here, too, people had abandoned their cars in despair of reaching home in them. Some were neatly parked, others stuck out into the road. In the darkness the fog seemed thicker.

Hugh Drummond was suddenly taken with a fit of hiccups. They shook him every few seconds, as if he were being given electric shocks. The sound was distinctly audible.

Shorty was disgusted. "Hold your breath. You'd wake the bleeding dead."

Drummond opened his mouth to say that he had been holding his breath, and let out a sharp hiccup. "Do it now. Good place," he said.

"All right. You ready?"

"Got my little—*hic*—carver." The carver was a metal strip that went around the palm, with razor blades set into it on the slant. Drummond had bought it from a man in a pub, who said he had worked for the Kray gang. Drummond had frightened Chrissie by waving it in front of her, but apart from that had done no more than make passes at himself with it in a looking glass. Now he fitted it on his right hand.

Shorty had a small club with spikes sticking out of it. The club was very light, made of aluminum, and closed up so that it looked like a long shiny case, of the shape that might be used for holding cigars. When it was opened out, the club had on it small chains like a dragging net. The spikes had hooked ends which caught in anything, and when you pulled on the club they tore the substance they were embedded in, whether it was cloth or flesh. He did not much like using the club, but he did what he was told.

Now he said, "Let's go," and they went. Carefully, because it was not easy to see more than a yard or two, they began to run, or at least to trot.

Within seconds they were up with Lovesey. They saw him just in time and separated to pass him, one on either side. The sight of two men trotting in thick fog reminded Lovesey that his brief was not only to watch Haynes's movements but to look after him. In what might be called a policeman's voice he called on the men to stop, and took one of them by the sleeve. As though the action had prompted an inevitable response, the man gave a loud hiccup. Lovesey did not relinquish his grip. "Now hold on a minute," he said. "I want to talk to you."

When Drummond felt the hand on his sleeve he panicked. He shouted to Shorty for help, and brought around his right hand, with the carver in it, striking up at Lovesey's face. The detective ducked aside, took the blow on his shoulder, heard cloth tear and realized that the man had a weapon. He brought up an elbow into his assailant's face, heard his teeth rattle, and with the other fist punched the man in the stomach. Drummond gave a really tremendous hiccup and sank to the ground groaning.

Shorty, turning to help his companion, stumbled over Drummond's outstretched foot. The foot sent him sprawling, but also cast him unexpectedly into Lovesey's arms in the parody of a loving embrace. Struggling together, the two men staggered off the pavement, bounced onto a parked car and came back again. Drummond clutched at a pair of legs and brought them down. They were Shorty's, but the detective, still in his grip, was brought down as well.

Lovesey had realized that it was not a matter of reading the riot act to these men, but of getting away from them and taking one with him if he could manage it. Shorty tried to get an armlock around his neck, but he broke free, got almost to his feet and aimed a kick at Drummond's groin. His intention was to disable one of the men, lay hold of the other and try to get reinforcements, but although the kick hurt Drummond, he took the force of it on the inside of his thigh, not on his genitals. Crying out with anger and pain, he got up and slashed the carver across Lovesey's face.

The detective felt nothing for a moment, then there was a sensation of warmth. He put up a hand, encountered the stickiness of blood, tried to wipe it away, and felt terrible pain in his eye. As he screamed, Shorty shouted, "Come on." They left Lovesey on his knees, a hand to his face, crying out something.

A woman walked by him a couple of minutes later, but thought he was drunk and made no response to his cry for help. He staggered out into the road, and a car crawling along York Street just managed to avoid hitting him. The driver got out, prepared to be angry, but when he saw the man's condition put him in the car and took him to St. Mary's Hospital in Praed Street.

Shorty and Drummond ran along for fifty yards without speaking, aware that they had lost Haynes. Then they stopped a man walking toward them and asked if he had passed a tall, thin man in the last couple of minutes.

"Passed him. No, haven't passed him." The man was small,

waggish, in his fifties. "Thick fog right enough, but still I'd know if I'd passed a man, wouldn't I?"

"If you haven't seen him, he must have gone into one of these houses," Drummond said wildly.

"I didn't say I hadn't *seen* a man such as you're describing, now did I?" The man actually wagged a finger.

Drummond raised his hand threateningly, but Shorty stopped him. "It's a friend of ours, and we've lost him in the fog. If you've seen him—"

"Yes, I've *seen* him but he's not *passed* me, if you take my meaning. He crossed the road just before he reached me. Stepped right out. If there'd been anything coming he'd have been hit. People get more and more thoughtless, you know that? And in this fog."

They ran recklessly across the road in their turn. A small side road turned off York Street here. They went down it and found themselves in Marylebone Road. There were more lights here, and there was traffic. They were in luck again. Twenty yards ahead, momentarily visible as he passed under a lamp standard, stalked the raglan-coated figure of Sheridan Haynes.

The girl had gone into the cabinet swathed in blue-and-black silky material from head to foot. The magician winked at the audience and said, "Now for the trick, the most extra-ord-in-ary di-vest-ment trick you ever saw." Above the cabinet was his name and occupation: "Professor Porno Graff, the Great Lubrician." Through a hole in the cabinet no bigger than the eye of a large needle he pulled a thread of blue-and-black stuff. As he pulled the thread was a strand, was finger thick, arm thick, then cascaded out of the hole as he pulled it, more and more, until the magician had fairly wrapped himself in the material.

The door of the cabinet flew open. The girl inside was naked. The spotlight focused on her extreme embarrassment as her hands moved first between her thighs, then up to her breasts.

Then she stepped out, turned and bent down to show her buttocks and the cleft between them. Turning again, she made a V sign at the audience, said distinctly, "Up yours." The stage blacked out.

The baldheaded man with thick side whiskers on Val's right had been trying to make contact throughout the show. Now his thigh moved unequivocally against hers, and a hand touched her breast as he leaned over to say, "At least we know she's not wearing falsies."

"No, but I am," she said. "I'm transsexual, but I only do it with women."

He withdrew his hand as though the tip of the breast had been a bee. She got up and walked out, wondering why she had gone to the show. "Makes *Oh! Calcutta!* look like a vicarage tea party," said a placard outside, but what had attracted her about that? She found it hard to admit that rejection by Willie had been a blow to her sexual pride, and that she had gone to the show with the intention of being picked up. Well, that was no problem, but the whole thing revolted her, its unromantic coarseness and the way in which the men in the audience assessed the women as if they were cuts of meat. She felt a real distaste for Willie and a longing for Sher. What did it matter if he played at being Sherlock? She could not imagine how she had ever left him.

The car was in a multistory garage, but she felt no inclination to get it out, or even to get her case from it. She pushed a way through the foggy, crowded streets to the nearest underground, and went to Baker Street. From there, even in the fog, it was only a few minutes' walk to the flat. She was disappointed not to find Sher at home, but the pleasure of being back was immense. She ran herself a very hot bath, and as she luxuriated in it knew that she would never leave Sher again.

Half past ten, Harry had said, but Sarah felt that she could not stay in the flat another minute. Thoughts of the cat oppressed her, the cat and the completed Curse of Scotland and the telephone call. What did it matter if she got to the club early? She would get some chips, charge them to Harry and play roulette.

Outside in the mews she was surprised by the denseness of the fog, and decided that it would not be a good idea to take the car. There must be taxis about, and she would get one to the Carrousel.

She had almost reached the exit of the cobbled, silent mews when the figure moved away from the wall. "Miss Peters?" said a voice unknown to her.

She said that it was, before she had thought that to answer at all might be foolish.

"I've been waiting for you, Miss Peters. You killed something. You have to pay for that," the voice said.

She knew then that she was in danger. Her instinct had always been to fight trouble rather than run away from it, and now she sprang at the man, screaming at him to get out of her way. He grappled with her, her nails raked away at him, her shoes kicked his shins. Then he had twisted her around. She knew that something terrible was about to happen, and then the something came, a blow somewhere on her neck, a tearing, a breaking, a conclusion.

"If one of us went in the public bar I don't reckon it would do any harm."

"You're the greatest man for feeding your face I ever did see. I don't know where you put it."

Shorty and Drummond had walked half a mile along the Marylebone Road. It was not hard to keep Sher in sight, even when he crossed a road and they were held up by a red light, but there were too many people for them to make a move. Now they were outside a pub called the Bear and Staff, a couple of hundred yards away from Marylebone overpass. On the sign above their heads the bear danced, a staff in his hand. Mellow light shone through the windows; there was the sound of a piano. Sher had gone into the saloon bar five minutes earlier.

"All right, you go in. I know this pub. If you're in the public, nobody in the saloon can see you."

"I don't want anything. I'm waiting for Sherlock." Drummond's right hand moved in an upward arc. He saw the blood on his hand and licked it. The blood was not his own. "Bulldog Drummond strikes again. Didn't I crease that copper?"

"You're a fool."

"Ah, come on now, it was beautiful." Drummond's hiccups had gone and he was in high spirits. He patted his pocket. "My little carver. I can hardly wait."

"Do you think Harry wanted us to cut a policeman?"

"How was I to know? By the smell? Anybody who stands in Hugh Drummond's path is swept aside." He began to laugh.

"You know what you are? A nutter. I'm going to tell Harry."

"Tell him what you like." Drummond's hand moved again in the arc. "Beautiful."

"If you don't want a drink in there, I do. Tell me when he comes out. But watch which way he goes first."

Shorty pushed open the swinging door that said "Public Bar" and was gone. Drummond stamped his feet and blew on his hands. It was cold but he could not see his own breath, which merged into the fog. He heard the rumble of traffic on the overpass.

Shorty, inside, ordered a ham roll and a half of bitter. By standing right at one end of the counter, he could see Sher in the other room. He sat at a table on his own, staring into space. Once get him outside and in a dark street, and the job wouldn't take a minute. If he stayed in the main road with the lights and people—well, they'd have to take a chance on rushing him. In this weather it shouldn't be difficult, although you never knew where you were when you had a nutter for a partner.

In the saloon bar, Sher looked at his watch. Ten minutes to nine. For the first time it struck him that the appointment he had made might not be kept. It occurred to him also that he had no real evidence of any kind, and that there was not much he could do in the face of a flat denial.

The pianist in the corner was playing schmaltzy tunes from the forties and fifties. For some reason they made him think of Val. A voice behind him said, "Mr. Haynes. I got the message you left in the center to join you. Here I am."

It was Cassidy, overcoated and mufflered, his long face pinched with cold.

"Cassidy. What are you drinking?"

"A drop of Scotch would go down well. I haven't known a night like this in years. Scotch and water." Sher brought back a large Scotch and the water jug, and watched as Cassidy poured water with a steady hand. "You wanted me? I ought to tell you, I haven't got Miranda."

"Miranda?" Sher was momentarily confused. "Oh, yes, your car."

"I've left her near the center. It isn't a night for her, though I might take her home later if it clears."

"Home. That means Purefoy Road."

"Yes."

"I know the address because I took an envelope from your car to make a note when we were following that van. And then I had a dream. Do you believe that we see real things distorted in dreams?" Cassidy did not answer. " 'Pure,' the dream said to me, 'pure.' And I dreamed about a dog that looked like the Hound of the Baskervilles. So then I remembered something I'd been told, that the Moles had an accident in Purefoy Road. Or they thought they had, but there was no report in the papers, not even the local one. And I remembered something else, fragments of conversation I'd heard at the wardens' center about an accident to an animal, and somebody being morbid about it. It was your dog, wasn't it, the one I saw in those pictures in the car. That was what Mole hit, that was why there was nothing in the papers."

"Lassie. Dear old Lassie. She never went over the road except at the traffic crossing. I'd trained her." It was with incredulity that Sher heard the name. That the bitch should be called Lassie was too much, but then what is too much in life? "She was thirteen. She'd slept at the end of my bed for years. What harm had she ever done to anybody?"

"No harm, Cassidy."

"They ran her down and never stopped. I was still at the door and she'd gone on in front as she often did. They killed her, killed her on the crossing, Mr. Haynes, and they never even stopped. I picked up my Lassie and took her in the house and cradled her in my arms. I just couldn't believe she was dead, but she was. I made up my mind then."

"You'd taken the car number, and it was easy for you to find the owner through the wardens' center. And you killed Mole."

"I punished him. He deserved punishment." Now Cassidy looked up, his eyes bright with certainties. "Should a man be able to knock down a dog in his car and drive away, and nothing happen?"

"Should a man be allowed to put himself above the law?" Cassidy did not answer. "And the others, Cassidy, the others. They hadn't killed anybody." He was about to add, "not even a dog," but caught the words in time.

Cassidy spoke earnestly. The scarf around his neck came loose. "I did not act except where I had seen things with my own eyes. A car is a machine, neither good nor bad; it is the man in the machine who is guilty. I saw Gladson knock over that poor old woman. It was only chance that she was not killed. I saw Halliwell when he hit the other car. He drove over a red light, and he was drugged. The other man was badly hurt. Should Halliwell have gone free?"

"You could have given evidence in the case."

"What would have been the use? Halliwell was a pimp and a homosexual." A quick shudder went through his body. "He was able to bribe witnesses. The law can do nothing with people like that. They had to be punished, and I did it. They called them the Karate Killings, but they should have called it the wrath of God."

"I know how you did it, Cassidy. There was no karate. You hit them with that truncheon I saw in the car. If you knew just where to hit, the blow would be a killer. And you knew—you'd been in the army as well as the police. The only thing that showed would be the mark of a blow."

Cassidy seemed to shake his right sleeve, and the piece of wood was in his hand, polished and gleaming. "This is teak, specially made for me. I don't know karate. It was the papers that talked about it."

"You had no right to punish them yourself."

"I have thought that. But then they would have gone free."

"You said to me that there must be rules. You've broken the rules." The scarf had fallen completely away, and Sher exclaimed at what he saw. "What are those marks on your neck?" Cassidy mumbled something. "What are you saying?"

"She killed a cat. Last night. I saw her. But it has troubled me. I think perhaps I was wrong and that she didn't mean to kill. I punished her, but she fought. I didn't like it. I'm afraid I was wrong."

Sher looked at him in horror. "You did it tonight? And the woman's dead?"

"Yes. I was following her. For you."

"Sarah Peters?"

"Yes. She was no more than a prostitute, but I'm afraid—afraid I did wrong." He put his face in his hands, weeping.

"Cassidy, you need help. You can't go on."

"I can't go on," Cassidy agreed, still weeping.

"We have to go to the police. Together. Now."

Cassidy wiped his eyes, nodded, got up. They went out of the pub together.

When Johnson got to the center, they told him that Mr. Haynes had left a message for Cassidy to join him in the Bear and Staff. In the pub he learned that the warden had left in the company of a tall gentleman just a couple of minutes earlier. Where were they? There was a tangle of road junctions beside the overpass, with barriers put up to make sure you did not cross the road but went through the underground passage. If they had gone back to the center, he would have met them. There was only one thing they could have done—gone into the underpass.

"The police station's over there." Cassidy pointed in the direction of a dimly visible central island of stone. All the streets here were one way, and some traffic moved along them. The overpass reached almost directly above their heads, and it was possible to see the tops of lorries moving along it, turned by the fog into shapes like lumbering animals.

"We have to go through the underpass." Cassidy led the way down the ramp into what looked like total darkness, and Sher felt a twinge of anxiety. As if he had sensed this, the other man said, "No need to worry, Mr. Haynes. I don't have anything against you. Why should I? Anyway, I've done enough. Too much." When they got farther down the ramp—it was a ramp that he had descended in his dream—small bulkhead lights were visible ahead. "I shall be glad it's finished. Everything has got out of hand since Lassie was killed. I'm not in control any more."

When they entered the underpass itself, Shorty and Drummond were coming down the ramp. For once there had been no difficulty in getting Shorty out of the pub, but he had been shaken to find that Haynes now had a companion, and that the man was in uniform.

Drummond, on the other hand, was exultant. "Number two's as easy as number one, my mother used to say. And look what I've got for him." He took his switchblade out of his jacket pocket, flicking it open to show a long stiletto point. "My knitting needle."

"If he's fuzz I'm packing it in. We'll have the whole force on our backs. Wait a minute, though." Shorty had seen Cassidy's peaked cap. "He's not fuzz; just a bloody traffic warden."

"Nothing to worry about."

"Nothing to worry about." Shorty saw Haynes and the warden enter the underpass. "Come on, this is it. We won't find anything better."

The passageway smelled musty, but the fog was thinner here, with better visibility than up above. As Sher and Cassidy went on, the tunnel branched out and expanded. A sign said "Bakerloo Line. Buses to Victoria and Oxford Circus." Where the tunnel widened there was a shop that called itself a boutique, and another that said "Rings an' Things." Both were closed. Three tunnels led off in different directions, and with a consciousness of absurdity Sher asked Cassidy which way to go.

"I'm not sure. I've been down here before, but it was daylight and there were people—"

He broke off at the sound of running footsteps behind, and they both turned. Drummond and Shorty were within a few feet of them. Drummond was grinning, holding his right hand in front of him and waving it occasionally in the air. He said as he advanced, "Mr. Sherlock Holmes, I presume. We've got some unfinished business."

Shorty spoke to Cassidy. "Get out. We don't want any trouble with you."

"Mr. Haynes?"

"You'd better get out, Cassidy." It was extraordinary advice to give to a murderer, but what else could he say?

"And leave you with this rubbish?" Cassidy drew the truncheon from his sleeve. Shorty, as if enraged beyond the point of no return, shouted, *"All right,"* and moved forward with his weapon in his hand, showing silver. At the same moment Drummond lunged for Sher, his right arm describing an arc. His left held the switchblade.

What followed was like a ballet. Sher, used to facing Riverboat, evaded Drummond's rush with ease and turned to meet Shorty. The aluminum club caught in the cloth of his sleeve as Shorty threw it, and tore the cloth as he pulled it away. Drummond had been left off balance, and Cassidy brought down the miniature truncheon on his exposed right arm with a *thwack* like an exploding tire. Drummond's arm dropped to his side and he whimpered with pain.

Shorty backed away from Sher and threw his club again, aiming for the face. He missed, but the hooks caught in the other's shirt where it showed above his raglan overcoat. Cassidy, confident now that he had neutralized his opponent's right hand, closed with him. He caught his man a blow with the truncheon that broke his kneecap, but at the same moment Drummond used the stiletto, striking deep into Cassidy's chest and then turning the knife for maximum effect. Afterward, he dropped to the ground, screaming.

Cassidy stood for a moment apparently unhurt. Then blood welled from his mouth. He tried to speak and failed. Slowly he sank to his knees, with both hands held in front of him as though in supplication.

At the moment when Sher saw this, he was conscious of agonizing pain as Shorty pulled downward with the chain. The hooks, piercing through coat and shirt, raked the front of his body from chest to stomach. Before he succumbed to the pain, he heard feet running toward him and saw Johnson. He saw also in these last moments Shorty looking disgustedly at Drummond before he started to run, and Cassidy's body unfolding slowly from the kneeling position to curl up on the ground. A coil of blood came from his mouth, like—what was it like?—like the plastic blood that had come from Sarah's mouth in Hyde Park. He wanted to make a joke about this, but felt his eyes closing.

SHERLOCK LIVES!

Voices, among them a voice from the dead. Sarah Peter's chiseled articulation came through the veil of unconsciousness, although the words were not distinguishable. Were they both dead, joined in a permanent squabble in some Sartrean hinterland? Another voice alternated with hers, and this was surely the voice of somebody left alive. Listening carefully, he heard a few words: "Mr. Haynes . . . the message . . . lucky I got there. . . ." Johnson! Of course, Johnson had arrived on the subterranean scene, but what was he doing here in the hinterland? To be the companion forever of Watson-Johnson and Irene-Sarah might be more than he could endure. At the thought he chuckled, felt a pain in his chest and opened his eyes.

"He's awake." The two faces looking down on him were undoubtedly real. Sarah's head was swathed in a black-and-white scarf. Johnson looked cherubic as ever.

"You're dead. Cassidy said so," he said to Sarah.

"Not me. I clawed him, and it must have put him off his stroke. I was knocked out, that's all. Cassidy's dead, though. Drummond knifed him."

"I remember." He said to Johnson, "You came up, saved me."

"Oh, I don't think so, Mr. Haynes—"

"Sher."

"Though perhaps it was as well I arrived when I did. After our talk on the phone, see, I got to thinking about those questions you'd asked about Cassidy's old dog, and where could you find him, and it worried me. So I came along to the center."

"In the fog. Good old Watson."

"Johnson, Mr. Haynes."

"I know. What happened to Shorty and Drummond?"

"Cassidy broke Drummond's kneecap and he couldn't move. Shorty got away." He produced a square box. "Emmy made you a cake."

"Very kind. Thank her. And thank you." He felt the scene slipping away from him. "My wife. Does she know?"

"She was here at the hospital all night. She's resting." That was Sarah, who came close to him now. "Sher, I'm sorry for everything. That joke in Hyde Park, and mucking up the show, and everything. Can you forgive me?"

"No need. Behaved badly myself." He summoned up his last resources of energy for a couple of lines from Blake:

> "And throughout all eternity
> I forgive you, you forgive me."

His eyes closed, but he felt the touch of her lips on his, the first and only kiss by Irene Adler to Sherlock Holmes. Then he was asleep.

Val and a nurse were by the bed. The nurse said, "You're with us again, then, hero. I'll leave him to you, Mrs. Haynes."

"What did she mean, hero?"

Val was wearing a dark-blue suit, and looked neat and competent as ever. "I wasn't going to show these to you yet, but I daresay you're up to them. You're big news." She showed him two headlines: "SHERLOCK GETS HIS MAN" and "SHERIDAN HAYNES CATCHES 'KARATE KILLER.' "

"What's happened to the fog?"

"Gone. It's raining. And warmer."

"How long have I been here?"

"Since last night. It's two in the afternoon. Do you want to know your injuries? Lots of lacerations, some of them fairly deep, but nothing serious. And some shock, of course. But they're letting you out tomorrow. Mind if I smoke?" She lighted a cigarette. "I came back yesterday evening. If that's all right."

"I've missed you."

"It turned out Willie didn't want me, and I didn't want him either. And do you know what I did then? Went to a sexy revue; I don't know why. Nasty. I'm back for good. You're sure you want me?"

"Of course I want you. Shall I tell you something, Val? Sherlock Holmes is finished—the series, everything. And I accept it."

The late afternoon brought Willie, accompanied by a gigantic mass of roses. "One thing you must accept, Sher, you must take it like a man. Sherlock Holmes is finished. *Finito. Kaputt.*"

"I do accept it."

"I have done my best. I have talked to Dryne, said to him that this publicity is marvelous, incredible. But that man is a monster. A machine. He has figures inside him, not blood. He is made of statistics. He would not listen. Sher, I must tell you something else that is finished, too. The apartment, Baker Street. Since there is no show, they say there is no point in it any more." Willie bounced out of his chair, walked around quickly on his short legs. "I tell you, Dryne is not human."

"When does he want us out?"

"He said a month. But of course if you need longer, you will take it. I shall insist." His open arms made a present of extra days. "And now I must say something very personal. About Val."

"There's no need."

"What happened was an aberration, a misconception, a few moments of madness." He put his hand on his heart. "I regret it deeply. But it is you she loves, you she has always loved."

"Willie, you've been reading all that in a novel." Willie looked offended. "Anyway, you needn't go on. I'm not sure that sex is so important to most people, after all. Not after they're forty."

"I am sure you are right. We are still friends, Sher?"

"Still friends."

Willie going out almost passed Devenish coming in. "Just a few minutes," the nurse said. "None of your interrogations now."

"No interrogations, just congratulations." He pulled a chair up to the bedside. "So Sherlock beat the professionals. By inspiration, I suppose you might say."

"In a way. Although of course I had some clues. And you might say I was helped by the unconscious." He told Devenish about the dream. "It struck me that if Mole had knocked over a dog, that wouldn't have been reported in the press. And I knew Cassidy was very keen about his dog. So when I learned that he lived in Purefoy Road, I put the two things together. Of course, if you hadn't told me about the Moles' accident—"

"I did a bit more than that. I put a man on to keep an eye on you. He got done up by those two villains, but he very likely stopped them from getting at you in York Street." He saw no reason to tell Haynes that he had been considered as a suspect. "It was smart of you to think of the truncheon as a weapon."

"Yes, but then I'd seen the thing itself in Cassidy's car," Sher said modestly. "He's dead?"

"Yes. Just as well in a way. We could never have made a case stand up in court."

214

"You wouldn't have had to. He was on his way to the station to make a confession."

"Is that so?" Haynes was a man who had a comeback for everything, but Devenish was determined not to leave him with the last word. "It's worked out very well all round. We've picked up Shorty, and although *he* won't talk, Drummond has spilled his guts. With any luck we'll put Harry Claber where he belongs." He got up, those menacing thumbs very visible as he shook hands. "A word of advice. It worked out for you this time, but I shouldn't try it again. Stick to being Sherlock on TV. It's safer."

When Sher went home on the following day the lacerations on his chest and stomach were much less painful. He had to return to the hospital for a change of dressings, that was all. Mentally, however, he had suffered a relapse, and his depression increased at the thought that they would soon have to move from Baker Street. Perhaps Val's sensing of this was responsible for her suggestion that they should go on a cruise. After all, she said, they had saved money, there was no need for Sher to work for some time, he could think about what to do next.

From the depths of his Holmesian chair he asked, "What am I fitted to do next? Go back to provincial rep?"

Before she could reply, the telephone rang. The voice at the other end had a mid-Atlantic accent, classless and enthusiastic.

"Mr. Haynes, my name is Chester Franklin. You won't have heard of me, but I operate the Chester Franklin Bureau, which is the only lecture agency that covers all five continents. I have a proposition I want to put to you. Can you give me two minutes of your time now, Mr. Haynes? It's in connection with Sherlock Holmes. Shall I continue?"

He told the voice to continue, and it did. "You'll remember the readings that were done from Dickens and Oscar Wilde in recent years? Very successful; real money-spinners. Now, what I want to ask is whether you would consider doing a series of such readings from the Holmes stories, acting the parts and telling the stories. Can you imagine *The Hound of the Baskervilles* done like that, with the atmosphere of those dark moors conjured up, and the great hound striding over them? But of course you can, Mr. Haynes, much better than me. Now, there's tremendous enthusiasm for this idea. We'd start in the States, go on to Canada and Australia, and that's only the beginning. I mean, I don't see any end to the demand for Sherlock Holmes. Not to beat about the bush, I'd be ready to sign a contract now, and then get the show on the road in three months' time, say, when you've had a chance to work out a program. And terms —obviously I'd like a chance to talk about them with your agent, but at the moment you could almost write your own. . . ."

He put down the receiver, dazed, and, still in the daze, told Val.

"But of course," she said. "It's what you want, isn't it?"

"Yes. Val, he said he could see no end to it. Sherlock Holmes might go on forever."

"And what's wrong with that? I'll tell you something I've realized. There's nobody I'd sooner live with than Sherlock Holmes."